Praise for **Lucas Alves**

"Alves gives us a nicely-put together novel with a hint of romance. Reminiscent of Cormac McCarthy's writings."

- Audrey Davis, The Independent Book

"Alves has an influential writing style that captivates readers. writes sentences that are often succinct, direct, and devoid of unnecessary embellishments. With his concise prose and economical use of language, Alves' writing style embraced a remarkable combination of simplicity and depth. He skillfully employed short, declarative sentences that communicated a sense of immediacy, lending a powerful impact to his narratives."

- Suzann Maddox, Two Books For You

"Like the keyboard depicted on the cover of the book, Alves taps out his words throughout the story, challenging readers to ask Landon to break a smile, or cry a tear – because that is the time, we like him best. This was a wonderful debut novel from a natural storyteller."

- Karen, Goodreads

"A triumph of storytelling that begins with uncertainty but culminates in a profound impact. Alves skillfully turns initial hesitation into genuine attachment, showcasing his narrative prowess."

- Paige, Reviews by P

SIGNATURES

Lucas Alves

First edition

ISBN: 979-8-9883381-0-9

Cover art by Jason Anscomb

Editing by Samantha Giles

To my wife and daughter, my everything.

Out of all the things you could not have there were some that you could have and one of those was to know when you were happy and to enjoy all of it while it was there and it was good.

Ernest Hemingway

SIGNATURES

The sun casted a translucent fog over the fertile Texas hills. Bulbous and cobalt. Earthworms, flecked with dirt, drawn out by the inviting rains, writhed across the torrid pavement. Blue jays and blackbirds sang in dulcet notes. Along dew pebbled lawns, Pumpkin-bellied robins jabbed their charcoal beaks to feast on those that dwelled beneath the softened earth. Lights flickered awake across this vast landscape, echoing the fading stars. An old retriever hollered in aging cries. Potholes lesioned the roads. A wet coat of lilac garnished the breeze.

Under ocherous skies and crepuscular twilight, they pulled into a small gas station along the town's perimeter. The truck doors creaked sharply through its rusty hinges. Five of them in blue jeans and plaid pearl snaps, aging Ariats and Tecovas, stepped out. Permanent crowns of sweat outline the interior of their Stetson hats. One of the men wiped his brow with a grimy red and mangled Indian motorcycle bandana, a memento from long ago, never once a lover. The driver walked to the front door, his boots hard across the crunching gravel. The door chimed as he entered.

The small Shamrock had three rows of snacks, microwave meals, cleaning supplies, assorted toiletries, red gasoline cans. An illuminated panel of transparent doors, lightly brushed with frost, containing cold beverages and ice cream. He looked towards the front counter. Untouched packages of chewing gum, assorted candy bars. Behind the skeletal, black haired clerk were rows of cigarettes and off-brand electronics.

Café? he asked.

Without taking his eyes from the cheap literature between his hands, the clerk pointed towards the third aisle, where four large black canisters stood on the counter.

The driver pulled a large cup from the sleeve and pressed the silver pump as if drawing water from a well. Steamy black liquid emitted from the faucet, filling the insulated cup. He slid a cardboard sleeve up its gray trunk and clamped a white top to its rim, sealing with his thumbs. He clapped a cardboard tray onto the counter and twisted in the piping cup then repeated the process four more times.

He walked back to the clerk, paid for the coffees, plus an extra ten dollars for gas.

The clerk asked the driver if he'd any news of the world. The laborer stared at the man, not understanding his intentions. After a while the clerk shook his head, muttered to himself and stood and walked into the stock room. The door jingled as the laborer pressed the handle with his back.

He handed the tray to one of the workers. *Le puse diez*, he called out.

A short, thin laborer with leathery skin and beautiful long black hair, uncorked the gas cap, plugged the hose in and began filling the tank. The numbers slowly rose. The other men sat in the truck with their legs dangling childlike, watching the morning bloom forth in swaths of vanilla and apricot. A coyote yapped across the highway. One of the men thought he'd spotted the almond eyes aglow in the distance. He blinked, rubbed his tired sockets and looked again. Nothing stirred, save the rippling feathery grass.

The pump handle snapped metallically. The thin laborer unlatched the nozzle, replaced it, screwed the cap shut and closed the hatch.

Listo? the driver asked.

Listo, the thin man replied, getting into the back seat. He wiped his hands on his chest and closed the door.

Café? the driver said, offering the tray as he started the engine.

Si, the men said.

The passenger took the tray and doled out the cups to the other riders. One of them took a sip.

Cristo, he exclaimed, *su ebullición.*

The men laughed as the driver put the truck into gear and rounded onto the highway.

I

A truck passed along the road below the small stone house. A small structure there, with a back porch and a pair of mirrors on each side. A flock of ebony crows emerged from the lower trees and balkanized in numbers too inumerable to calculate. The motor's roar ripped the silence, waking her, and was gone.

Her black and white body laid outstretched on the large burgundy chair in the corner of the room. She stared out the window with rich hazel eyes, head propped on the chair's arm, legs prone like a sphinx. Her cream tipped tail was folded beneath her. She lifted her head, hearing another vehicle pass in the distance. She looked left. Then sharply right. Her pink collar tingled like a baby bell. She gazed at the lush landscape before resting her head again with a breathless wheeze.

Not long after, he awoke from another restless sleep with the same throbbing pain in his lower back. The alarm was on its sixth rendition of Simon and Garfunkel's Homeward Bound. He was straddling the disordered blankets watching the light seep horizontally through the slotted shades. The fan revolved in calm circumferences as he peered about the cold room. A cherrywood armoire, matching dressers and drawers. The closet mistakenly alight.

He heard Maple's collar chime from the other room.

He sighed and pulled the covers from him and swung his legs over, finding the floor. He massaged his lower back as he stood. The floorboards creaked as he made his way to the bathroom. He sat, urinated, washed his hands then spooned several palmfuls of water into his mouth. He opened the dryer and pulled out his bathrobe and slung it around him, tying the waist strap taut. The freezer blew across his brow as he cracked cubes into a glass then filled the glass with pitcher water. The ice clinked against one another, floating quietly. He drank. The water stung his throat as he looked at his oblong reflection in the refrigerator door. He set the glass down and picked up Maple's periwinkle porcelain bowl. He twisted the large tub's cover free, grabbed the gritty scoop and poured a cup out then resealed the cap and set the bowl back as before.

The backdoor swung open, displaying a ripe sun rising beyond the smooth tangerine skyline. He walked along the back deck, dried a steel chair with his sleeve and sat, holding the glass to his forehead. The highway snaked far below, his nearest neighbor not far from it. A flock of mallards in perfect geometric formation bark overhead. Their emerald wings flapping over the treetops, fading westward.

The razor slid the bristles from his cheeks, his neck. He wiped the sink out with his hand then rinsed his face with cold water. He showered quickly afterwards. Then pomade his hair and dressed in a yellow button-down with a pair of old Levi's. He peered at the clock on the bedside table. Five till noon. The rocks glass dangled from his fingertips as he made his way to the couch, the generous amount of Johnny Walker sloshing back and forth. He stretched out, took a long drink and let out a long exhale. The glass waited on his stomach. Waited.

The clock over the mantle chimed the new hour, then his phone rang.

Hello? he answered, taking a drink.

Hello Landon, the lighthearted voice replied.

Good afternoon Dolores.

How are you my dear?

He eyed the amber whiskey.

Doing fine, he answered.

How's the little one?

She's doing fine. Sunbathing on the back porch, I believe.

That's good to hear.

How are things in the big city?

I

Noisy as ever, busy as ever.

Sounds about right.

Did you ever get that new mattress?

Not yet, he mumbled into the glass.

You'll continue to have back problems till you do. Do you still have my recommendation or did you lose it? she chuckled.

I have it jotted down somewhere.

How's the book coming?

Fine, he lied. Almost finished.

A pause.

Hello?

You said that six months ago. And an additional three before that.

And I was telling the truth.

You have yet to send me anything.

I can send you my most recent draft by the end of the day, how's that sound?

Dolores, tawny haired and ivory skinned, wearing a beige blouse and black pants that furled as she paced around her office in ponderable silence, ignoring the vast collection of local art adorning the walls. She stopped, canted her head and produced a thin smile.

Sounds wonderful, she replied.

I'll call you when I send it, Landon said.

I'll be here.

Landon Cassidy pulled up to the Thorny Vines Winery just as the sun set beyond the blistering marigold hills. He got out of the red Chevy single cab, smacking his lips to taste the whiskey through the mouthwash. Maple jumped onto the gravel as the hollow thud of the locks engaged and followed behind him as he ascended the small wooden staircase.

The deck was strung with tiny, overhanging round lightbulbs. Pine needles, brown and orange, cracked underfoot. He could see houses alight among the darkening trees. Like constellations off an oceanic mirror. A couple stood from their chairs, and carried their empty glasses to the bar. The old bartender nodded to the couple and bid them farewell.

How's the night going, Tom? Landon asked, taking a seat at the end of the bar.

Mister Cassidy, Thomas exclaimed. Good to see you.

Thomas Thornton was a lackadaisical man in his twilight years with strangely long legs below a short torso. His feet sported a pair of leather strapped sandals. He had snow white hair, cropped tight to the sides, and his eyes twinkled like blue Akoya pearls against his deeply wrinkled skin.

You as well, Landon replied.

We've been a revolving door since opening, but not enough to tire me out of a good late-night bantering.

They laughed.

Come on and sit, Thomas said. We got a nice Riesling. Two types of Merlot and a Cabernet. If you stay long enough, I'll let you try our experimental batch, made with Argentinian Malbec grapes.

Sounds like a pleasant enough proposal.

Thomas set a clean stemmed glass in front of his guest, took out an opened bottle of Riesling and gave him a generous pour.

Cheers, he said.

Landon lifted his glass, smelling the fragrant apple notes, swirled the wine till it became almost transparent in the deck lights, and drank.

How is it? Thomas asked, a look of confident curiosity lathered across his complexion.

Very clean, he replied. Quenches a parched throat. That's what we like to hear.

A table away, another couple departed. They glanced at the two men in passing, nodding their farewell.

Have a nice night, Thomas said.

Maple laid beside her owner, taking in the night air in long drawls.

Thomas filled a steel bowl with cold water, rounded the bar and placed it beside the dog. He patted her on the head, stood and returned to the bar.

Maple sniffed the bowl then took several mouthfuls.

Susan Thompson walked from the house wearing a long, flowing blue and white dress with sandals that showed of ten freshly painted opalescent toes.

I

Her hair was thin, long and gray. The diamond adorning her bony finger glistened as she moved in casual placidity. She saw the familiar face at the bar and walked up and kissed him lightly on the cheek.

How are you, my boy? she greeted.

I'm well, Susan. How are you?

When you live out here and do what you love, who can ever complain?I'll drink to that.

How do you like the Riesling?

It's wonderful.

Good.

She peered across the deck at the dwindling tables of customers. Excuse me while I do the rounds. Be back in a jiffy.

Susan drifted off and generated light conversation with those still in attendance.

So, what's new with you? Thomas asked.

Finished the damned book, he said, taking a drink. We're out celebrating.

Good for you.

They drank.

Are you a writer? a guest beside asked.

Landon nodded.

What do you write?

Fiction, mostly.

Mostly?

Sometimes I assist, unofficially, with those bold named writers you see in the checkout line at the grocer.

How so?

How so what?

How do you assist?

If I'm offered, I might ghostwrite a chapter or proofread one of their novels.

Anything good?

He turned and looked at the inquisitor, irritation corroding his gaze.

Less questions, Thomas interjected. More drinking.

The guest turned away without his answer and went about his business.

Thomas leaned over the bar. It's funny when people hear that someone else's a writer, he whispered. They love to ask so many damned questions.

Landon smiled and let the last globule of wine slink down the glass and settle on his tongue. He savored it then set the glass on the bar.

Thomas took the glass and replaced it with a wider model, then poured it full of darkly rich wine.

Try this, Thomas said, sliding the glass to his friend. This is one of our new Merlots. After this, you can try the other and you can tell me which one you prefer.

Landon took the glass, swirled, sniffed, and sipped. He held the wine on his tongue, examining the flavors. Plum, oak, blackberry. It was very dry. Not bad. Not his favorite. After he swallowed, he felt an arid tug at his throat, and asked for a glass of water.

Thomas poured a glass and handed it to him.

He drank, cleansing his palette before taking another sip. Slightly better. He licked his lips then nodded to Thomas.

What do you think? Thomas said.

Not bad, Landon answered. Very dry. But not bad.

I see, Thomas said with a demeanor of defeat.

Was that not the answer you were looking for?

We all have our opinions.

Is this a favorite of yours?

Maybe.

Landon laughed.

Then for people that enjoy dry wines, I highly recommend this one.

Thomas chuckled. That's a better way to put it.

They touched glasses and drank.

Susan patted her husband on the shoulder. She rounded the bar and sat next to Landon and told her husband to pour her a glass of Riesling.

Did I overhear that you finished your book? Susan asked, watching Thomas pour out the wine.

I did, Landon replied.

When can we read it?

Most likely early next year.

That's a ways away.

He shrugged.

Susan sipped the wine, licked her lips, then pinched the corners of her mouth with her thumb and forefinger and took in a large lungful of pine air.

It's a beautiful night, she said.

Yes. Couldn't ask for a better one.

Around eleven o clock, the last guest departed. Landon helped Thomas rearrange the table and chairs, clear glassware to the sink and dispose of trash. When he was done, he sat at the bar, reached over, plucked a half bottle of Cabernet and dislodged the cork with a hollow pop. He poured his glass full then sat back and took a long drink. He massaged his heavy eyes, his tight forehead. When he stood and crossed to the railing and peered out over the country, a cold wind blew across his face, tinkering with his equilibrium. Distant cricket chirps. The pines and elms rustled in gentle waves as the wind rolled off the hillside in silent prayers. He watched a vehicle pass far to the east along the highway. Like a falling star gone towards its death. Final witness, this chance encounter. The thick fragrance of wet earth filled his lungs. He wanted to sleep. He turned and walked back to the bar, grabbed the glass and threw back the violet dregs.

Thomas was wiping down the tables when two stocky, cotton haired elderly men in matching taupe khakis, chartreuse polos and herringbone flat caps, appeared. They peered about the establishment, brows rumpling like puss caterpillars, as if they'd taken a wrong turn and hadn't realized it until that moment. When they saw their bemused audience at the bar, the taller one gave a slight jolt, as if he'd hit a wall. The old man smiled, tapped his comrade on the arm and moseyed over.

Can I help you, gentlemen? Thomas inquired.

Came up for a drink, one of the men said. You still open?

Where'd you come from?

Houston, the other said. We're here for the weekend.

You just get in?

Yes sir.

Well, Thomas said rubbing his hands together, we'll stay open for two weary travelers.

The old pair smiled and sat.

Thank you very much, the first one said. The drive gets longer and longer each year.

I bet, Thomas replied, setting two wine glasses in front of them. He uncorked a fresh bottle of Riesling and poured a smidge into each glass. Give this a try, see if you like it.

The old men lifted their glasses synchronously. They sniffed, and drank in one throw.

Landon watched as they savored the wine.

They nodded to each other in agreement, then to Thomas.

It's really good wine, the first one said.

Yes it is, said the second.

Glad to hear it.

Thomas filled their glasses then poured himself a glass. He corked the bottle and set it on the shelf below the bar.

Cheers to your travels, he toasted.

All in attendance raised their glasses, clinked and drank.

So, what brings you both here at this time of night? Landon inquired.

We come out once a year, the first man said. We left late and hit the downtown traffic.We tried a bar not too far from here, but they were closing. They suggested we come here. Said you might still be open.

And sure enough, you were, the other exclaimed.

You caught us closing up for the night, Thomas said.

Well, we do appreciate you keeping the place open.

Of course.

The name's Samuel, the first man said, extending his hand to Thomas.

And I'm Marlow, said the second, shaking Landon's hand.

They crossed over one another, shaking the other's hand.

Pleasure to meet you both, Landon said.

He twisted the stem between his fingers, examining the sediment settled at the bottom of the glass.

This is a beautiful place you have here, Marlow said. Do you both own it?

No, Thomas chuckled. My wife and I do. My friend here is a loyal customer.

Landon laughed, turning to see the lights glisten on the hills.

You come here often then? Samuel asked.

Not as often as I'd like, Landon replied, turning around.

What do you do?

I'm a writer.

A writer? Marlow repeated.

Yes.

What do you write?

Fiction. Mostly.

What kind of fiction?

The fabricated kind.

The old men and Thomas laughed.

Landon finished the rest of his wine and wiped his mouth with the back of his hand. He looked down to see Maple fast asleep.

Do you want to try that Argentinian now? Thomas asked Landon. Sure.

Bring her out.

They howled with laughter.

Get me some water, and a new glass.

Thomas took the dry water glass, refilled it, and handed it back.

Thank you, Landon said.

Thomas took the wine glass and replaced it with a fresh replica.

You're going to love this, Thomas said, twisting off the cork. He held the bottle to Landon's nose.

After he smelled, Thomas held it to the other noses.

I'll have one of those afterward, Marlow said.

Same here, Samuel agreed.

Thomas poured the glass slowly. Thick plum and tobacco notes filled the night air.

Landon closed his eyes and felt himself rolling back. When he opened them, he grabbed his glass and took a long drink of water.

I had a dog like yours once, Samuel mused. Only she was brown all over. A bit bigger too.

What was her name? Landon asked.

Cheyanne.

That's a good name for a dog.

Sure was. She was a loyal girl too.

Hard to find one of those these days.

They laughed.

Thomas finished pouring and slid the glass across the bar. You enjoy that, he said. If you like it, I'll give you a bottle. A gift to commemorate your new novel.

You don't have to do that, Thomas, Landon said.

You wrote a new book? Marlow said.

I did.

When? Samuel asked.

I sent it in earlier today.

Well, isn't that something, Marlow exclaimed. Congratulations.

Thank you.

Another toast, Samuel proposed.

The quartet raised their glasses.

To your success, Samuel said, looking at Landon then at Thomas. And to your success. May we all find the simple pleasantries of life in this merry drink.

The glasses chimed loudly.

Susan came outside to investigate the commotion. A look of confusion came over her as she spotted the elderly couple at the bar, filled glasses in hand. Who are these night owls? she inquired on approach.

This is Samuel and Marlow, Thomas introduced.

Sam, please, he corrected. Good evening ma'am.

Pleased to meet you, Marlow said.

They're from Houston, Landon reverberated in his glass.

Houston? Susan replied. That's a bit of a drive this late at night, isn't it?

Miscalculated our departure time, Marlow said.

I see.

We won't be much longer, Samuel reassured.

That's quite alright. Can I get anyone a sandwich or something to snack on?

A sandwich would be great, Landon said.

Anybody else?

No, thank you ma'am, Marlow replied.

I'm alright, Samuel said.

Thomas shook his head.

Susan kneeled down and picked up Maple's dry water bowl. She filled it in bar sink and set it back then went inside.

Landon looked to see Maple's right ear erect, twitching like a submarine periscope as she drifted back to sleep.

Saw an accident on the way out here, Samuel said.

Landon and Thomas turned curiously to the old visitor.

Old truck, couldn't make out the model or year. A Ford, most likely.

Looked like it fell from a mountain, tattered to pieces. The bumper was twisted and hanging like a busted lip. Metal, bits of metal, glass and whatever junk from the inside streaked down the road for at least a quarter mile. Must've hit something then dragged or rolled its way to where it eventually stranded. Whatever it was that hit it did some number on it. We didn't see any driver or passengers. Not sure how many there were, if there were any at all. But from the look of it, I doubt any of them would've made it. Crazier things have happened, in the realm of miracles, that is. And those people live to tell about it. He sipped his wine. That truck sure was busted good, though. I doubt anyone could've lived through it. I truly doubt it.

Susan came out with the sandwich.

Here you go dear, she said, placing the plate in front of Landon.

Thank you, Susan.

That looks good, Marlow admired.

Would you like one?

No. Thank you ma'am.

Y'all don't stay up too late.

She kissed Thomas on the cheek and went back inside.

He took a large bite of the sandwich. Mayonnaise soaked turkey pressed into his teeth. The white bread, soft and chewy. The lettuce crunched as he tore away a good size. The scalloped ridges from where his bite impacted looked like a child's interpretation of flower petals. Inside, he could see the missed ripe slice of tomato, peering at him like a precious stone.

So, how long have you been a writer? Samuel asked.

He chewed and swallowed, washing down the remains with the water. He coughed to clear his windpipe.

I've been writing since high school, he said. Nothing publishable. Just stories and such. I got into screenwriting when I went to college. Wrote a few screenplays here and there.

Anything good? Marlow asked.

Nah. But I did get drunk one night and mail one to a studio. Never heard back. Probably wrote down the wrong address. Or tossed it in the waste bin.

What was it about? Thomas inquired.

Landon sipped his wine and shrugged. I don't remember.

What's your new novel about?

He took a long drink, swallowed, and titled his head back to take in the night air.

Honestly?

Yeah.

I have no idea.

The old men looked at one another. They sat in silence for a while. Samuel began to giggle. Marlow joined. Then the others started doing the same. And one by one, they burst into crescendoed hysterics. They drank and laughed as the stars grew brighter, and the night wafted into morning.

Two days later, the trembling touchdown of the plane's rear wheels on the JFK tarmac shook Landon from his inebriated slumber. He belched gutturally, and saw the tiny twin bottles of empty Jim Bean nestled in the backseat pouch. The window had a thick smudge from where he'd laid his head. He passed his palm in circles to clean it, but only made it worse.

He ambled through the terminal like some out of place miscreant, darkly eyed, back aflame. He purchased a large coffee and made his way towards baggage claim. The passengers scuttled around the carousel, like worshipers waiting for their god to speak and spew gifts. They read the carousel board, looking left and right to find the numerical direction in order to follow. Children sat on their backpacks, their chin in their palms. Several stealing a page from their literature, hoping the buzzer never sounds. A man tore into his baggie of in-flight peanuts, poured them into his cupped palm and tossed them all at once in mouth. A shrill cry. A little blonde girl in a long princess pink dress ran brokenly through the doors, her soundless footfalls echoing across the pale linoleum. Her trajectory, a young man in a navy blazer, bent down and scooped her in his arms, kissing the plump cheeks. Onlookers ogled, smiled and clapped. Landon shook his head and drank as the revolving luggage siren wailed for all's attention.

An hour later, the driver pulled up to The Literary House Publishing Company. He opened the door and retrieved his passenger's luggage. Landon tipped the man, grabbed his two curry leather bags and went inside.

The Literary House was established in 1928, after founders Horace Clifford and Benedict Kilns purchased a small reprinting company, a side hustle, from oil magnate James Hammer. They'd go on to represent local writers through the First World War, but during the Depression, they stood on the brink of bankruptcy. When the men realized that the only way to save the business was to sign writers from outside the state, they ended up becoming, what is now, one of the top literary agencies in the world.

The elevator doors divided, revealing along cerulean hallway. Men in slacks and white button downs with rolled sleeves and cheap ties. The women wore long skirts and monochromatic tops, their hair short or pinned up in elegant knots. They strode back and forth, wielding stacks of paper, manuscripts and drafts. He'd never seen a place where everyone had somewhere to be, something to do. Mechanical movements, blank stares, rehearsed expressions. Drones on preprogrammed trajectories until the day's end.

Landon rounded the corner and saw Dolores's secretary behind her desk, dialing the phone.

Good morning, Danielle, he greeted with a smile.

Good afternoon, Mister Cassidy, she replied.

Afternoon? Already?

As of an hour and thirteen minutes ago, she said, checking her thin wristwatch.

He nodded.

Please have a seat. I'll let her know you're here.

I appreciate it.

He turned and sat in an intricate auburn leather chair.

Can I get you anything?

Coffee would be great, Landon replied. A water too, please.

Danielle laughed and nodded. She called in the order. When she was done, she hit the switchhook and dialed another number.

The drinks arrived ten minutes later.

As he reached for the water, Dolores opened the office door.

Mister Landon Cassidy, she exclaimed.

She wore a black dress with a short sleeve ruby top, several gold bracelets dangled from both wrists. Her voluminous, dark hair waved about her crown, scent of iris.

Landon stood and hugged her.

She kissed him on both cheeks.

Danielle placed the drink tray on a small table at the far end of the office. He sat in a tall egg-shaped chair, opposite his publisher. They turned to look out at the cityscape, watching the scuttling New York street life below. Traffic moved and halted, moved and halted. Flashing streetlights, vehicle brake lights. Crowds making their way in every direction like ants in a farm display.

Landon lifted the mug and took a sip of coffee. It was rich and good, taming his hangover.

How was the flight? Dolores asked.

Fine, he replied. Up early. Fell asleep right after takeoff.

How's Maple doing?

She sleeps a lot.

Dolores laughed.

He set the mug down and drank the water. He looked at the walls and studied the art. Large canvases in thick black frames. Impressionistic daubs with vivid colors of blue and yellow. An image of a sailboat pointed towards a distant storm. They complimented the alabaster walls well. He looked at her and smiled.

How've you been, Dolores?

You're looking at it, she replied with a smirk. A new novel from one of our emerging, young talents. Plus, we signed another bestselling veteran last week. We're only going up.

How's Paul and the kids?

Paul is Paul, and the kids are growing too fast.

Landon chuckled. That's how it goes, I suppose.

I suppose.

He set the glass down. So, you wanted to talk about touring dates?

Yes. We need to finalize those.

Fire away.

Do you have any objections to the ones I proposed you yesterday?

No. Those are fine.

Do you want to add any more?

Do I need to?

It's up to you.

I'd rather not.

I'd rather you did.

Then why'd you ask?

Courtesy, she shrugged.

He nodded.

We discussed four cities?

Right.

As of this morning, I've taken the liberty at added seven more. My goal by the end of the day is to have fifteen or sixteen.

Sixteen cities? he exclaimed. Yes.

That's more than I've ever done.

Correct.

You don't think that's too many?

If you're worried about Maple, I've already planned days where you fly home to check in on her. You would fly out again, of course. Collectively, it's six weeks.

Six weeks, he lambasted.

Yes.

When and where would I start?

Friday. In San Francisco.

Landon shook his head, mulling over his situation.

Danielle came in with a pitcher of water. She crossed the wide floor space, her nude heels soft along the rug. She filled Landon's glass and placed the pitcher at the center of the table.

Thank you, he muttered.

My pleasure, Danielle replied. Can I get you both anything else?Another coffee, please.

Same, Dolores said.

Of course.

Danielle slinked out, closing the door behind her.

Tell me something Landon, Dolores said earnestly.

He leaned back and looked at her.

I noticed something unsavory after I read your book.

Unsavory?

Yes. I'd say you didn't seem particularly thrilled when you were finished. I know you're never one to be over the moon about such things, but I always saw a hidden sense of prideful accomplishment when you did. Even though your novels don't bring much in terms of sales, they continuously receive generous amounts of praise.

I thought you had a question.

My question is, why did you turn in a book without your heart in it? It's a fine enough story but a far cry from the last two. It's puzzling.

He sat silently for a long time, listening to the light ticking from the desk clock on the other side of the room. The traffic seemed to have grown louder.

Landon?

He looked at her.

I'd like an answer.

He cleared his throat. I just wanted to be done with it, he muttered.

What?

I said I just wanted to be done with it.

Done with it? Dolores said, confused. What do you mean?

I lost interest. Towards the end I—

You lost interest?

I couldn't think of an ending I was satisfied with.

I'll agree with you on that, she said, adjusting her blouse. You ended it like a fairy tale.

You're disappointed in the results, is that it?

Disappointed is a word for it.

Sorry, he mumbled.

It's alright dear, she said, waving of her hand. I think if we give it enough head traction we can still see positive enough sales before the critics have their way with it.

Is that why you want me on the road for six weeks?

If we're to have any luck selling this one, yes.

Landon nodded.

Tell me something else, if you don't mind, Dolores asked, sipping her water.

Yes?

For all those months you told me you were almost done, had you actually been sitting on the completed manuscript? Hoping to never send it to me?

He ran his hand through his hair, crossing his legs.

Yes.

Why did you not contact me for help?

I don't know.

Dolores hummed to herself.

He waited. A lump of immense uncertainty, hard in his throat.

She sat there, studying him.

What are you thinking about? Landon asked, hesitantly.

We may need more cities.

He hired a sitter to stay at the house and tend to Maple, leaving her a list of numbers to call in case of emergency. The refrigerator was stocked, and he told her to save any receipts upon his return. He gave Maple a massive marrow bone and a long embrace.

The machine spat the ticket out. He tossed it over the dash and proceeded to search for a vacant spot in the expansive, populated lot. He parked the truck, got out, slung the leather briefcase over his shoulder dropped the bed door and retrieved his navy suitcase and set it on the ground and extended the handle and latched the rear and engaged the locks and headed to the nearest bus stop.

He got through security quickly, dodging the morning rush. He made his way through the terminal, breakfasting at a small Mexican cantina, waiting for the nearby newsstand to open.

The clerk unlocked the gate and slid it overhead like a garage door. Landon perused the shelves of new releases, classic literature, newspapers, magazines. He read the back of Michael Crichton's newest novel, The Lost World. Nicholas Evans, an author he'd heard about from Dolores, had finally released The Horse Whisperer. He picked it up, read the back cover twice over, and walked to the cashier.

The book swayed inside the white plastic bag as he made his way to the gate.

He was halfway through Evans's book when the plane touched down on the San Francisco runway. He'd forgotten how frightening it was to land in the Bay Area, since all you saw until the last forty feet was water. He bookmarked his page with the receipt and returned it to the bag.

His suitcase came, he hailed a cab.

They drove haphazardly through the morning traffic. Horns and sirens blared down the 101. Motorcyclists weaved between vehicles like stuntmen. The driver muttered curse sunder his breath while Landon continued his reading, avoiding all conversation with the man. The car crawled down Market Street towards Kearney. Landon watched a homeless woman walk lackadaisically through a green traffic light, screaming at whoever dared sound their horn at her. They turned on Sutter and worked their way towards the Francis Drake Hotel. The driver slammed into park while they were still moving, causing his passenger to fly forward.

Sorry, he grumbled.

Landon got out and was greeted by a man in a ridiculous beefeater coat.

The driver sat the bags on the bellhop's polished brass cart and snatched the tip from the passenger's hand on his way back to the cab and closed the door and sped into traffic.

The hotel was luxurious. Ivory marble columns with stunning gold archways and wrap-around leather seating. Obsidian granite. Tall white chairs and low sapphire loungers. Extravagantly hand-stitched carpets and rugs adorned each room. Crystal chandeliers coruscate against the brass light fixtures, flashing cameras of newly acquired tourists. Men bantered at the bar, drinks in hand, at lips, empty, asking for another.

A receptionist called him forward with a welcoming smile. He gave her his name and affiliation. She plugged the information into her computer, confirming his stay. She scanned two keycards, slid them into a sleeve and handed him the small manila envelope. She turned to the bellhop, and gave him the room number.

Landon looked over the lobby once more before ascending the fine carpeted steps to the second floor to catch the elevator.

The small brass box on his door beeped as the lock disengaged. The temperature was set to an inviting 72 degrees. A king bed with white linens beckoned to Landon as he closed the door and looked about the room. He placed his briefcase on the floor, and put the plastic book bag on the walnut varnished dresser. Over the desk, hung a large canvas of a weeping soldier, English in origin. He sat on the bed and removed his shoes, observing the painting for some time. He crossed to the window and peered down onto Union Square. High enough to not hear the traffic banter below.

A knock came on the door.

He opened it to find the bellhop with the luggage cart. The bellhop smiled, pushed the cart in, and placed the bags as directed.

Staying long? the hop asked.

Just the weekend, Landon replied, watching the two bags being carefully placed on the luggage racks.

First time in the city?

No.

Want some advice?

Okay.

If you see lines for the small joints, go there. Best food in town.

I'll keep that in mind, he said handing the hop a ten-dollar bill.

Thank you, sir. If there's anything else you need, or want to know the real good places in town, dial nine. Ask for Mister Collins.

Alright.

Have a pleasant stay, sir.

Thanks for the bags.

Of course, sir. Of course.

The bellhop pulled the cart into the hallway, closing the door behind him. His steps and the shrill squeak of the cart faded like the wind.

He opened the drawers and set his clothes in and hung his dress shirts, jackets, and pants in the closet. The honey hued toilette bag gave the alabaster bathroom a decadent splash of color. The digital clock on the bedside table read one in the afternoon. He retrieved the book from the bag and collapsed onto the bed, the covers wafting in response. He turned, set the alarm for two hours, opened the book and picked up where he left off.

When he awoke to the alarm's irritating frequency, it was from a heavy sleep that caused him to slam the alarm with the heel of his hand. The book splayed prone at his feet, the pages fanned like dress creases. The room was dark. Light faded outside, the square coming alight through various street lamps, headlights.

He showered and changed into a fresh set of clothes. The citrus scent from the hotel shampoo gripped his nostrils as he double knotted his brown chukka boots. A startling growl emitted from his stomach.

A homeless man, cologne in an abhorrent scent, outstretched his mangled hand on the corner of Powell and Sutter while doling out grotesque obscenities, laced with Dijon tinted spittle.

I

The cold night was made colder by the hefty breeze off the bay. The night dwellers blossomed through rich saxophone notes. In the nooks of skyscrapers, hidden alleyways nestled with romantic dinners, sipping expensive wines, cocktails. Fashion statements from club hopping college students. The intoxicating fragrance of vodka and cigarettes.

He walked along the Embarcadero, passing boats and channel ships, lovers and artists, college students and tourists, beggars and officers, his own reflection in various art installations. Along a plot of well kempt greenery, blissed by twilight and streetlight, children and dogs scampered about, their effulgent laughter loud as they chased one another. A group of students sat huddled, easels in lap, smeared colors on wooden platter boards, cups of gray water. They peeked up at the evolving sky, studying its resplendence. The stained wooden brushes firmly held, lightly gliding. Lathering of paint, dabs of water, observing eyes. What was there? Did they know? Do they care?

On the outskirts of AT&T Park, tucked away on a narrow side street, was the growing line towards a small bistro. He crossed the road at the stoplight and inserted himself. By the time he arrived at the hostess desk, the line had rounded the corner.

The restaurant was quaint, comfortably seating a little over forty guests. Dim lumens in austere fittings of brushed black brass. Dark leather booths, chairs and stools. White tables. A cool breeze. The staff looked like floating heads in their dark slacks and dress shirts. Their trays held bowls and plates of translucent plumes of succulent odors.

Good evening sir, said a slim, busty waitress. Her hands crossed behind her, standing tall and prim. Have you dined with us before?

No, answered Landon. First time.

Well, we're glad to have you. Here's our menu, she handed him a thin paper pamphlet. What can I get you to drink?

Your recommended bottle of red.

Very good, sir. I'll give you a few minutes to browse and be back with some water.

Thank you.

She turned the red wine glass on the table over and took the white as she departed through the tables.

He browsed the menu, reading the options in the low amber light. Muttered conversation filled the space. Slow classical music played quietly overhead. White napkins in laps, like flags of surrender. The menu featured a prefix. He read it several times over, convincing himself that that was the better option.

She returned with a small glass of water and a bottle of 1987 Sauvignon Blanc.

Landon looked over the label and smiled. Very nice, he said. Thank you.

Of course, she replied.

He slid the glass towards her.

She produced a corkscrew from her back pocket and, with little effort, twisted, turned, and popped the cork. She held the purple stained stopper to her nose and respired deeply. She nodded and splashed the glass. Landon clasped the stem and swirled the wine under his nose. He sipped, savoring it wholeheartedly and swallowed.

Good? she asked.

Very.

She smiled and poured the glass full and placed the bottle on the table.

How do you see in here?

The waitress laughed. You get used to it after one or two slip-ups.

How many have you had?

Slip ups?

Yeah.

I think four.

He chuckled and sipped the wine. Are you visiting or new to town?

Visiting. For work.

What kind of work do you do?

He picked up his water glass and drank. Warm, slightly metallic. I'm a writer.

You're a writer? she exclaimed.

Yeah.

What do you write?

Novels.

I

Anything I would have read?

I'm not sure. Do you read?

I do, she giggled. Not as much as I'd like, but I get through one every once in a while.

Well done.

A loud shrill combusted through the room. Hysterics from a nearby table.

So, what can I get for the writer? she asked.

Do you recommend anything specific, or should I do the prefix?

The prefix is really good. We're trying it for the first time this weekend.

Perfect. Prefix it is then.

Very good, she softly replied, taking the menu, flashing a smile in her departure.

The meal started with a pleasing chartreuse spinach and pea soup with a crème fraîche swirl. The spoon split the smooth texture like fine, whipped butter. He poured his glass full, then corked the bottle as she brought out a plate of scallops. Plump. Brushed with fire. Drizzled with a citrus ginger garlic sauce, the color of daffodils. The pearly meat glistened in the steam, like balefire in a dense fog. Ripe lemons, bite of ginger, coating his tongue in a buttery crescendo. A sip of wine interlude, an exhale of ecstasy. The entrée was an immense, spice encrusted New York strip steak topped with bleu cheese and garlic herb butter. Caramelized braised carrots and asparagus.

Another? the waitress said, pointing to the bottle.

Please.

She smiled and poured the remnants into his glass and departed with the empty bottle.

The steak bled thickly scarlet upon first cutting. He bedaubed the piece in the topped mixture and ate. Charred, ripe garlic licked his tongue as he chewed.

She returned with a fresh bottle, opened it, and poured.

How is everything?

I don't think I've ever had a steak this good before. She

laughed. I'm glad to hear it.

He nodded, sipping his wine.

I hope you left room for dessert.

I'm sure I'll manage to find some.

He sopped the remaining juices with a wedge of pumpernickel and ate, leaving the plate close to clean.

Dessert was a flawless segment of cheesecake, raspberry drupelets orbited like moons. She handed him a small fork. Landon delicately carved from the rind. He slid the shaving into his mouth and chewed with closed eyes.

How is it? she asked.

Indefinable.

Good.

Would you like a piece?

We're not allowed.

Are you sure? he said, waving his fork at her.

I'd love to but can't.

Shame.

He cut another small bite and ate.

After a while she brought him the check. When he opened it and scanned the bill, he noticed the cake was missing. He finished the wine and left the largest tip he'd ever done and signed the receipt and closed the leather pamphlet. Beneath the receipt was a folded cocktail napkin. He opened it, turned it over and read: *Wait for me,* in red ink.

She'd told him her name, but he had long forgotten it since they'd ascended the grueling hills. When he asked her again she laughed.

Her apartment was loudly bohemian. Several conflicting units of furniture, artwork, decorations. Odor of burnt incense. Beaded doorways. A small bookshelf fetched his eye. He walked over, bent to one knee, and read the spines. She offered him a glass of water, to which he obliged while taking rest on the lapis couch.

Nice place, he complimented.

Thank you, she said, pouring his glass.

How long have you been here?

Almost two years.

Is the rent good?

I

It's fixed. Got a decent enough price for it. The owner's old school. Not many of those left in the city.

I bet.

She walked over and handed him the glass.

Thanks.

You're welcome.

She walked into her bedroom and started to change.

A faint metallic aftertaste. He wiped his lips with the back of his hand, catching sight of a light ruby hue streaked across the top. They'd fissured from the sharp bay breeze, the brittle pain made him wince.

Do you have any chapstick or lip balm? he called out.

Yeah, she replied. Hold on.

She emerged, wearing only a teal bra and panties. Her hair was long and messy down her ivory back. The muscles popped and faded with each strut. Her breasts shook with each step and with each step he couldn't take his eyes off her.

She opened a drawer and tossed him a tube of Burt's Bees.

Landon caught the tube unblinking as she crossed back to her room, a small grin along her lips.

Forward, he muttered to himself, uncapping the chapstick and rolling it across his lips.

The head shop window with neon lettering shone brightly in his eye while he held her tightly against the brick with his body. Her breath hot down his throat. Four legs in spasmodic thrusting twitches. Cool pats of sweat where their thighs hugged. A mulberry welt at the top of her breast, misshapen and margined by teeth, where he loved her too much. Remnants of Dior perfume on their tongues.

By the time they arrived at the third club, it was two in the morning. Freshly groomed bartenders in bespoke vests with rolled sleeves and dark slacks were showcasing their mixology skills in a barrage of movements. Like some celebratory tribal worship to an unknown deity. They danced while they drank from thin straws. The flashing pink and purple lights stirred recollections of alleyway copulation in their minds and soon were at it again in the bathroom. She saw someone she knew over the stall wall and said hello.

They summited Sutter street, arriving at the Francis Drake. He fumbled in his inner coat pocket and handed her the spare room key. I'll be there shortly, he said. She threw her arms around his neck, pulled him into her, and kissed him inclemently on the lips. Her tongue circumnavigating in wild circles. When she turned and walked inside, he wiped the gin infused slobber from his mouth with the back of his hand.

Lori's Diner was loaded with drunken college students and early morning tourists. Waitresses garbed in 1950's uniforms strutted with large trays of food. A bright red jukebox playing Elvis Presley's Moody Blue album. Black and white checker tile, dusty and heel scuffed.

Landon plucked a plastic menu from the holder on the counter and scanned the breakfast options. The waitress walked over, caught his musty scent, winced, asked what he would like, listened, scribbled the order on a notepad, tore the sheet, and stuck it beside the fellow slips on the cook's silver merry go round.

About fifteen minutes, hon, she said through cheap scarlet lipstick. Thank you, he replied drunkenly.

He sat in front of a glowing dessert case, mesmerized by the cake's hypnotic revolutions. Wedges of chocolate and carrot cake. Their frosting dry and cracked.

A man in the corner snored loudly, his ticket slip dangling from dirt riddled fingertips.

All of a sudden, he heard a shouting match outside. A young couple, a tall brown-haired man and a short blonde woman, both fancily dressed, trudged up the street. She darted into the road. He grabbed her, lifted her flailing body off the ground, and set her on the sidewalk. They exchanged vulgarities, slurred and incoherent. Halted traffic blared their horns in long drones. She turned and swore at the drivers as the frazzled man tugged her along the sidewalk, continuing their intense charade up Sutter street, until they were gone from view, but not from earshot.

She answered the door in her light blue bra and underwear, her dirty blonde hair furled like a mane. He placed the food on the dresser, then was turned and thrown onto the bed.

He rose five minutes shy of eleven. He looked around the room through painfully dry eyes. The waitress, along with her belongings, was gone. Dregs from the opened breakfast platter scattered atop the dresser. He turned to see a napkin and an uncapped pen bearing the hotel's insignia on the bedside table. He reached over and picked it up. On the napkin, scribed in broken cursive, was her phone number, and the message: *Thanks for the breakfast.*

He'd a pot of coffee delivered to the room. The tray came with two mugs, a bowl of brown sugar cubes and a small porcelain carafe of fresh cream. He sat naked at the table overlooking Union Square, sipping quietly, watching the city slowly come to life.

The San Francisco Book & Stage Company had been a city staple since the early fifties. They were known for showcasing local writers, poets, playwrights and artists. A quaint bookstore occupied the first and third floors. On the second, was a fifty-seat black box theater. Every two to three weeks, they showcased a guest that would draw a lot of buzz for the company, and for the local talent. Today, it was Landon Cassidy.

He opened the shop door to the intoxicating fragrance of mold and vanilla, a pair of looming oak columns, shelves upon shelves of classic literature and rare prints. He browsed the shelves in a slow two step, his mouth slightly agape as his eyes read off the works of all he'd read in the past.

Then a voice called out his name.

Landon turned to see a tall old man approaching. He smiled through an alabaster mustache, wearing a burgundy button down tucked into a pair of baggy Gap jeans. A pair of white New Balance sneakers. The old man embraced his guest, then shook his hand firmly.

We're thrilled to have you with us today, he said.

Mister Samuels, I presume? Landon said.

Yes sir. Andrew Samuels. But you can call me Andy.

You have a beautiful place here Andy.

Thank you, he chuckled. It's been in my family since the doors opened. We had a lot of good writers came through here. Founded a few great 'uns too.

Is that right?

Yes sir. But none you've heard of I'm sure, he laughed.

Landon nodded. So how are we doing this today?

Follow me.

He led him up the stairs and through a hickory varnished archway into a small theater. There were five ascending rows of ten black cushioned chairs. On the stage stood a podium, a black chair. The stage lights beamed in a reverenced glow.

We're expecting a full house, Andy said. Then standing room till we can't keep the doors shut.

Sounds good, Landon replied.

The signing will be upstairs. We cleared an area out for it.

Landon nodded.

You hungry?

I could eat.

They sat and ate bloated burritos outside a small Mexican cantina tucked on the corner of Kearney and Pine. The line was full of businessmen and women out on their lunch break. The four-person team behind the counter moved orders along as if they'd trained in the same position all their life. Outside, pigeons flapped and huddled for scraps. Loose napkins wafted away on rogue gusts. People stood and shot pictures at the intricate entrance of Chinatown, while stagnant traffic inched along the thin singular street.

How is it? Andy asked.

Good for a downtown burrito.

I've been coming here for years. Seen a lot of establishments come and go in this area. I would've never thought that this one would stick around. Not sure how they do it, with the rent increasing each year and all.

It's prime location too.

Sure is.

They ate and watched the line slowly dwindle.

How do you all stay in business? Landon asked.

We take advantage of certain tax breaks, Andy replied. For years we weren't. Then I hired this smart girl who knows about that sort of thing. She was flabbergasted when she found out I wasn't privy to them. She's saved us thousands each year. So, with the influx of independent authors that we advertise, it gives us the cushion to keep the doors open when nobody wants to buy books. Computers are taking over thanks to the boys over in Silicon Valley. I'm not sure what will come when that fateful day rears its ugly head. We got close to calling it a day a few years ago. We made this big announcement, stating that the business was to be sold. But when word spread, the community stepped in. Authors we've hosted, and ones we've never heard of, donated. Then came the tax breaks. Rich philanthropists from all over the Bay Area pitched in because of that. Turns out, a lot of people love our store. More than I ever thought. They're the ones that saved us. Now they donate annually. All in all, it's been quite humbling.

That's incredible, Landon said.

Andy nodded and bit into his burrito.

Are there many other bookstores in the city like yours?

Not as many as there once was, Andy replied. More used bookstores are closing their doors each year. Its the electronic book plague that's taking over. More and more books are being accessible, for cheap I might add, on little tablets. You can carry a whole library in your back pocket. I know print wont go out of style, but bookstores will definitely feel the brunt of it.

I hadn't thought about that.

Can't fight that kind of progression. If you try, you're wiped out before you can take up arms.

Landon thought about this, looking aloft towards the passing traffic.

During their absence, a line had formed around the store, some of them hugging Landon's new novel. Most, his older works.

After shaking their hands and exchanging small talk, he headed through the archway and onto the stage, eyeing a crisp copy of his new book. A red page maker peeked from the top. He looked towards the stadium seats. The black carpet separating the rows. He listened to his loud and hollow footsteps echo off the wooden stage. He smoothed out wrinkles on his shirt, turned, unbuckled his belt, unzipped his pants, tucked his shirt anew, zipped up, and fastened his belt. He crossed to the podium and picked up the book. He examined it closely, then held it to his nose. His fingers fanned the pearly pages as he inhaled deeply. He did this several times, unaware that Andy was watching him.

Are you ready, Mister Cassidy? Andy said from the archway.

Landon turned, smiled, and nodded to his host.

The auditorium was enveloped in myriad colors, clashing fragrances. He waved to the smiling, giddy faces. The seats were filled within minutes with faces that reminded him of a Guess Who game. After thirty minutes, Andy shut the doors. Then walked on stage and stood behind the podium, calling for silence. The attendees policed one another as they giggled into placidity.

Ladies and gentlemen, thank you for coming out this afternoon to see our featured author, Mister Landon Cassidy.

They applauded.

After reading his first two books, I knew that we were witnessing the emergence of a special kind of talent. A talent that the literary world has already begun making way for. A talent that each of you have witnessed through the beauty of his work.

Applause.

When we reached out to Mister Cassidy's publisher with the interest to host him whenever the chance should occur, you can imagine how floored I was when I received the call about booking the date. There are many authors writing today that I enjoy, as I am sure you all have your favorites, too. But there are seldom authors I believe in. Those whose work does something to you. That as soon as you lay the cover shut, you sit there, marinating. That is what Mister Cassidy's work does for me. And with that, it is my honor to present to you, the newest voice of modern literature, Mister Landon Cassidy.

The crowd erupted to their feet in applause.

Landon stood and embraced Andy. He crossed to the podium as Andy exited the stage.

Thank you, he said.

The crowd's applause quieted after another minute, amidst the shuffling of reseating.

Thank you for that great introduction, Mister Samuels, he repeated, clearing his throat. He poured a glass of water from a pitcher, drank, and set the glass beside the book. He opened the book to the red marker, looked into the crowd, and smiled.

Good afternoon.

The reading lasted twenty minutes.

When he closed the book, the room was deafened by applause. Andy retook the stage and announced that the Q&A would begin in ten minutes, followed by the book signing.

Bathroom lines materialized within seconds. Ubiquitous conversation reverberated along the walls. Several guests purchasing copies of his new book, ready to be freshly signed. The horde began to make their way back to their seats,waving to Landon as they passed.

The theater doors shut. All vocalizations faded into tranquility.

After the talk concluded, he made his way to the first floor. Landon sat at the table and laid his head on the cool surface. He was clammy all over, the adrenaline countering the hangover began to dissipate.

Are you alright? A voice asked.

He looked up and saw Andy standing at the top landing.

Yeah, Landon replied. A little dizzy is all, but I'm fine.

I'll bring you some water.

Thank you.

He did not know when he drifted but when he opened his eyes, Andy was placing a glass and water pitcher on the table. Landon thanked him and drank. The water was cold and refreshing.

Are you ready for them? his host asked.

Landon nodded, finishing the water.

Andy crossed the floor, descended the stairs, and instructed the crowd like a school teacher. One by one, they crossed the wide space awaiting their personalized messages, the author's signature. The pen died with seven people to go. He rifled through his coat pocket, producing an old, short ivory fountain pen. He twisted the cap free, securing it in his opposite hand. The ink flowed black and brilliant. He closed the last cover and set the pen down and massaged his stiffly, clawed hand. The front doors shut. Murmurs of the outer world beyond the walls. A dissipating silence settled in. A long sigh drained from his lungs. He leaned back, shut his eyes and was almost asleep when he heard Andy's voice echo from below: You hungry, Mister Cassidy?

They hopped on the cable car at Post Street, made their way portside, and hitched a hand to a hanging leather loop for support while children cheered and laughed each time the car darted downward. Landon's stomach tickled as it did when he was a child swaying on the swing set. He closed his eyes and felt the gravitational metronome shift through his body, the evening's breeze twirling his hair. The car's wheels whirred in their slots. Contained currents clicked and snapped along suspended wires. Pleasant bell chimes, signaling their crossing to busy intersections, waving bystanders. The tinted windows reflected the fading sun's amber glare, as they snaked towards Fisherman's Wharf.

They left the station at Beach and Hyde and walked along the tourist littered sidewalks, discussing the works of Conrad and Melville. A chrome painted man moved robotically among myriad spray paint artists and their crude celebrity canvases, slipshod self portraits. A drummer bashed fractured oak branches he trimmed into crude drumsticks over worn and stained plastic buckets like some tribal being free from whatever shackles contained it, conducting a melody egregious and alien to any all musical worlds save his own. Landon watched these theatrical movements like a scientific observation before walking on.

They came to the crest of the industrial district, where a peculiar shack stood. Andy led his guest passed the quarter mile long line towards the hostess stand, and waited.

He watched the mountains across the bay blacken against the ruby skyline. The vast establishments across the shoreline sparked alight one by one. Alcatraz ferries carrying the day's final passengers back from their guided tours.

Can I ask you something, Mister Cassidy? said Andy.

Sure.

Do you think the book will do well?

I

Landon began to turn then stopped. A light sigh vented through his nostrils before he returned his gaze to the flexing and straightening waves. The hostess appeared, crossed their names from the reservation list and escorted them through the ten-table shanty and sat them at a rickety table balanced by a thick cardboard cutlet. The chairs were dull, black paint faded to pewter. The floor had several open knots that you could fit your heel through. Aged splotches of ominous liquids. Loud conversation. He refrained from thinking how the kitchen must look based on the appearance of the dining room or, for that matter, the establishment as a whole. The sound of the kitchen erupted beyond the swinging doors. Shouting and order announcements. Silverware clanked against cheap China plates. Bowls rustled atop one another as a busser cleared a table into his bin.

A waiter, hickory skin,black shirt, slacks flecked with white clam residue, arrived at the table with two waters. The hair greased back, shiny and flat. Once black shoes, now filthy, as if he'd trekked days through ancient clay, mires of another world.

Good evening gentlemen, said the server in a heavy Spanish accent. How are you both doing tonight?

Great thanks, Andy said. We know what we'll have to drink.

Landon chuckled.

The waiter plucked a small crumpled notepad from his apron. The pen fell from his hand. He bent down and scooped it up and wiped it on the stained apron. What can I get you both?

A bottle of the Napa Valley Chenin Blanc, two glasses. And sixteen oysters.

Perfect. I'll get that out right away.

The waiter turned and disappeared behind the kitchen doors.

He forgot the menus, Landon said.

Andy tossed his hand in the air, dismissing the comment.

Landon drank.

You're not allergic to anything are you? Andy asked.

No.

Good. Leave the ordering to me then.

I take it you're not new to this establishment?

I come here on special occasions. It's harder to get a reservation these days.

It seems like they do well, Landon said, observing the scene around him.

You saw the line, Andy said, nodding to the entrance. It's like that from lunch till close. Open four days a week, and one of those is dinner only.

When did you first come here?

I don't know. Late eighties, perhaps. One day the place was just here. No big announcement, no newspaper ads, nothing. Word of mouth was the only way people found out about it. And since then, it's been the best seafood in the city.

I'd never have given this place the time of day myself, Landon replied.

Never judge a book by its cover, Mister Cassidy, the store owner said with a sly grin.

Touché, he laughed.

The waiter returned. He set the wine glasses on the table and displayed the wine bottle to Andy.

I ordered it without looking, didn't I? he said with a whiff of sarcasm. Almost as if he was trying to be rude but failed to commit to it.

The young man quickly retrieved the opener from his apron and slid the sickle-shaped foil blade free with his thumb and rounded the tip, blooming the foil. He carved it away and sheathed the cutter and sprang the boot lever, erecting the worm. The point punctured and spiraled into the cork. He twisted till the lever sealed over the lip and dropped the crank onto the groove and gave a hard thrust and popped the cork free. He sniffed the purple belly and splashed the glasses and stood at ease.

They picked up their glasses, swirled the wine, brought it to their noses, and inhaled. Decadent notes of charred woods, black currant, dark chocolate. They sipped and exhaled as if taking a breath of untainted air after months underground.

Andy nodded to the waiter.

The young man poured the glasses full and set the bottle on the table. He twisted the cork from the corkscrew and placed it next to the bottle and returned to the kitchen.

Landon raised his glass and offered a toast.

Wait for the oysters, Andy stipulated.

He laughed and put the glass down.

The waiter returned with the tray of oysters. He arranged a small silver stand in the center of the table and placed the tray on top.

I'll be back to take your orders, he said, doling out two small plates.

Thank you, Landon replied.

Andy picked up his glass. To your success Mister Cassidy.

And to yours, Mister Samuels.

They touched glasses and drank.

Andy took the oyster fork and stabbed the lemon meat, bleeding it generously over each oyster. The air between them filled with citrus. He did this with the remaining segments then cast them aside, took up Landon's plate and placed three plump oysters on it and handed it back and laid three on his own. They sprinkled globules of scarlet cocktail sauce over each, then sucked them clean. They were silky and fresh and not too cold. Lemon juice tinged their tongues while the cocktail sauce cut the saltiness into a pleasurable sweetness.

Like clockwork, a runner carrying a black tub emerged from the kitchen doors. He hurried to a table, sat the tub down, flung the silverware in, glassware, plates, napkins, and sprayed the surface with a yellow disinfectant and wiped it dry with a moist gray cloth from his back pocket and replaced the cloth and picked up the tray and vanished behind the kitchen doors as the hostess seated the next couple.

The oysters were picked clean in a matter of minutes.

The waiter returned for their orders.

How were they, gentlemen? he asked.

Incredible, Landon said.

I'm glad to hear it. What would you both like to order next?

We'll have two bowls of chowder, Andy said, followed by a platter of fish and chips. Afterward, we'll have another bottle of wine, and then we'll order some dinner.

The waiter chortled and cleared the table.

Landon studied Andy as if he were some malnourished cretin. He sipped his water, pinching the corners of his mouth afterwards. Giving me the full tour of the menu? he said, putting the glass down.

You have to try it all, Andy replied. You never know what tomorrow may bring.

How true.

They traded stories and jokes while slurping chowder and feasting on a large platter of beer battered cod. It was late in the evening when they ordered a bottle of Riesling with dinner. When they paid, they were the only ones left in the restaurant.

Outside, the wind had picked up. They walked two blocks before Andy hailed a cab. The car sped hastily up the high hills while the two men laughed and made small talk with the driver. The cab pulled up to the hotel and Landon paid the fare.

They sat at the hotel bar, drinking Old Fashioneds, and trading heavily opinionated viewpoints on the state of southern Gothic literature.

This was the best night I've had with a guest speaker in a long time, Andy said, swirling his glass.

I appreciate that, Landon replied. It's been fun.

Should we toast to it?

Isn't the drink itself celebratory enough?

Andy laughed, picked up his glass and drank.

They shook hands and parted ways shortly after midnight.

When Landon emerged from the elevator, he took his steps slow through the hallway. At some point, his shoulder collided with the wall. He felt nothing. Do Not Disturb hung from the doorknob. He removed the place card and examined it, trying to recall when he had put it there. He rifled through his wallet, spilling crumpled bills, old ticket stubs onto the floor. He dropped to one knee and picked up the contents and the key card and slipped it in the slot till the green light glowed and opened the door and entered while stuffing his belongings back into his wallet.

I thought you'd never come back, said a soft voice.

His tired eyes shot up to see the waitress from the previous night lying in one of his large gray night shirts on the foot of the bed, twirling the remote control with her fingers.

How did you get in?

The waitress pointed to the other key card on the nightstand.

I still got your key, she smirked. Remember?

He stood and closed the door behind him. He retrieved his belongings from his pockets and almost put them in a plate of food scraps.

Did you order room service?

You were taking too long.

I didn't know you were going to be here.

That's no excuse, she chuckled.

It's late. Don't you have work or school in the morning?

Tomorrow is Sunday. We're not open Sundays.

Landon groaned as he slunk onto a chair. He loosened his shoelaces and tossed off the shoes with a violent flick of the ankle. They clattered woodenly against the wall. Then he staggered to his feet and crossed to the bathroom, shutting the door behind him.

She laid there thumbing through the channels, but nothing caught her interest. She heard the hissing water through the wall, his inebriated groaning followed by the metallic slide of the shower curtain. She tossed the controller on the bed, swung her feet to the floor, and walked into the bathroom.

Steam layered the windows. Landon's clothes sat in a pile as if he'd been spirited away. His tan silhouette visible behind the curtain. She hopped onto the sink and sat with legs crossed, watching him. After a long while she said: So, you leave tomorrow?

Landon recoiled as if sucker punched, almost losing his footing. He flung the curtain back and stuck his drenched head out.

What are you doing in here? he exclaimed.

Sitting here, the waitress replied. Asking if you're leaving tomorrow.

He rolled his eyes and shut the curtain.

Yes, at one, he answered.

Want to do something?

What?

I said did you want to do something?

Something? With you?

Yes.

Like what?

How about breakfast? Or we can walk around town.

I think in my current state that may be too much, Landon groaned. Then we can do something close by.

He didn't answer.

Scalding hot water rained over his pounding head. From how much the room moved, he knew that if he were to lay his head on the pillow in the state he was in, he'd wretch. If he stayed in the shower until the spins stopped, he would be able to sleep. He turned off the shower, sat, activated the bath spigot, and turned the water temperature with his foot. His drippy eyes stared transfixed on the rising waterline, the steam engulfing his perspiring body.

Are you alright? she asked.

Landon turned, lifted his arm and swung the curtain open again.

The waitress sat as before. Her emerald panties shadowed by her opalescent thighs. A seduction he wanted no part in.

What are you doing in here?

She laughed, clapping her hands like a toy monkey.

He came out an hour later. The waitress lowered the television volume as he sat on the edge of the bed, rubbing is temples.

How are you feeling? she asked.

Slightly better, he moaned.

She crawled towards him and ran her fingernails across his back.

That feels good.

Good, she whispered. How was your day?

You mean yesterday?

Yes, she chuckled, yesterday.

Fine.

I'd say more than fine.

Why's that?

Well, you told me you had a big turnout at your reading. That you met some nice people. Then you went down to the warf and had a nice meal, followed by drinks at the bar.

When did I say all of this?

When you were in the tub, she laughed.

He groaned, leaning against her.

Are you alright?

Is there a menu still here?

Yeah, hold on.

She rolled off the bed, he fell back. She slid the menu out from under the plate, pulled Landon back up, reclaimed her position, handed him the menu over his shoulder and went back to running her nails across his back.

Can you hand me the phone, please?

She leaned back, picked up the receiver and handed it to him.

He dialed the front desk. The dial tone sounded once.

Front desk, the receptionist answered.

Hello. Can I get three eggs, three sausages, three pancakes and rye toast delivered to my room, please?

Of course, sir. Which room?

Fifteen two.

Right away, sir. It will be up shortly.

Can I get you anything else?

A pitcher of cold orange juice and a carafe of black coffee would be great.

Of course, sir. We'll have that right up for you.

Thank you.

Have a good night, sir.

He handed her the receiver.

She hung up.

Oh, did you want anything?

The yolks were the color of sunflowers. Wafts of buttery steam filled the room while he ate. Plump sausage links exploded as he cut into their casings, spurting sage scented juice onto the plate. Centered on each of the pancakes was the square impression of the where the butter once laid, now a pool that leaked across the rounded surfaces. He cut each piece ravishingly and dunked it in the cup of maple syrup and ate.

I don't think you have enough butter on anything, the waitress said, biting into a slice of rye toast.

He snickered, pouring their cups full with the remnants of the coffee.

They laid gossiping till the sun rose.

When he awoke, she was not there.

He ate a large breakfast in the dining room in the clothes he slept in. Onlookers eyed the disheveled looking young man. Hunched over, eating like a prison inmate. The waiter brought a third cup of black coffee. Once it cooled, he drank it in three large gulps.

After along cold shower, he gathered his belongings and headed downstairs and checked out at the front desk and waited for the next yellow cab. Waiting under the awning, he saw the shouting couple from the first night at the corner. They were holding hands and laughing. She leaned her head on his shoulder. He canted his head onto hers and kissed it. The traffic light changed, and they crossed the street and went into Lori's Diner. A cab pulled in. They were only a block in when he saw the waitress fidgeting with her purse. Her hair was freshly curled and she wore a pair of sexy black heels. She retrieved a tube of lipstick and started applying in on her way to the hotel. He lowered in his seat as the cab rushed past.

He hiked with Maple along the Pedernales river. It was cool and the wind was calm and gusted in rapid intervals. Squirrels darted across the trail head, flinging their tawny furred bodies onto thick oak trees, twisting up the trunks onto the myriad branches overhead. Juniper shrubs, laden with sapphire berries. They came to the falls and set their belongings down and waded into the shallow river. Maple splashed upon the pebbles and gray shale. The water flowed clear into the pool. He palmed the water into his mouth, over his neck and head. It was very cold. He sat there looking across the silvery landscape. The cry of a warbler, though what direction he could not gather. He laid on the warm stone and dried in the sun, Maple by his side, panting happily. He reached in the bag and pulled out a turkey BLT and unwrapped it and shared it with Maple and listened to the calm babbling of the river. Sparrows and scrub jays spoke along the overhead airwaves. They stayed all day, drinking from the falls, watching the sun touch the oak and pecan spires.

He heard the phone outside the front door. When he answered it, the voice of Dolores Stemper spoke on the other line, requesting his presence.

Will speak more once you arrive, and that was all that she said.

At noon the following day, Landon Cassidy took in the sun-drenched streets of NoHo. Historical brownstones, black trim and masonry designs from a time when pride instilled everyman's work. Heavily modified housewives, walking with their girlfriends and children, large Starbucks drinks accessorizing each of their hands. Luxury vehicles, all shapes and sizes and color, aligned the curbs. Pretentious bistros and bars, filled to the brim with loud chatter and low hanging melodies. He came to her address and knocked loudly.

Dolores opened the door and gave him a tight hug and kissed him on the cheek. He could smell the fresh scent of gardenia upon her neck.

It's wonderful to see you dear, she said. Please come in.

The brownstone was beautiful for the exterior did not showcase the immensity of its insides. Vibrant white walls lined with priceless art pieces, tasteful nude images. Potted greenery on thin dustless wooden bookshelves. Hand-stitched Italian ivory furniture intermixed with Fisher-Price toys, Lego blocks. Freshly polished marble floors. Sun beams illuminated the staircase, accentuating the gold twisted railing up the four floors to bedrooms and offices. An immense Swarovski crystal chandelier gave off the impression of icy stalactite.

Dolores led her client to the kitchen, where Viking stainless-steel appliances greeted them. She pressed a button on a small panel and an elaborate trapdoor unlatched. She opened the door and he peered into her vast wine cellar.

I'll get us something to drink, she said, descending the steps.

Landon sat at a small table nestled between three towering windows. He looked out at the luscious gardens in the backyard. Tamed and tapered pink and scarlet rose bushes, stems long, hybrid breed, the thorns thick with intimidation. Alabaster lilies with mustard anthers. Bird houses on low hanging cherry trees, their watermelon petals spotting the fine Kentucky bluegrass. Alive to the tune of bee humming.

Where's the family?

Work and school, Dolores replied, from the cellar.

He nodded.

Do you have any preferences?

Whatever you like.

Oh, then we'll be here all day.

He chuckled.

Dolores emerged with a of 1990 Pinot Grigio on the counter and closed and locked the cellar door. She brought down two wine glasses from a glass cabinet, uncorked the bottle and poured the glasses full, crossed to the table and sat.

Here you are sir, she said, handing Landon a glass.

Thank you.

Cheers.

Cheers.

They touched glasses and drank.

How is it? she asked.

It's good. Refreshing.

Dolores nodded.

I'm glad you were able to come on such short notice, she said after a brief pause.

Sure thing. What did you need to see me about?

We had a meeting about you the other day.

Who had a meeting?

The company and myself.

Landon sat the glass down. About what?

After inquiring about the potential sales of your new novel, we're not seeing the increase of interest we were hoping for after the tour, which, don't get me wrong, you conducted very well. We thought by adding more cities would draw more readers. But, after speaking with various critics, they confirmed our suspicions.

Suspicions? he said, setting his arms on the table with grave earnest.

What suspicions?

That the book will flop.

Flop?

I'm afraid so.

You're serious?

Based on the statistics, yes.

Dolores took a long drink.

Landon was in a boxer's daze. He knew the book was not his best, but he never thought it to be a commercial failure. Most of the book was good, he thought. It was written during a short stint on the Amalfi Coast, after his second book went on a two-week run on The New York Times Bestseller list, garnering several Critic's Choice awards.

So, what does this mean? he asked.

Well, cards on the table. We just signed a slew of new writers these past couple weeks. We're going to give them a try.

That's it?

I"m afraid so.

That's some business model you got there. Cash in on the virgins.

I'm sorry Landon, but sometimes that's how it goes.

Yeah. That's how it goes.

He looked down at the table and rapped on it twice with his knuckles. He leaned back in his chair, sliding his palms down his face.

When are you releasing me?

End of the month.

What about my non-compete?

As a courtesy, and we don't do it for everyone, we'll rescind it. You'll be free to do as you please.

Lucky me, he scoffed, picking up the glass. He threw back the wine, swallowed without savoring out of spite and set the glass down.

How do I get paid?

Same as before. Nothing changes on that end.

Even the new one?

Yes.

Alright.

For what it's worth, they wanted you gone after I told them of my trepidation. But I was able to negotiate the non-compete in your favor.

How noble of you.

I really am sorry, Landon.

Everyone is until they're not.

Parfum de Page was housed in an old library that was stripped out and rebuilt in the early seventies. Cherry polished pillars greeted you upon entry. Swedish cut glass encased various rare and special volumes, both foreign and domestic. Reclaimed tobacco pine from decimated libraries in southern France served as the club's flooring. He perused the aisles, gazing upon the time scarred spines, titles and authors faded. He ascended the burgundy carpeted stairs to the lounge. At the head stood the check-in desk. An elderly man, liver spotted and pot marked by recent chemotherapy treatments, leaned over the desk in his newly pressed burgundy jacket and black slacks. A tremulous smile grew across his lips.

Good afternoon sir, the clerk said. Are you a member with us?

One way to find out, Landon said, sliding the black membership card from his leather wallet.

The clerk shot him a concerned look, taking the card. He opened the heavy ledger, checked his name on the card again and turned to the correct page for his name. His scrawny, crooked finger jittered down the list of names.

Found ya, he said.

Landon nodded.

The clerk pulled out a small gray box, fitted with a black card slot and two, small round lights. He turned the card over, checking the magnetic strip on the backside, then inserted it into the box.

They both waited.

The button flashed green.

I guess my canning hasn't gone into full effect yet, Landon muttered.

Sir?

Nothing. Thank you.

Enjoy your visit, sir.

I

The clerk handed the card back to Landon, and he walked onto the club floor.

The walls were lined with emerald wallpaper. A bar sporting the finest liquors and spirits. Several hand-stitched leather loungers populated the floor, all adorned with hickory lacquered tables. A sprawling fireplace, hand laid by a prominent New York masonry firm, had a short flame whisking about in its contained quarters. A large table of older men and women sat, speaking in secretive whisper sat the far end of the room, glasses of Irish whiskey perspiring in their hands. Landon walked to the bar and ordered a Scotch with a water back. The bartender nodded and fetched down a bottle of Dewar's 18. He set the glass on the oak bar and color edit with the amber liquor then splashed it with the water nozzle. Landon grabbed the glass, thanked and tipped the bartender and scanned the room for a spot he could be left to his thoughts.

The pale, thin linen curtains flapped mutely from the light breeze that slithered in from the cracked window. He sipped the whiskey, then set it on the nearby table. He walked to the window, held the curtain and watched at the traffic below.

By the end of the hour, the lounge was occupied by loud conversation. Writers from all over the city sat or stood with one another, discussing topics about which Landon had no knowledge of knowing. He ordered another whiskey, nodding to the other gentlemen at the bar. When he turned and started back to his seat, an old, ruggedly dressed man occupied the chair adjacent.

Hello, Landon said, approaching.

The man looked up and smiled. His azure eyes glowed in the retinas as thick crow's feet trailed into his hairline. He wore a burgundy button-down, faded blue Levi's, worn Lucchese boots, dry dirt on the heels. His cowhide leather jacket looked like something from an old spaghetti western.

I hope you don't mind if I sit here, his voice, rough like sandpaper, deep with age.

No, Landon replied. Not at all.

Thank you.

He sidled past the old man and sat back in his chair. He sipped the whiskey then leaned forward and placed it on the table while pilfering a glance at the old man.

It's been a long time since I've seen the city. Not much has changed.

When were you here last?

The old man tilted his chin towards the ceiling as if the answer was there. Nineteen-seventy.

That's a long time.

The old man turned and looked at him. Yes, it is.

Are you here long?

No. I head out tonight.

Where to?

Maryland.

That's not too long a flight.

No. Are you from the city?

No. Texas.

The old man's placid face turned to interest. Texas? Whereabouts?

Outside Austin.

Which direction?

West.

The old man lowered his head.

Landon watched the old man map out the coordinates in his mind. As if he himself were the architect of that land.

Johnson City?

Too far.

Oh, he said, lifting his head up. You're out in Dripping Springs.

That's pretty good.

The old man chuckled and shrugged. I was born in Marfa. I frequented Austin when I was a boy.

Marfa's out there.

It's as out there as it gets.

What brings you here?

To the city or this chair?

The city, Landon laughed.

Conference and conversation.

I see.

You?

Same.

How did you fare?

Not as well as I'd hoped.

How's that?

New book wasn't to their financial liking. Let me go.

I'm sorry to hear that, said the old man sincerely.

Could be for the best.

The old man shrugged.

How was your visit?

Fine.

No bad news?

If there was, it wasn't labeled.

Landon nodded.

He picked up the glass, sipped, then returned it to the wet ring it bore.

Why was your new book not any good? the old man asked.

A cavalcade of reasons. I should've told them I was going to shelf it and work on something else but I didn't have the guts to tell them.

Why not?

I wish I knew. I've always been this way when the stakes are out of my reach. But I try to get them anyways.

The old man hummed.

Landon felt a sense of unease waft over him. He looked over his shoulder and saw the conversations from other parties quieting. Their eyes fixated on the old man. Their lips moved, but heard no sound. When he turned back, the old man was looking out the window again.

What's the matter? the old man asked.

People are looking at us.

The old man looked and studied the room beyond them. His twinkling eyes roved to and fro.

You're right, he said, returning his gaze out the window.

Why?

Why what?

Why are they looking at us?

Beats me.

The old man eyed his companion's glass.

I'd venture to say that they're wondering why I'm speaking with you.

What?

I said they are probably wondering why I am speaking with you, the old man repeated.

I don't understand.

Me neither, he shrugged.

Landon picked up the whiskey and drank.

Are you afraid?

Excuse me?

Are you afraid? repeated the old man.

Of what?

Of what comes next.

He turned to the young writer.

Landon didn't answer.

The old man nodded.

I'll be okay, Landon murmured.

I wish I had your hubris when I was in your position.

What position is that?

The one right before the end of the world.

Landon fell silent.

I need to be getting on, the old man said, rising to his feet like an old marionette. He extended his hand and exchanged a firm handshake with the young writer. It was nice talking with you, Mister Cassidy.

Landon studied him quietly.

The old man smiled and nodded then crossed to the stairs, his boot heels falling heavily as he grabbed the railing and descended out of sight.

I

A chalcedony twine veiled the dark from the horizon. A faint rustle played amongst the trees. Flocks of Canadian geese slept like fat khaki eggs along the dew drenched grass. He dried the bench with his coat sleeve and sat. The coffee was hot and good. He peered at the blended buildings that bordered the park, their assortment of lights winking out as the sky ripened. The geese woke, barked, and shook spasmodically. Mocha beaks clapped at the lawn. After taking flight, their languid formations coasted along the brightening sky, ebbing beyond the tree line.

Landon watched the red lettered Delayed blink on the departure board. After looking out the gate window for the plane that would not arrive for another two hours, he began to walk the terminals, searching for an empty gate. Passing hordes of foot traffic, lost children, rolling luggage, he sought refuge in a terminal bookstore. He read over the new James Patterson novel, almost purchasing it. He bought a pack of Extra Original bubblegum, broke the wrapper, and slid out two sticks. Eventually, several gates cleared, the area vacant. He found the furthest corner away and sat in the window. Southwest, Virgin America, United Airlines drove around like some surrealist's rendition of a bus route. The planes sped down the runway, ascending into the sky in five-minute intervals. Different designs, same models. He pinched the bridge of his nose and massaged his eyes. Sudden whispers in his ear. No one around. Dolores Stemper's face flashed into his mind. Her gardenia scent returned in his nostrils. An image of his book aflame, the name charring in hot curled black. Then he lowered his head, and wept.

II

The following year he leased his house and moved into a small apartment in South Austin. He edited resumes, polished training manuals and simplified telemarketing scripts. Collection agencies phoned daily, sometimes as late as 8:00. There was no new story, no written word. Maple became twenty pounds heavier from inactivity. Veterinary bills piled up, all past due. One night, he found that a squatter had defecated and made artwork of it on the building wall. There was no new story, no written word. Every month a check from his book sales would arrive, enough for rent. Sales were lucrative, but would not last. Towards the end of the year, he started receiving rejections from the limited writing jobs that hired him. Tasteful replies stating lazy results, delayed deadlines. Eventually, proposals ceased altogether. His lease was terminated after the new year. They left Austin in early February.

The horizon set ablaze by the waning sun. Maple explored the plains on long, endless roads alongside her silent owner. They slept in the sheltered truck bed, huddled against one another under heavy blankets, among food wrappers and plastic water bottles. There were no night travelers. A flawless silence in an alien world. When the sandstone dawn appeared, he'd dig a hole, squat, and bury his business, a souvenir to remember him by. Neon illuminated roadside diners served their nutritional needs. Prying eyes from the morning's disheveled over their fried eggs and toast. At gas stations, he refilled the water stores and purchased assorted snacks. Mr. Goodbar. Payday. He cleaned himself in truck stop bathrooms with paper towels, keeping an eye on the pallid light below the locked door. Outside of Nashville, he purchased a small blue journal, a dozen Ticonderoga pencils and a box of straight razors. In the evenings, he'd lay on the hood of the truck and sharpen the pencil with the razors and set the razors back in their small sliding case and write about the world in which it was presented. Dreams, story ideas, words he'd heard that day. Maple laid across his lap, eyes aflutter as guttural snores escaped through her muzzle. One night on the border of Tennessee, he awoke to the deafening cries of brood cicadas. He dropped the truckbed door and slid out half-naked and peered into that endless dark. There was no moon to light the land. And nothing moved. From then on he would awaken each night and peer out into the dark to see what might call. He read over what he'd written in the dim overhead light and tear the pages from the spine and crumble them and break the pencils and walk out into the caliginous fields and dig a hole and bury them, cursing the onslaught of words in his head. Screaming in slurred prayers for all to stop. They were somewhere in West Virginia. National preservation country. He huffed the air, a lungful of soaked brown pine. He wrapped the blanket tightly around his shoulders and sat with his feet dangling, drinking the bitter lukewarm coffee from the steel enamel mug he purchased and filled at a 7-11 earlier that morning. He watched a gray fog drift along the tree spires. An arid moisture caused the blanket to stick to his backside. He studied his bearded complexion in the reflection of the coffee. He looked at the battered notebook and considered writing down his observations. Whispers cautioning him of the fallout. Movement through the trees. Shadowed shapes. He massaged the side of his head with his palm. Thunderheads formed far into the distance. Brief pangs of lightening. The wind communicated its ferocity by way of the veering forest. He sipped his coffee, watching their approach.

The next day the truck gave out.

He thumbed a ride for an hour before getting picked up. They watched the state flash by from the bed of a silver Toyota pickup. The day was clear and cool. His long oily hair, and wiry thick beard flapped against the wind. Maple's head leaned over the side, her jowls thick with drool. When they came to a stoplight, he felt slightly nauseous, as if he'd been thrown from a roller coaster. The driver dropped them off at a repair shop in Frederick. He thanked the man and tried to pay him but would not accept his money. They watched him drive out of the parking lot and pull away and out of sight on that busy strip of asphalt.

The mechanic behind the counter appraised the haggard man upon arrival. Pungent scent, clothes wrinkled and licked with dirt and grime, facial hair wild and matted. The dog sitting alongside him, feral with tired red eyes and hot breath, looked up at him with large brown eyes.

Does she bite? the mechanic asked.

No. She's a good girl.

The mechanic nodded. What can I do for you?

My truck died a ways out.

How far a ways out?

On three forty. Outside Jefferson.

Make and model.

Chevrolet. Red. Single cab.

Alright.

The man picked up a pen and wrote down the location on a yellow pad.

Anything of value in the truck? he asked without looking up.

No.

Is there a number I can call after we diagnose the issue?

When do you think it'll be in?

Should be by the end of the day.

I'll come back then.

The mechanic shrugged.

Leave the keys on the counter and take out whatever you wish to keep on your person.

An hour later, Landon came upon a creek, and followed it to an expansive, lush park. The grass had been cut early that morning. Teams of mallards floated along like paper boats. Gated tennis courts with all the nets utilized. A dry, leaf clogged community pool. A bell signaling the half-hour. They followed the sound to an alabaster brick tower, as if drawn by some phantom frequency. Amidst its beauty, he found it out of place.

They continued along the creek, walking the brick pathway that fenced it, occasionally spying multitudes of marigold Koi that swam beneath plump lily pads. He untucked his journal from the rear of his pants and took note of the sight. Passersby sped past him with their heads down, eyes affixed upon distant subjects in order to avoid contact with him.

On Market Street, all was quiet. He heard the wind blow between the brick buildings. Flags bearing the state insignia ruffled from the light posts. Painted murals along the alleyways, a man with angel wings. They crossed the narrow street to a coffee shop in its final hour, where he helped himself to pastry remnants and lukewarm coffee from the self serve. He filled two cups and bagged a cherry Danish and blueberry muffin. They ate on the stoop, watching the traffic go by. A young woman with an enormous nose piercing smiled at him, dragging her dog along. One of the bakery workers brought out a steel bowl of water and set it beside Maple. She lapped it dry before the door shut, then laid on the cool concrete. Slow strings of Bach wafted from an open window over the adjacent toy store. He listened for a long time before making his way up the street.

A small bookstore caught his eye. He peered through the windows, scanning the newest releases, colorful notepads, leather-bound journals, flat packs of writing utensils, stands and shelves of paperbacks. The tiny bell overhead chimed his entrance. A tall, portly man stood erect, the underside of his gut peeking from beneath his black striped shirt. He had thick glasses in thin frames, and was badly balding.

Good morning sir, he said with a slight lisp.

Hello, Landon replied.

Can I help you?

Just came in to browse.

The portly clerk nodded.

Alright. Let me know if you need any help.

Thank you.

Maple sniffed the air, strolling down the short walkway towards the back wall. A castle entrance cutaway. Children's books inside. A semicircle with three plastic chairs in yellow, red, and blue. A tie-dye bean bag chair. Maple smelled the air again, then plopped down in the center, exhaling loudly.

He set the coffee and pastry bag on the window lip and looked through the books on display. There were authors he'd never heard of, nor subjects he cared for. Town history, cooking, politics. A small staircase led him to a wall of classics. A thin smile crept across his lips as he read titles from Hemingway, Melville, Shelly, Nabokov. He passed his fingertips across the spines, feeling their virgin smoothness. The sparse mystery and science fiction section was a surprise. Stephen King, Arthur C. Clarke, others he couldn't have cared less about. A cardboard stand that housed employee recommendations through phrases like: Dave's Fav or Sophia's Choice. He was returning to the entrance when he saw it. Nestled under the checkout counter, among a random assortment of books by random authors in random genres, comedic calendars, religious self help, and five-cent bookmarks, was two copies of *Sandstone Harbor*, his new novel. His eyes studied the gaudy Halloween orange lettering of his name. Untouched, minus the exception of the hand that had placed them there. He lowered and slid one of out, stood, and stared at the softcover, the lifted texture of the title. A solemn smile formed on his lips as he brought the pages to his nose, flipped them with his thumb, and inhaled its fragrance. The clerk watched him.

Sorry, Landon laughed embarrassingly.

That's alright, the clerk replied. I do it too.

I wrote this.

What?

This, he held the book to the clerk.

That came out a while ago.

I know.

Are you a local author?

No.

Did you want to buy it? Landon laughed.

The clerk gave him an odd expression.

I could sign it for you. And the other one, too. Make a little more on it.

That's alright.

Really?

Yes.

Alright, he scoffed, taking one last look at the book before replacing it.

He whistled for Maple and she sprang up and trotted down the aisle to him. He grabbed the coffee and pastry bag, opened the door, glanced toward the books, thanked the clerk, and walked out.

They were sleeping under the eaves of cherry blossoms when the bell tower harmonically sang from several blocks away, then chimed four times in long pangs as three o clock struck. The shadows had waned, the sun white under their lids. He wriggled, stretched and yawned widely. His back throbbed from the hard earth. He pulled out his wallet from his back pocket, counted his bills, and rifled through the last four months of uncashed checks. He tallied their totals in his head then tucked them away and slid the wallet back. They wandered south of town, inquiring about the local banks. Within the hour, he cashed one of his checks for four hundred dollars. The money came in a clean white envelope. He slid the money into his wallet and balled up the envelope and tossed it into a waste bin outside a vermilion structure shaped like a barn, the pale trim long faded into a deep beige. He studied the structure, engrossed by its charming demeanor. He held the door for Maple and followed.

A small grocery with walls the color of buttermilk. Long hazelnut beams strung across the high ceiling. A makeshift café, tucked in the corner with two unoccupied, mustard colored tables. On a counter ledge sat three percolators containing the morning's coffee dregs. A wall of freezers with bags of ice, vacuumed sealed cuts of meat, cartons of locally sourced eggs. At the back was a trio of men assembling sandwiches on an assembly line, reading tickets from telephone orders. A young woman with pumpernickel skin and long brunette hair answered the endlessly ringing phone. She wore a long, plain black shirt that covered her jean shorts, elongating her thin toned legs. He was privy to the judgment in her greeting as he closed the door behind him. The sandwich menu was painted on a long wooden board that hung from the ceiling on thin silver wire. He saw the outline of dust creeping over the top edge as he read the options. A paper sign taped to the glass shielding told customers that all orders were to be made and paid at the cashier. He stood and watched the young woman scribble an order on a mangled yellow receipt pad, announce the pick-up time and replace the phone on the receiver.

You ordering something? she said, irritatingly.

I'd like a large and small cheesesteak, Landon replied.

She bent over and wrote down the order.

Anything else?

He scanned the aisles, walked over and grabbed bag of Utz potato chips and two bottles of cold water and placed them on the counter.

She rang up the items.

He handed her twenty dollars.

She made the change and dropped it into his palm, making sure not to touch it.

Thank you, he said.

She nodded.

He slid into one of the booths and slapped his journal down on the table and propped his feet on the adjacent chair. Maple walked over and laid on the cold linoleum tiles. He pinched the Utz bag with both hands and opened it to the smell of freshly fried potatoes. A chip fell and bounced off Maple's head. She sniffed it, then chewed as if it were scorching. He poured a pool of water into his palm and held it to her snout to lap dry, then dried his hand on his pant leg.

The wait made him drowsy. His head bobbed back and forth until he involuntarily rocked himself to sleep.

He awoke ten minutes later to the sound of the door opening. An elderly man came in. The sun flared, obscuring his features. When the door closed, he had disappeared behind the aisles. The man's boot heels were slow and hollow against the wood flooring. One of the sandwich makers greeted him, but he couldn't make out the somber tone of the customer. He rounded the nearest rack and came smiling towards the cashier.

Hello dear, the old man said.

How are you doing, Mister Granger? she sweetly replied.

Landon rubbed his eyes and stared at the old man. He wore an evergreen button down with dark faded jeans, calf hide Lucchese boots, the soles dusted with gravel. A camel suede bomber jacket. He spoke in a low droll to the cashier for some time. Trading laughs, town gossip.

Maple sneezed.

The old man turned and saw the disheveled man sitting at the table, the dog at his side. Bless you, he croaked with a smile. He paid the girl, held his palm supine for the overage, and slid the coins into his pocket. He sat at the table across from the man and leaned back and folded his hands in his lap. The only sounds were the hiss of steam under chopped onions and the murmur of passing traffic outside the wall. The phone at the cashier rang.

Landon's gaze never left the old man.

Can I help you?

You're much older than when we last spoke, the old man said.

The young man's eyes widened.

Yes, he smiled. Under all that long hair and scraggly beard. The dirt. The grime. And your querulous scent, I remember you.

And I you.

The cashier brought their sandwiches and placed them in front of the men.

Landon broke the beige tape strip and unfolded the thick deli paper. The cheesesteak was soft, glued to the bread. The inexpensive chopped meat and provolone oozed from every side. Shards of white onion and hot shriveled peppers were interwoven in a saporous harmony. He took an enormous bite, then hurriedly unscrewed the water bottle and drenched the fire setting his mouth ablaze.

The old man laughed.

What are you doing here? Landon strained.

Having lunch, the old man replied. Same as you.

Right.

I live here, remember?

He paused, chewing, recalling their exchange those years ago.

The old man chuckled then bit into his hoagie. He chewed close to the table, not allowing any juices to spill onto his shirt. He wiped his lips with a napkin then sat up.

Who are you? Landon asked slowly.

The old man cleared his throat. My name's Harrison Granger, he said, wiping his lips with a napkin. And your name is Landon Cassidy.

How do you know that?

I asked the bartender when I first saw you. He took another bite.

Bartender?

In New York.

Why did you ask about—

Are you going to eat?

Landon looked past the old man's shoulder, locking eyes with the cashier. She jerked around quickly, shifting her attention to something he couldn't see.

Their hoagies have a splendid oil and vinegar blend, but they never tell me the formula, Granger said.

Landon bit into his cheesesteak, thinking about how long he'd been on the road. How he picked up all that was needed and leaving without thinking twice. Thwarting reality long enough for it to only catch up with him in the end. He thought about the truck. The repairs. The cost. The checks in his back pocket were getting smaller and smaller. He'd been lucky thus far with Maple staying healthy, but how long would that last before he couldn't provide for her anymore? Where did the road lead to? Paradise? Oblivion?

What's that? Granger interrupted.

What's what?

The old man pointed to the notebook.

Landon looked at the oil stained notebook on the table.

A notebook, he said.

May I?

He picked up the journal, stood, reached across the table, and gave it to his inquisitor.

The old man set the notebook on the table, wiped his mouth with a grease-soaked napkin then daintily opened to the first page and read silently. He flipped through the pages in a silent, rhythmic fashion.

This is quite good, he said.

Landon took another bite and chewed.

The doorbell rang and a man entered and hurriedly picked up his order and paid the cashier and was gone before the jingle could finish.

Might I ask you something? inquired Granger, closing the notebook and sliding it aside with delicate care.

Sure.

How did you come about being here?

Truck broke down.

Truck broke down?

Yes.

Where?

Outside Jefferson.

Really?

Yeah.

You didn't walk into town, did you?

No. Thumbed a ride with a guy who took us to a mechanic.

Where's that?

Where's what?

The mechanic.

A few miles from here.

Did they say when you get it back?

No, Landon said. He's supposed to call me when they get it in later today.

When will they do that?

We're heading back after this. No other way to know unless I'm there. No phone?

No. No phone.

Maple had sauntered over to the old man during this exchange. He leaned over and patted her on the head, her black slouched ear perked with delight.

This' a good girl you have here, Granger said.

Thank you.

How bout I give you a lift back?

Where?

To the mechanic. We can see what he says.

We?

Yeah.

I don't think that's a good idea, Landon mulled.

Why not?

I'm filthy, for one.

Granger laughed.

And second, he paused, thinking of another excuse. She's filthy.

Granger laughed again, waving the comedian off with the back of his hand. Finish your sandwich and I'll meet you outside.

He stood, balled the trash together and tossed it into the waste bin and turned and picked up the notebook and slid it next to the dirty man and traded farewells with the cashier and headed out the door in the same blinding white flare he'd entered with.

Outside, parked around the corner, was a cherry red 1975 Ford Bronco with white trim, 31-inch tires. The engine, a prowling six-cylinder Ford Coyote with a 2.9L Whipple supercharger. Polished silver bumpers and chrome exhaust. Chestnut brown upholstery. No watermarks. No blemishes. A tall, slender man with brushed silver hair, gold-rimmed aviator Ray Bans, navy plaid shirt with rolled sleeves and blue jeans, was leaning against the brick, newspaper in hand. Landon observed a pair of leather driving gloves waving out of his back pocket. A faded Marines insignia tattooed along his forearm.

This is Ben, Granger introduced. My driver.

Ben looked up at their approach.

Who's the vagrant? he inquired, rolling up his paper.

A castaway.

Is that right?

Landon introduced himself and exchanged a firm handshake.

What can we do for you, Mister Cassidy? the driver asked bluntly.

The auto shop on the mile, Granger said. His truck is there.

You want to drive him there?

Is that a problem?

Ben eyed the vagrant.

Do you want me to put a blanket down?

They pulled into the auto shop parking lot. Landon looked around and spotted his truck. The trio parked beside the sad looking single cab and got out. Axles look alright, Granger observed aloud. He kicked the tires, and stood pondering for a moment. The other two in attendance stood behind him, waiting. He slowly went to his knees and looked under, his head swiveling in study. He stood and brushed his jean legs and walked to the front of the truck and stared with pursed lips then turned and headed inside. The others followed. Maple laid on the cool leather with the windows cracked and the air condition blowing, fading fast asleep.

How can I help you, gentlemen? the mechanic asked as the party entered.

My truck was brought in earlier today, Landon said. The red Chevrolet.

The clerk looked out the window, stared at the truck for a moment, and nodded.

Oh yeah, he said. Transmission's shot to hell on that one, unfortunately.

Swell.

New one'll cost you around three grand. With the cost of labor, you're looking in the range of five altogether. Not including tax.

He rubbed his eyes, letting out a long sigh.

How long can she sit here? Granger asked.

Depends on what you want to do with it, the mechanic replied, shrugging. We can keep it in the lot for a few days, but after that, we'll have to move it somewhere in the parking lot. It wouldn't be under our protection anymore, it'd be subject to fines or impoundment.

Can I sell it? Landon asked.

You got a seller?

No.

The clerk studied the haggard man, theorizing his status in the world. He removed his smudged glasses and pinched the bridge of his nose, massaging his eyes.

I could ask around, he said. See if anyone's interested.

Thank you.

Do you have a number I can call you at?

My driver will write one down for you, Granger interrupted.

Alright.

Thank you, Landon repeated.

Sure thing.

After they made it back to the Bronco, they realized he was not with them. Granger turned and saw Landon Cassidy standing alone in the lot, the gray sky beyond him, a cool breeze wafted his long hair as if he were afire.

Where are we going? the young drifter called out.

The old man glanced at Ben.

Ben sighed.

You're coming with us, Granger said.

Where?

My home.

Why? You don't know me.

Granger approached the man, his hands tucked into his pockets. He stood before him canted to one side. A gentle, thin smile across his lips.

To know thyself is to know the world, he said. The terminus that stations our choices only harbors those previously mapped. You think you're in uncharted waters, but you're not. Far from it. You're simply aboard a vessel beyond your comprehension. The fog will part, the sky will clear. But in order for you to see the sun, you must pick up the oar and ferry forth.

Landon thought about this, then nodded.

Gather what you need from the truck. We need to be on our way.

He unlocked the Chevy and gathered clothes and other assorted belongings. He gave one last look around, recalling the moment his father gifted him the truck upon graduating high school. Then closed the door, locked it and walked to the Bronco and got in.

The Bronco roared to the tunes of Waylon Jennings. The supercharger hissed and wheezed in peculiar intervals. The radio crackled as the frequency thinned through the thickening trees. A sleeve of 8-track cassettes rested beside Granger's leg. Vibrant shades of evergreen and umber swathed in every direction. Long curvatures of road where further away stood grand houses with tamed acreage. Sprawling farmlands. Grazing livestock. Garish gates with fictitious family insignias. The remnants of a house, blackened by blaze decades before. The skeletal struts stood splintered and soot-stained over piles of gray, charred wood. Packs of white-tailed deer grazed along the side of the road, their heads snapping erect to witness the growling truck pass by. They pulled up to a large metal gate, fairly new. The dashboard clock read 5:20. Ben dropped the visor and pushed a small gray button on a black box clipped there. The gate slowly opened. As Ben put the car in gear, Landon saw the sign warning away trespassers.

The sun blinked behind brushstroke clouds. A black paved road wove like a serpent through the dense forest. Browned maple leaves with crab curled edges tapped across the asphalt. Ben slowed the truck as they came upon a small cobblestone bridge. Moss etched bracken. Light poured through tightly packed crevices overhead. The creek, merely a glass fissure among pebbles and mud and shattered slate. Landon looked skyward to view the silver backed elm leaves. Their thick rustling scintillated like emeralds. Deer bounded far into the thickening distance. Granger switched off the radio and worked the window crank, dropping the glass. He reached out, parted his bony fingers, and glided his hand against the wind. They listened to the timbered dialogue. Crimson cardinals and navy jays and blackbirds and carrot-chested sparrows fluttered across the branches, giving chase to one another. And giving chase to nothing at all. He inhaled the cool mountain air. Wet and earthy. Maple lifted her head and peered at the glistening foliage. The trees thinned. A clearing formed. Landon leaned forward and gazed upon the breathtaking spectacle.

Welcome to my home, Harrison Granger said, smiling.

The ranch sat in the middle of the clearing. Mountains sheathed in cobalt lie westward. A large brick house centered around a gravel road, orbiting like Saturn's ring. The pathways were lined with yellow and white daisies. Towering sunflower fields plotted throughout the land, tenanted by brown belt bees, hummingbirds, tiger-striped monarchs. Rich oak and cherrywood buildings, barns. A stout windmill gracefully rotating on the breeze. Structures barn shaped, an expansive livestock pen. The horse stable was unlike anything he'd ever seen before, the mammoth size of it.

As they drove in, a white fence showcased the vastness of the horse grounds. Miles upon miles of summer green fields. Studs and mares, prancing freely in patterned coats foreign to Landon's knowledge. A lake reflected the peach glow of the postmeridian sky. They circled the road and parked in a large garage.

Good driving Ben, Granger said.

Ben chuckled as he shut off the engine. He got out, rounded the front, and helped Granger down.

Thank you, Landon said.

You're welcome, Ben replied.

He gathered Maple and placed her on the ground. She whiffed the air and ran to look about. He shut the door and stood outside and listened to the quiet and watched the wind bend the grass. Distant horse cries. Ranch hands eyeing the foreigner in passing. Their clothes stained in patches of sweat and dirt. The gravel crunched and rolled underfoot.

Granger came up beside him and patted him on the shoulder.

Care for a shower?

The water turned black beneath him. The soap bar looked like a hunk of coal as he scrubbed himself incessantly. His fingers became entangled in his long, knotted hair. After five minutes, the water finally ran clear, and he smelled clean for the first time in months. He palmed the steam from the glazed mirror. He opened a drawer, a razor, a pair of hair clippers, a can of Barbasol. Tufts of facial hair slowly twisted into the small trash bin he'd wedged into the sink. He set the razor to warm in the torrid pool he'd collected in the bowl. A hiss of air, a cough of foam. He lathered his face with the mint-infused cream. The blade left clean streaks of bare skin after each pass. Menthol stung the fresh cuts along his neck, his cheekbones. He repeated the process in the opposite direction, wiped his gaunt face and slapped on a palmful of aftershave. The comb tugged at his knots. After he got each strand unfurled, he cut the split ends with novice fragility, pleased to see his entire face once again.

Folded on the bed was a fresh outfit: navy button down, jeans, white wool socks, a used pair of Tecovas. He opened the door and peered down the hallway to find who'd left them but nobody was there. He dressed and checked the musty cedar drawers, the closets. All were full of clothes. He measured them against his chest, his legs. A few ran slightly bigger than his current, withered state, but for the most part, they would fit.

The bed was soft, with a bevy of creaking from its oak frame. Adorned by a thick maroon comforter. A small desk by the window overlooking the ranch. He headed down a long corridor of rooms. Small chalkboards hung by the doors, most of them erased with dusty residue.

One read: *Chambers*. Another: *Staff.*

The main staircase led to a large living space that looked like something out of a hunting lodge magazine. Leather sofas encircled a large stone, soot-stained fireplace. Fresh cedar logs stacked in a pile of pewter ash. A set of brass pokers at one end. Identical, round tables. Mocha lacquer, the sun's fading incandescence illuminating the wooden striations. A deck of cards on one, poker chips on another. An oak-varnished pool table, the balls resting triangularly at the emerald felt center. Racks of half a dozen cue sticks, tipped with various levels of blue chalk. The bar on the far wall contained liquor and spirits in assorted states of consumption. The kitchenette and pantry were clean and newly stocked with dry goods.

Outside, the windows winked alight. A blue hue emitted beyond the jagged horizon. Birds in black silhouette traversed the sky, vanishing from sight. Cricket chirps and insect cries. Sound reminiscent of Louisiana bayous. He made his way to the immense ivory house, his feet loud across the hollow porch. The front door opened and shut behind him. Laughter and conversation reverberated off the walls. French designed light fixtures illuminated the rooms. He peered into the living room. Long chocolate-leather settees with accompanying armchairs and ottomans under a crystal chandelier. The wall wide fireplace's dim flame pirouetted over the quartered oak logs. A long black table, ornamented with a yellow humidor, the color of daffodils. Thick exposed beams loomed overhead like the ribs of a great cetacean. Further down the hall was a lavish spiral staircase, looping three floors aloft. Detailed carvings of forest wildlife etched by austere hands. Almond polish, vanilla redolence. The walls were lined with pictures, some with frames, some without. All shapes, all sizes. Histories from dim memories. Do we remember these occurrences? When the details fade, what purpose do these happenings yield then?

Their conversations fell silent when he walked in. A room full of strangers looked up at him with bemused eyes. Granger at the head. Platters of pork chops, bowls of green beans and buttery mashed potatoes and sweet carrots, towers of cornbread, boats of umber gravy, steamed corn on the cob. They smiled in various forms, then beckoned him to sit. Maple walked person to person, scamming scraps with her bright brown eyes and hot breath. The men laughed and slid her bits of pork, salted green beans.

How do the clothes fit? asked Granger.

Fine, thank you, replied Landon, sitting down. How did you know my size?

I didn't. It's the staff house. Most of the rooms are stocked with outfits because the men work on rotating shifts. It's a useful system that saves the expense of luggage.

What happens when the guy comes back? Landon inquired.

Jorge may not come back. Sick mother. We'll figure something out if he does.

Alright.

Granger introduced him to the ranch staff. Most spoke Spanish, but understood English fairly well. They shook his hand and inquired about his occupation as they ate and listened to his story.

An older woman, hair pinned up, pursed pink lips, accompanied by an older gentleman with short, gray combed-over hair, entered through the kitchen door. They wore white dress shirts and dark slacks, and moved with rapidity to remove the empty place settings. The older woman returned, filling glasses of water, inquiring about drink requests.

Red wine please, Landon said.

What kind? she replied sternly.

Whatever's open.

She scoffed and exited.

They can make you a cocktail if you like, Grayson said.

Wine will be fine. Thank you.

He ate as if there were no tomorrow. The man beside him said to slow down, ensuing laughter among the others.

The food is incredible, he complemented, wiping his mouth.

Thank you, Granger replied.

How long have you been here?

A little over fifteen years now.

What is it you do, exactly?

Granger chuckled.

Qué es lo que no hace? said one of the men.

The men laughed.

What did he say?

He said what do I not do here, Granger replied.

Ahh.

We can discuss that later. But for now, please enjoy yourself. Eat and rest. You've traveled some distance to be here.

Wherever here is.

Granger smiled.

The moon cast a pale glow across the fields like a burning spotlight. The black trees swayed against the atramentous sky. Beyond the faint rustlings, silence mastered the land. He descended the front porch steps with the workers, eavesdropping on their mumbling Spanish. Maple followed in a bloated saunter. Granger behind her.

I'd say she's plenty full, he laughed.

I'd say you're right, Landon replied.

The old man leaned against a pillar, stuffing his hands into his back pockets.

Thank you. I You sleep in as long as you need.will.

Tomorrow we can have our discussions.

Alright.

Alright.

He nodded and headed inside.

Mister Granger, he called.

The old man turned and stood erect in the bleeding yellow hall light.

Thank you. For your help today.

He chuckled. No need to thank me, son. The world has a peculiar drollery about how it goes about weaving lives into one another. You and I are together once again, contrary to mathematical oddities. That requires not thanks or forgiveness, but beauty. Let's leave it at that.

Okay.

Get some sleep. I'll see you tomorrow. He turned and closed the door behind him.

The men sat around the poker table, enveloped in a thick gray smoke.

Cigarettes flickered up and down between their lips as they spoke like fireflies attached to a string. Cigars smoldered in communal ashtrays. Conversation loud, full of jokes unintelligible to his comprehension. He circled the table, studying the men there.

Come on over, *chico nuevo,* one of them said. Pull up a chair.

He obliged, taking a chair from the adjacent table.

The man who called him over was handsome with jet black hair, walnut skin, and reeked of cheap cologne and sweat. His hands were riddled with fresh cuts, caked with coagulated blood. Scars from past trials. The plaid overcoat accentuated his squarely shaped, broad shoulders. When he looked at his cards, the thick carotid artery pulsed ominously. Smoke teemed from his nostrils as the cigarette breathed like a faint coal on the prairie.

Your name is Dominic, right? Landon vaguely recalled from dinner.

Si. Call me Dom. Everybody does.

Alright.

The men went a round tossing in white clay poker chips. Of what significance the colors held only they knew from these nightly rituals.

You want to play? Dom asked.

No, thank you. I've had a long day.

More like a long life from what you said at dinner.

The men laughed at this.

Yes, Landon chuckled. You're right about that.

One of the men omitted a card then placed the next one up, laying it next to the other three along the river. The first betting next man folded, the next tossed in a green chip. Dom and the rest called.

There's not a lot of you here, the newcomer said, observing the room.

Tomorrow there will be. We work in large shifts. Right now, there are not many horses, so we don't need as many men. But tomorrow, they'll be here, you'll see. A lot of horses show up this week.

How many shifts are there?

Two. We are the main staff so we stay permanently, tending to what needs to be done on the grounds. Repairs and such. The two rotating teams work with the horses.

How long have you been here?

Ah, mucho tiempo.

The men laughed.

I met *Señor* Granger fifteen years ago, Dom said. He was scouting for trainers in Texas. I asked a friend of mine about the man. He told me what he knew, or rather, what little there was. I called and asked for an interview. After we spoke, he hired me on the spot.

Landon nodded.

Señor Granger is a great man.

Si, si, the men muttered.

The dealer laid the final card down. Jack of clubs. The man to his right upped his ante with a blue chip. Dom raised. The next one folded. They showed their hands. Dom had three jacks, but the man across flashed a straight flush.

Hijo de puta, Dom cried.

They all laughed.

They smoked their cigarettes as the winner huddled over his winnings, drawing them in. He stacked the chips methodically, smiling ear to ear. Two of them took up their cigars and ingested a deep, long draw. Translucent smoke, hints of violet, oozed from them. The dealer caressed the cards back to the deck, shuffled twice, and slid the deck to his right for the next dealer.

What do you know about Mister Granger? Landon asked.

Many things, Dom said. *Señor* Granger is a great admirer of all that is beautiful in this world. He's a worldly man, without having seen much of it. Look around. The livestock, the buildings, the gardens, he designed them all. He speaks in poems about the trees, the wind. Words that make you question everything you know about anything.

Does he talk about writing?

No. *Nunca.* He despises the subject. We've spoken on other books, but he prefers to talk about other things.

I see.

The dealer dealt out the cards.

Have you ever ridden? Dom asked.

Ridden what?

A horse.

A horse?

Si.

No.

Well, he said looking at his cards, you will learn. I'll teach you.

The men looked up and chuckled like a clan of hyenas.

Tomorrow?

No. Not tomorrow. Later. You have other plans before we do that.

Such as?

Dom chuckled and took a long pull on his cigarette. He turned to the newcomer and exhaled slowly. You'll see, he said with a Cheshire grin.

The men chuckled again, tossing in their ante. I'd better get some sleep then.

Si.

Where will I find you?

Find *Señor* Granger first. After you speak with him, come find me.

Alright.

He stood and shook hands with the men.

They bid him a good night's rest.

Dom called out to him as he ascended the stairs.

He looked over the railing, seeing the smoke coil around poker players.

We're happy to have you with us.

Thank you, Landon replied. Goodnight.

Buenas noches.

III

He awoke at ten thirty the following morning to loud commotion on the other side of the door. He tossed the blankets aside, swung his feet over, and stood. The floor was icy, jarring to the touch. Maple peered from the foot of the bed, following him with her rich amber eyes as he shuffled to the window and surveyed the hitched trailers and horse boxes along the gravel road. Crowds of Stetson wearing men and women running in all directions, taking inventory of the unloaded studs, mares and equipment on yellow ledger pads. Granger, sipping coffee out of a silver enameled mug, stood in the company of the other owners, watching the whole ordeal take place around them.

Flawless equine purebreds of alabaster, pewter, and hickory. All led out on steel ramps onto the fenced grounds, their legs covered with thick cloth wrappings. The wranglers removed their lead ropes and slapped them on the hide. They took off into the late morning sun, their manes furling behind them like fine silk fibers, tails gliding along the wind. The handlers rested against the fence and watched the horses in blissful silence.

Landon made his way through the hordes of laborers claiming their rooms.

They regarded the newcomer with curiosity, whispering amongst themselves in languages foreign to him.

Breakfast had already been served. The older woman and gentleman from the night before were cleaning in preparation for lunch. They nodded to him as he entered.

Would you like some breakfast, Mister Cassidy? the older gentleman asked.

Yes. That would be nice.

Please sit.

He sat at the table and watched the older gentleman prepare his breakfast.

What would you like to drink?

Water, orange juice, and coffee, please.

The man nodded. He turned and opened a cupboard and brought down two glasses and a mug and opened the refrigerator and filled a glass with water from an icy cold pitcher and another with orange juice and set them in front of Landon.

Thank you, he said.

The older man nodded.

He fried up thick strips of bacon, filling the kitchen with the salivating scent of bubbling salty fat. As the bacon cooked, he opened a pantry door, retrieved a bag of Purina One, filled a steel bowl with kibble, closed the bag and set it back in the pantry. Maple inspected the bowl but made no advances towards it. She walked over, sat by the cook's side and peered up at him. He chuckled, turning the strips over and prepared the coffee.

Landon sipped from the perspiring glass.

The older gentleman returned to the bacon and clasped them with silver tongs and set them on a plate and set the plate down and cracked three large eggs against the pan and drooped the contents into the pork fat to sizzle and pop. He marinated the eggs in the oleaginous fluid with a spoon then turned them over in one motion with a spatula. Once done, he slid them alongside the bacon and dusted them with salt and pepper. He nestled two wedges of rye bread into the toaster right as the coffee percolated. He filled a cup, walked over, and set it on the table. The toaster sprung. He buttered the toast thickly, halved them and placed them on the plate and handed the plate to his guest.

This looks great, Landon complimented.

Enjoy, the older gentleman replied with a smile.

By the time he'd made his way outside, most of the trucks had gone. The hustle and bustle of the morning had died down. Tranquility had returned to the land. Granger was leaning against the fence, surveying the grazing thoroughbreds.

Morning, Landon said approaching.

Morning, Granger replied without taking his eyes off the horses. Sleep well?

I did. Thank you.

Good.

There seems to be a lot going on this morning.

Always a ruckus these first few days of every new shift. As you can see. Is this all of them? he asked, leaning against the wooden slats opposite.

Not even close.

When do the rest get in?

They will trickle in throughout the week. That's how we have to plan it. If they all came at once, it'd be hell on earth. We'll have all the stalls occupied by this time next week.

I see.

Granger nodded and spat.

I spoke with Dom and some of the others last night.

Is that right?

He seems like a nice guy.

That's because he is, the old man said with a wry smile.

He said he'd be teaching me a few things while I'm here.

Granger nodded.

Landon studied the heavily occupied fields. Do you own all these horses?

Most of em. We have our own stock that we breed with others throughout the east coast. Some even go as far as Tennessee. Sometimes owners might bring their prized thoroughbreds here for training.

Really? Landon exclaimed.

Granger nodded.

Are they all thoroughbreds?

If not, they're purebred. Mainly the mares. The finest stock.

They're beautiful, he said, watching them graze.

Yes, they are.

The horses peered up at the rustling trees. Their ears twitched as if responding to some phantom frequency. A flock galloped far into the distance, their incandescent coats uniting into one as they dwindled into the distance.

Come on, Granger said. I want you to meet some people.

A quartet of men, all in their late fifties, sat on bench under a sun-stained umbrella, glasses of lemonade sweating in their hands. Juniper notebooks and short grubby pencils, jotting notes, muttering to one another in Spanish. One chortled. Two chewed on cigars with frayed and gray smoldering ends. When their employer and the new face approached, they stood and greeted the pair, exchanging handshakes.

Good morning, boss, said a man with a long, thin graphite mustache.

How's the morning, Mister Ferns? Granger inquired.

Beautiful as the day is, the mustached man proclaimed. With weather like this, the horses will never want to leave.

The men chuckled.

That's good to hear, Granger said. Any trouble yet?

Ol' Gal was being stubborn after breakfast, but Javier got her right.

Good, good.

Granger turned and looked across the grounds at Ol' Gal. A dark chestnut mare with a long gait, muscles glistening against the sun. Her mane was the color of Hawaiian sand, resting on her right side. The ripples along her chest, legs and haunches flexed tightly with every movement.

Who's the new guy? one with a cigar asked.

His name's Landon Cassidy, Granger replied. Found em in town.

Found em? the man asked, looking at his peers. Found em doing what?

Having lunch.

The men stared perplexed at one another.

I'm a writer, the new guy explained.

A writer?

Yes.

What do you write?

Fiction. Used to, at least.

They went silent gain.

The quartet studied the gaunt, long-haired man through squinted placidity.

These men are my top trainers, Granger explained. This is Stu Redson, Javier Graves, Frank Ferns, and Todd Childress. All men I've known for years, and deeply trust.

Nice to meet you all, Landon said.

Alright gentlemen, let's get to it.

The quartet finished their lemonades and set the glasses on the table. They closed their notebooks, and slid their pencils behind their ears. Frank, a man with shoulder-length hair, thin legs, and a short gait, opened the gate for the group. As everyone made their way in, he closed and latched it behind. They walked slow and calculated across the grounds. The men opened their notebooks and shared their observations with one another, informing the old man. The horses stood obediently as the group inspected them and scribbled notes. Landon watched and listened intently. Halfway along, they came to a lake where several of the horses stood watering. As the men approached, the horses looked up and studied their movements, water dribbled in glittering flares from their rubbery muzzles. The men stopped. The horses watched them for a long time. Then scoffed and continued to drink.

How deep's the lake? Landon asked.

Not deep at all, Redson replied. Five feet at its the deepest.

Should they be drinking from it?

Why wouldn't they?

Chemicals. Or something.

We treat the water. The fish in there help with nutrients and so on.

I see.

They made it to the end of the grounds. Beyond the fence line stood the elms, the pines, myriad of foliage. The horses looked like menagerie figurines from the hilltop vantage. A caressing wind wafted through the grass as the rising sun canted off the lake's silky surface. Everyone stood quiet, lost in the beauty of that world.

Never gets old, does it gentlemen? Granger muttered.

No sir, Javier agreed with a thin and black smile, exposing the large misplaced molar. His long hair hanging down his jawline.

The others nodded.

Makes you wonder how a world exists outside this one. When all that's needed in life is a cool breeze, the scent of the woods and the sight of those horses. Running.

They returned to the bench. The men sat as before, opened their notebooks and resumed their scribing.

Granger turned to Landon, I'll meet you in the stables in ten minutes.

Alright.

Granger headed into the house.

So, new guy, Childress said.

Landon looked at the slump-shouldered man with streaky dark hair and salt and peppery beard. The bottom teeth askew, overlapping into a jagged point.

How did *Señor* Granger come about you?

What do you mean? Landon replied.

I mean, where did you come from? Why are you here?

Not sure. I guess he wanted to help me.

Eso no tiene sentido, he muttered to the men.

Si, si, they each replied.

What? Landon said.

Señor Granger does not hire just anybody, said Childress. Each of us here have a certain specialty in order for the whole operation to work.

Landon looked at each of the men. Their eyes hard on him. What are you asking me?

He's asking you, Redson said slowly, leaning his elbows against his knees, the long and bony fingers intertwining, what specialty do you have to help the operation run?

They stared at one another silently.

I was a writer, Landon said. Then I wasn't. Now I'm not sure what I am.

They nodded approvingly.

He backed away slowly, keeping his eyes on the men before turning for the stables. When he reached the doorway, he looked back. Their eyes were still on him.

Blonde straw covered the floors. Sunlight peeked through the panel cracks, the scuzzy windows. Four purebreds were being washed and brushed, filling the air with the potent stench of wet hide. Flies circled the horse's ears, causing them to jostle their large heads. The groomers smiled, nodding to their onlooker in passing. Granger entered through a sliding door on the opposite side. He plucked a carrot from a hanging bag and underhanded it to Landon. Feed em, he said. He walked to a stall gripping the carrot by the shamrock stalk. An auburn mare stood, its rounded white eyes finding him as the groomer gently brushed its mane. She snorted. Pulsating veins ran like divaricated rivers down her broad face. He side-eyed the old man before he approached her. He reached the carrot out slowly. The mare sniffed. Her lips drooped over his fingers and snatched the carrot away. He wiped the bubbling slobber across his pants.

Well done, Granger said, nodding.

They circled the gravel road towards the rear of the house, coming upon a two-story cedar cabin with a glass circumvoluted balcony. Rich chocolate gloss, an ebony roof. The tinted windows reflected the woods as if they were painted there. A single, white rocking chair occupied the front porch.

What's this place? Landon inquired.

My study, Granger replied.

Your study?

Yes.

It's beautiful.

Thank you. I worked with an architect for several years on it. I told him my specifications, and he, in turn, produced a wealth of drafts. I couldn't tell you how many drafts I looked over. Then one morning, the lad told me he wanted to show me a new sketch. So, I went over to his house, and there it was.

The old man gestured to the study.

I asked him how he came up with the design and he told me that he drifted off to sleep working on a concept one night, and when he awoke, he drew for six hours straight.

He saw it in a dream?

He saw my patience wearing thin.

The old man spat.

Degenerate gambler. Good architect, though.

I'd say so, Landon agreed.

The porch creaked as they walked up.

Maple's collar jingled towards them. Her tongue hung like a raw strip of bacon, eyes bright as the woods. Granger bent down and scratched behind her ears. When he stood, she shook like a wild wind chime before darting off and disappearing around the bend.

Granger produced a small key from his shirt pocket and unlocked the door. The hinges rang sharply through the massive floor space. Beige sunlight flooded the room to where you could make out the knots at the far wall. Pictures, awards, bookshelves, literature memorabilia populated the walls. A kitchen and full bathroom along the left side. A leather settee, matching recliner, an oak lacquered coffee table opposite. Billowy clouds washed over the sun, sending the room into pewter shadows. The polished, expansive desk contained a rusted Autocrat coffee can with a pair of scissors, various pencils and red pens, a ruler, a sharpener, several fountain pens, and a pack of erasers. A Meylan stopwatch. Sitting front and center, was a 1963 Olivetti Lettera 32 typewriter, the color of an Italian sun.

You built this? Landon asked, breathlessly.

A long time ago, yes, the old man replied, removing his jacket and hanging it on a hook by the door.

He crossed the polished floorboards to the kitchen, his boot heels filling the room. He opened a cupboard and took down two clay mugs and sat them on the counter and opened another and brought down a tin of ground coffee beans and filled the reservoir with cold water from the refrigerator and spooned the hickory scented grounds into the small basket. He clicked the gas stove alight and set the percolator to heat.

Landon made his way down the wall, studying the history there. It looked like something you might see in a small-town museum. His desk was lit by amber sunlight. He wanted to run his hand along the cold steel case of the typewriter, to press the black, inviting keys like a curious child, but he refrained.

Have you written all your stories on this? he called out.

Yes, the old man replied, his voice low and far.

How many have you written?

Ten novels, four collections of shorts, three screenplays and a stage play.

He turned to Granger. Really?

Yes.

He scanned the bookshelves but could not find the old author's name. Do you use an alias?

No, chortled Granger, his eyes affixed on the percolator, the stream slowly thickening through the silver port.

I don't see your books on the shelves.

They're tucked away.

Why?

One should be surrounded by the words of great writers, not the words of one's great writing.

They must be really good if you have to tuck them away, he said, turning to him.

Granger shrugged.

I'd like to read them.

Suit yourself.

He returned to the pictures on the wall. He saw a younger Granger with several women, different celebrities, a handful of politicians, nothing in no particular order. Scenes of sunsets in Mexico and Texas. Wildflowers. Wildlife. One with him signing a book for President Ronald Reagan. A wedding portrait. Another.

Are you married? Landon inquired.

Separated.

I'm sorry.

It's alright.

How many times have you been married?

Four.

You've been married four times?

Mhm.

The percolator started to wail. Granger removed it from the stovetop and twisted the gas off. Thick plumes of steam vomited from the spout in translucent tendrils.

Do you take cream or sugar? he asked, setting the percolator on a cold grate.

Just a splash of cream, please.

He took out a small carton of half & half. He opened the drawer and retrieved a spoon and filled the spoon with the cream and dumped it into the cup and stirred. He flung the spoon into the sink and returned the carton and grasped the handles in one hand and turned and crossed to the settee.

Mary was my first wife, he said in stride. I met her when I moved to New York for the first time.

He set his guest's mug on a coaster and sat in aspiration. Then slid his boots off.

At the time, I'd written several drafts of my first novel, chronicling my travels from West Texas through the South and up the eastern coast.

Landon walked over, picked up the mug, and sat on the recliner.

I took a job as a janitor at the New York Public Library and got myself a closet to sleep in with what money I'd saved. I shopped the manuscript around town for a few weeks, this was before agents were a necessity. When you could bring unsolicited material to publishing houses and they would actually look at your work.

He sipped his coffee.

Anyways, someone finally picked me up. Mary worked as a typist at the company, that's how I met her. We grew close. Within the year, we were married.

How long did it last?

Nine years.

What happened?

We were young. And quite poor. I drank a lot in those days. Landon sipped his coffee.

A few years later, I moved to Westport in Ireland.

Why Ireland?

I wanted to get away. Felt like I had to. I was writing poorly. I thought it'd be a good idea to see some of the world. A friend of mine told me about the town. So, I went.

Was it worth it?

In a way, he said, sipping. I was there two weeks when I fell in love with Annalise, who would later become my second wife. She was married to an abusive man whom I was trying to convince her to leave. She worked at the local pub. I tried courting her every night for a whole year.

How'd that go?

Not well. One drunken evening when I was sulking back to the place I was staying, someone behind me gave me a good go around. He tossed me over a bridge, and I waded down to the shore.

A bridge? Landon exclaimed.

It was nothing, really. A couple cobbles over a thin river. I swam ashore and passed out in a drunken daze among the weeds till morning.

Did you go to the hospital?

Eventually. My face was all blue and swollen. Had myself a cracked rib to go along with it. During my recovery, I got sober enough to finish my novel. Within six weeks, I felt good again. I decided to head stateside. And to give Annalise one last shot.

How did you get her to go with you?

I pleaded. Not begged. Pleaded.

A loud scratching came at the door.

Landon set his mug down, stood, walked over and opened the door. Maple trotted in. Her nails clicked like plump raindrops across the floorboards. He went to the kitchen and searched for a bowl.

Far right cupboard, Granger croaked.

He took down a ceramic bowl and filled it at the tap then set it down.

Maple lapped up several mouthfuls, then sauntered to where they were sitting and laid on the floor where the warm sun draped across her back.

Landon took up his mug and sat.

She's tired, Granger said.

She hasn't had this much excitement in a while.

The old man chuckled.

So, Annalise left with you?

Yes. We took a cab back to her house. She packed while he slept. Then we were gone.

You brought her back to New York?

Yes.

That must have been quite a change.

It was. She never cared for it. Always wanted to leave.

Why didn't you?

Because I'm a stubborn mule. Even when I was younger, I was always acting like some old croon. But I did write some of my best work when we were together.

What happened to her?

Returned to Ireland. Who can blame her. I was belligerent most our entire marriage.

Are you sober now?

Yes. Been that way for over thirty years.

And yet you have wine and liquor on the premises?

Just because I can't drink doesn't mean nobody else can. All I ask is for the staff not to work with a load on.

Has it happened?

Not often, but it has happened.

Are they still here?

No.

Landon pondered this as he drank.

Any children?

No, Granger replied, scratching the fine bristles on his cheek. I never wanted any. That's what killed the third marriage after only four years. Judith was an amazing woman. Got me to drop the bottle. I find myself thinking about her from time to time.

Landon nodded.

Meredith, my current wife, is the one who's been by my side for thirty-six years.

Thirty-six years, he exclaimed.

A long time.

But you separated from her?

She separated from me.

Where is she?

Elsewhere.

I see.

Granger sucked his teeth and stood.

He took the mugs and walked to the kitchen and tossed the dregs into the sink and refilled them. He filled another spoon with cream, stirred it in one of the mugs and tossed it in the sink with the other and walked back.

Thank you, Landon said, taking the mug.

The old man smiled and crossed to his desk and set the mug down. He knelt and opened a large drawer and grabbed a stack of paper and stood and pushed the drawer shut with his toe and walked back and handed the slab of pages to his guest.

What's this? Landon said.

I need a reader.

For what?

Do you have a blank notebook? Granger said, ignoring the question. No.

The old man grumbled and walked over to a closet. He opened it and rifled through the drawers within.

Landon flipped through the pages with fascination. The language was beautifully structured. Simple and elegant. Masterful.

Here, the old man said, holding out a blue composition notebook. Use this.

What for?

For writing.

But I have one.

Not an empty one, you don't.

Landon took the notebook and flipped through the pages. Blank, faintly lined.

Thank you.

Once you're done reading, go find Dom. He told me he's got some work for you.

Work?

Granger chuckled and walked back to his desk and sat. He opened another large drawer and retrieved a stack of paper and set it on the desk. He sipped his coffee and slid the top sheet into the typewriter and leaned back. He didn't move for a long time. Then he took up the stopwatch and started it. The ticking was loud, reverberating throughout the room. He stopped it, looked at its face and reset it. The ticking began again. Longer. Stop. Quick glance. Reset. Then he set the watch down and began typing.

Tap tap tap.

The mid-afternoon sun glistened off the trees as the frequent breeze shed from the mountains, wavering the branches. Maple had relocated her nap to the sofa, her chest rising slow in contrast to her epileptic eyelids. He stood and washed the mug in the sink. He picked up the pages, straightened them, and walked to Granger's desk and set them down and left.

The breeze was cool and inviting. Aromas of pine and cedar filled his lungs. He heard the horses whine in the distance, the jawing cattle. Far down the back road, through a tunnel of trees, a woman rode a gigantic beast of a horse. Black, or a deep chestnut brown. Her dark silhouette shimmered with tinges of beige light, fractured by the raining yellow leaves along her path. The Stetson she wore thwarted her long hair from swaying about. Her posture was immaculate. Then she was gone.

There were platters of sandwiches on the table. Pitchers of lemonade and coffee. He poured himself a glass of the tart, sugary citrus, grabbed a sandwich and ate. Shuffling on the floor above. The sound of furniture being pushed into location? He finished the drink and set the cup on the counter and opened the back door. He eyed the ceiling once more, listening for further sound. Nothing. He shut the door behind him.

The horses lied meditative in the grass, their coats soaked in sun. They watched the workers shovel and bed the gardens with their manure. An auburn mare stretched her legs and sneezed a plume of translucent mucous. Her neighbors turned their heads in freight, their wide white eyes placing the genesis of their disturbance. They whined at one another and went about surveying the land. Landon made out Dom's silhouette in the distance. He opened the gate and closed it behind him and walked past those resplendent creatures. They watched him with an aura of ancient sagacity. They watched for a long time, never moving.

About time you showed up, Dom called out.

Harrison wanted to show me around.

What did you see?

His study.

Ahh. It's beautiful, no?

It is.

Está Bien, follow me.

They made their way across the grounds.

When I first came here, most of the land was still overgrown, Dom proclaimed with swaying hand gestures. Only the stable and the big house were built. The windmill was under construction. Myself and a few others worked on excavating these grounds. Eventually, many years later that is, we got to what you see before you.

Only the stable and the house were here? Landon said.

Yes. But the windmill is what fuels this place. There is a generator underground that connects to all the buildings.

A generator?

Si. State of the art.

That's clever.

Señor Granger is a smart man.

Where did you stay?

In the main house. There are several rooms.

Do they do a lot of furniture rearranging?

Que?

Never mind.

Landon wiped his brow with the back of his arm.

How did you end up here?

I was born in Mexico, Dom answered. A small town outside of Durango. When I was eighteen, I got a job on a ranch in Odessa.

And you were there when you met him?

Si.

They came to a small gate. Dom unlatched the lock and swung it open. Wait here, he said, latching the gate behind his pupil. He walked toward a small shed and disappeared for some time. When he emerged, he was toting a long spool of rope. He coiled it tightly and held it out.

Show me your best knot.

My best knot? Landon replied.

Si.

I don't have a best knot.

Everyone has one.

Not me.

Try.

He sighed, grabbing the rope. He held the ends in each hand and began tying the only knot he knew.

Zurdo, Dom mumbled.

What?

You're a lefty.

Landon nodded as he worked the rope like a pair of thick shoelaces. He yanked the rope taut and handed it to Dom.

There you go, he said.

This? Dom asked, confused.

My best knot.

Dom rubbed his eyes. *Temenos trabjao por hacer,* he mumbled.

What?

Nothing.

I double knotted it.

Dom burst into a bout of shrill laughter.

Si, si. You did.

Dom untied the knot with no trouble.

Landon shook his head.

Now, watch carefully, he instructed. He examined the rope with squinted umber eyes and measured it with his thumb against the coiled surface, counting the grooves in their separations. He fastened a small double loop in a flurry of hand movements. He pulled both sides, diminishing all the gaps of light peeping through. Then he created a wide knot above the tightened one and passed the tight knot through the new loop. He fastened the new loop, funneling the limp rope into a tight noose. With the opposite end, he slid the rope through the loop and held the final product to his pupil as if showcasing a rare breed of snake.

This is a Honda knot. We use it to rope livestock.

A lasso? Landon confirmed.

Si. A lasso.

Dom yanked the lasso apart, returning the rope to its original state and handed it back.

Try again.

Landon took the rope and did his best imitation of Dom's movements but could not recall the later arrangement.

His instructor laughed.

After an hour, he was able to tie the Honda knot in the correct sequence. He spit and spent another hour repeating the steps, tying the knot better each time.

Dom straddled the top fence railing and drew a pack of Winston Reds from his shirt pocket and rattled out a cigarette. He untucked the lighter from the pack and lit the end in an orange flicker and replaced the lighter in the pack and replaced the pack in his shirt. He watched Landon tie the knot with growing confidence. He pulled slowly on the cigarette, tasting the toasted tobacco on his tongue.

You still got family back in Durango? asked Landon.

No, Dom replied. My mother and father died years ago. I have two brothers, but I don't know of their whereabouts.

When did you last see them?

He scratched the gritty stubble along his chin with his thumb. I saw my younger brother two years ago. My older one, six.

What happened?

Same thing that happens to everyone who wants to complicate their lives. They got married.

Landon chuckled.

They both married the wrong women and hurried away. He drew on the cigarette, turning to the meandering horses along the hill line. The wind had shifted, blowing towards the northeast. His pewter smoke plumed like a great fungi cap over his head. Spreading, thinning, gone.

Where did they go?

I don't know, he shrugged.

Was it because you told them you didn't approve?

Yes.

Of their wives.

Yes, of their wives.

That didn't bode well, I assume?

Does it ever when you tell a man that the woman they are about to spend the rest of their life with is the wrong person for them?

Landon nodded.

I don't know how Señor Granger ever did it.

Did you know her?

Señorita Meredith?

Yes.

Si.

When did she leave?

Almost a month ago now.

What happened?

I'm not sure, Dom said dragging the cigarette to its midpoint.

He tied the knot one last time and set the rope down and walked over to the fence and rested against it. The sun teetered atop the shale mountain peaks. The sky dwindled into shades of amethyst, magenta. Peach-bellied clouds thinned overhead. A few stars blinked to life.

Dom peered at the knot on the ground. That is good work, Mister Cassidy, he said.

Thank you.

Want the next step now or save it for tomorrow?

Why not.

Buen hombre.

Dom slid from the fence and picked up the rope. The cigarette was to the filter, but he held it in the crook of his mouth, puffing slowly.

See the loop you made?

Yes.

It's meant to slide. Like this. Dom demonstrated by sliding the loop back and forth along the slack. See?

Yes.

That is to tighten it against the animal's neck. Then you can rope his legs afterwards.

Alright.

But first, you need to know how to swing it properly. Once the loop is around the steer's neck, you only have a few seconds to get it tight, or else you risk hurting the animal, or getting yourself hung up.

You don't rope the horses? Landon asked.

Just the livestock. They're performance horses, remember? They don't need wrangling.

Landon nodded.

Now, watch carefully.

Dom held the rope in his hands. Measured with his thumb like he did before and began to swing the loop in his right, over his body several times. He released and caught the top of the fence post and moved like a fencer, drawing the knot tight around the wood. The thin veil of dirt he stoked settled. Dom inspected his work. Then turned to his partner.

See?

Well done.

Dom chuckled.

Did you learn that when you were a kid?

No. I learned it when I got to Texas.

You're really good.

Everyone's really good at something when they do it for long enough, he said, loosening the knot.

I suppose.

Were you really good at writing?

I thought I was.

Why think? Why was?

Lack of talent. If I had to put a name to it. Confirmed by rejection.

Dom hummed and nodded at this. He rounded the rope in his palm and turned to his student. That does not mean you are not good at writing.

It doesn't? Landon replied.

No.

Then what does it mean?

It means you have some work to do.

Or it means I'm not as good as I thought.

But you had success at it, no?

Beginner's luck.

Que?

A little, sure.

How so?

I had three books published.

And you made money just from writing? Not working any other jobs?For a time.

How much time?

Almost seven years.

Then perhaps you are good at it. Perhaps you grew stale.

Stale?

Si. Perhaps all you need is a new approach. Like an animal does in order to survive. Adaptation. Create new ways to live. Like all species after decades of destruction, or they die off. Old tricks won't work in your world anymore. They are gone. Like all things that come to pass.

I have not read your stories, Mister Cassidy, so I cannot say whether or not you are a good writer. Maybe you will come to find it was another means to another end. But what I can say is that when you do something well for a longtime and what used to work does not anymore, it does not mean you were never good to begin with. It simply means you must change your ways.

Adaptation.

Si.

Is that why you left Texas?

No. I left Texas because of Señor Granger.

Was that the only reason?

Among other things.

Such as?

Dom chuckled.

He handed his inquisitor the rope and patted him on the shoulder. Let's focus on your lassoing, Mister Cassidy.

The dinner table was set with bone china plates and sterling silverware. Silver trays and glass bowls in a variety of shapes and sizes. The staff were all in attendance, eating and laughing. The older woman and gentleman shuffled around, refilling glasses, removing plates and bowls, pouring wine, replenishing food. Conversation was loud and overlapping. Dom and Landon arrived. They filled their plates with steamed green beans, grilled chicken, warm buttered pasta, shaved corn, and charred asparagus. Dom grabbed two beers from the refrigerator and twisted the caps free and tossed them in the stuffed trash bin and handed one to his pupil and clinked his glass. They drank standing there. The beer was cold and good.

Trabajas duro con el escritor? a ranch hand asked.

Si, Dom replied. *Lo hizo bien, pero tiene mucho más que aprender.*

The men laughed.

Entonces fue capaz de hacer un lazo adecuado? Granger said.

Si.

Muy bueno.

He felt a sharp sting on his hands. He looked down to see fissures, bloody and blistered. Compliments from the ropework. He set his plate down and clenched his fists and walked to the bathroom.

Manos virginales, one of the men said.

They all laughed.

He lathered, scrubbed, and bandaged his hands best he could. He felt his heartbeat in his fingers. He made his way back to the dining room before being halted by a picture of a teenage Harrison Granger along the wall. The picture was small, easily overlooked. A frame old and splintered, plagued by black mold scarring. The photograph itself, ancient. A rugged teenager sound asleep on a bus. His head leaned against the glass with a bundled jacket serving as a pillow. His hair was long and mangled as if he'd been on the road for years. A copy of Albert Camus's *The Stranger* lay prone and split on his lap. His sleeves were rolled to the elbows, exposing think blankets of black hair. His jeans were besmirched, or perhaps time had corroded the ink. A tan rucksack peeked from the seat beside. And that was all.

When he returned to his seat, the staff were finishing up. They brought their dishes to the sink and thanked the staff and exchanged their goodbyes and waded out the back door leaving the old man and the newcomer at the table. Sink water streamed silently. Clatter of dishes and glassware. She mumbled to her partner while scrubbing in elliptical motions.

How're your hands? Granger asked.

They'll be fine.

Good.

How's your book coming?

The old man did not answer.

The pages I read were incredible.

He nodded.

When can I read some more?

You can have at it tonight. But the pages will have to stay in the study.

Thank you.

We'll head over once you finish.

Alright.

He opened a new beer and drank. The foam bubbled and popped on his lips.

How long have you been working on it? inquired Landon.

Some years now.

Are you almost finished?

It's been finished.

It is?

Yes.

Then what are you working on?

Maintenance.

When do you plan on releasing it?

Granger sighed deeply. Let's talk about something else.

Of course, Landon replied. I'm sorry.

It's alright.

The light on the study's porch was like a beacon for lost ships. A world of dark. A pair of workers crossed along the gravel. Low grinding beneath their boots. Abrupt. Then silenced as they stepped onto the grass. He watched them fade for a moment. Then caught sight of them again as they approached the yellow lights at the ranch house. Black silhouettes, hunched and swaying. Granger unlocked the door. He turned to see the old man enter the house. He mounted the porch and turned towards the night to find the men but they were not there. The door closed behind him, sealing the eternal solitude that awaited us all in the end.

Granger flipped a switch and the lights flickered on. He walked to the desk and opened the large drawer as before and returned with a handful of pages.

When you're done, leave them on the table.

Alright, Landon replied.

I'll see you in the morning.

Goodnight.

Granger closed the door behind him.

He could hear the crunching gravel under his boots fade into the night. He considered reading the new text on the second floor, but no stairway existed. The room creaked endlessly. Drifting winds swayed the house as if the foundation had been uprooted. He filled a glass from the tap and leaned against the counter and drank and looked over the study in its entirety. He set the glass in the sink and walked to the couch. There came a soft tap on one of the windows. The sound stopped him in his tracks like a spooked deer. He looked out every window but never found the source. An untamed limb from one of the flower bushes, he thought. He read on the couch, glancing over the perimeter of the page to silence his wandering imagination.

In the dark, early morning, the stable door had been left ajar. A faint, bronze glow spilled onto the ground. He stopped and looked around. Nothing stirred. He could not tell where his feet fell, where his arms swung. A nervous tightness in his throat. The trees rustled, but he could not gauge their direction. As he made his way closer, the ground began to lighten. He saw the sharp frames of grass manifest before him. The door creaked as he opened it slowly. He slipped in and saw the horses sleeping. They sniffed the air as he crossed, snorting once he passed. The light he saw came from a single bulb that hung in the center of the walkway. Nothing amiss. He sighed and turned to leave.

Hello?

He whipped around.

Nothing.

Hello? he said hesitantly.

Who's in here?

The voice belonged to a woman. Stern and young.

He was stock still, unsure on how to proceed.

I saw a light on in here, he said.

Her head peeked over the railing at the far end of the stable. A beautiful tan face with black hair falling around it. Do you work here?

Landon relaxed, chuckling to ease his tension.

Not necessarily, he said.

She opened the stall door and came out to meet him. She was tall and leggy. She picked up her chocolate Stetson hat from a nail in one of the posts and held it by the brim and walked towards him, shadows darkening her figure. Her eyes were the color of chrysocolla. Caramel freckles peppered her delicately round cheeks. Her legs donned a pair of custom-made ostrich Lucchese's. And her hands told old tales of a hard life lived all too young.

Who did you say you were?

I didn't, he cleared his throat. My name's Landon Cassidy.

What is it you want, Mister Cassidy?

I saw the light on.

Are you a moth?

Excuse me?

Are you a moth? she repeated slowly, as if he were a dunce child.

No, he laughed, understanding the quip. I came in the other day.

How's that?

Your boss invited me.

Invited you?

Yes, ma'am.

Invited you for what?

I'm not entirely sure.

Are you a ranch hand?

No, ma'am. I don't know anything about working on a ranch.

She fell silent. She studied him all over, this gaunt figure in baggy clothes.

What are you doing out at this hour anyway?

Heading to bed.

Heading to bed?

Yes, ma'am.

She pinched the bridge of her nose, as if her brain was tired of the inquisition. Then turned and walked back to the stall she came from and petted the horse there.

I'm sorry to have bothered you, he said. I'll leave you to it.

She didn't turn around.

He left the door as it was when he arrived and trekked once more through the darkness of that cool night.

The guest house was loud and buzzing with the arrival of the second shift. Both card tables were occupied. Ashtrays already polluted by mashed filters, brown black ash. The loud crack of breaking billiard balls. Shouts and laughter. Whiskey and smoke. He entered, and they all cheered as if he were the final butt of some unspoken joke. He smiled and shrugged and walked over to Dom at the pool table as he was dusting his cue with blue chalk.

Mister Cassidy, Dom said with a smile. How are you this evening?Sure is loud tonight, he replied.

Yes. On the first night of new shifts we have a small celebration. It's tradition.

I can see that.

Can I get you a beer?

Isn't it your turn?

Of course, Dom laughed. I meant afterward.

I can get it while you play.

The ones on the top shelf are mine, he said, patting Landon's shoulder.

Alright.

Gracias.

De nada.

Dom and the men at the pool table whistled and cheered. They slapped the newcomer on the back and joked in drunken syllables about how they'll turn him into a fine Mexican by the end of his tenure. He smiled and crossed the room to the refrigerator and opened it and plucked two beers from the top shelf. They were lightly frosted, sticking to his warm palm. He cranked off the caps with a silver bottle opener and tossed them in the waste bin and walked back to Dom. The balls cracked ferociously. Dom tipped an orange striped ball into the far corner pocket and picked up his chalk cube and dusted the tip and rounded the perimeter to his next target. He set the cube on the table ledge, leaned over, hooked the cue in his extended hand and shot.

The men laughed and took their turns.

Cheers to your first day on the job, Dom said taking the beer.

Thank you, Landon laughed.

They all touched bottles and glasses and drank. The beer was ice cold and it numbed the back of his throat.

Why are you back so late? Dom asked. You get lost in the dark?

I might as well have. I was on my way over when I saw a light in the stable so I went to check it out.

Ahh, like a moth.

What?

We keep a few lights on for the horses.

Why?

Comfort.

Is that true?

Dom shrugged.

There was a woman there.

Yes. *Señorita* Chambers.

Who's that?

One of the best horse trainers around. She's been with *Señor* Granger longer than I have.

Really?

Si.

How long has Harrison been breeding and training horses?

A long time. He told me he learned all about horses when he was a boy. Even had one himself. Said that there are few things in this world that encompass the true meaning of beauty. And a horse was one of them.

Landon sipped his beer, pondering the thought.

I always knew horses were beautiful, but the way he talks about them, *es como si viera a Dios en ellos.*

The men around the table nodded in silent agreement.

What does that mean?

It means he sees God in them.

The game ended. One of the men gathered the balls from the pockets and racked them. The triangle lay at the center of the fine green felt. They chalked their cues and drank their beers.

Do you want to play? Dom asked.

No, Landon replied. I'm going to turn in.

Bien.

Thanks for the lesson today.

Por supuesto. Get some rest, Mister Cassidy.

You too.

Buenos noches.

Buenos noches.

The men chuckled.

He finished his beer and dropped it in the trash. He walked up the stairs, over the translucent cloud of various tobacco smoke. The lights were obscured as if a heavy fog had rolled in. The forms there took on the shape of long forgotten phantasms. A scene at the edge of one's dream. Will you remember this when you wake? He mounted the top landing when the door opened and Chambers came in. The room burst into cheers, whistles, whoops and cries. She said something inaudible and went around greeting the faces she'd not seen in a while. They stood and hugged her, making small talk. Like a politician making the rounds. When she looked up, he was there. He waved but she didn't seem to notice. He lowered his hand and turned and walked down the hallway to his room.

The chalkboards along the wall listed their occupants. Chicken scratch, playful art, elegant penmanship. His door was open. He flipped the light switch and found Maple curled behind the pillows. She grunted, trying to hide her bay eyes from the light. He closed the door, took a shower and collapsed onto the bed and was fast asleep, forgetting to close the blinds.

In the morning, a tangerine sun pierced beyond the forest. Its beams darted into the room. The air was frigid. He bundled the blankets around him as he swung his feet to the floor, trying to tuck the blankets underfoot. He slid towards the window and peered out.

A collection of ranchers, groomers and trainers were already up, walking towards the house for breakfast. He watched as they gestured to one another, their lips moving with muted chatter. The horses trotted out of the stable. They broke into full gallop across dew crystalline grounds. A flock of geese flew over the building, heading into the ripening sunrise.

He closed the blinds and laid back in bed. He checked the time on the desk clock and rolled over and slept again. Thirty minutes later, he was awake.

The house was warm, filled with the fragrance of charred cedar. He fed Maple in the kitchen and followed the scent to the expansive living room. A fire blazed in the chimney. All the draperies were pinned back, flooding the room with porcelain light. Granger sat on the couch with a cup of coffee and a half-eaten bowl of watery oatmeal. A banana peel, squid sprawled, on the table.

Good morning, the old man said without looking back.

Good morning.

Sneaking up on me?

Landon chuckled.

III

I smelled the fire.

I like a big fire on a cold morning, the old man said.

Isn't it May?

These days, the cold doesn't care about the time of year. When it's cold, it's cold.

I won't argue with that logic.

Did you get yourself some breakfast?

Not yet.

Go get some and join me.

He returned to the kitchen. Maple had finished her food and was sitting by the older gentleman, who was frying sausage links. On the table, a glass of water, orange juice and mug of coffee awaited him.

Thank you, Landon said.

The older gentleman nodded and slid the sausages onto a plate. He spooned a hunk of congealed pork fat from a jar and tapped it into the skillet, the heat quickly liquifying it. He cracked two eggs into the fat to bubble like boiling water. He toasted three slices from a fresh baguette, buttered and halved them and set them on a plate. Then he slid the eggs and sausages beside them and handed the young guest the plate.

Please enjoy.

He finished his breakfast and cleared his plate and filled his mug anew and headed back to his host.

Evelyn told me you stumbled into the barn last night, Granger said hearing the approaching young man.

Who's Evelyn?

Miss Chambers.

Oh.

She said you spooked her.

I saw a light in the stables and I thought I should check it out.

Why would you do that?

I don't know. I thought someone may have left it on.

It's a nightlight—

—For the horses. I know.

Granger chuckled.

Does it work?

What?

The nightlight.

I haven't the faintest idea.

Landon sat, sipping his coffee.

You should talk to her today. Get to know her.

Alright.

Alright.

You said all the horses were for racing?

Breeding mainly, Granger corrected. Most of them are studs. Got a few mares, too. We pretty much send them off to ranches to mate with other racing or show horses.

Do they pay you for that?

Of course.

Do they pay well?

They do, Granger said with a sly grin.

Landon smiled and sipped his coffee.

Each one was a prize-winning horse at one point or another. All have strong bloodlines. That's what the customers are really paying for, in a nut shell.

No pun intended.

The old man laughed.

I never understood horse breeding.

It's an expensive hobby.

Yet you enjoy it?

Absolutely.

What does Evelyn do then?

She conditions them. Mainly the performers.

Performers? Landon said.

Dressage, we call it. Steeplechase once in a while. She's the best I know.

Steeplechase is where they jump over things, right?

Obstacles, yes.

Dom told me you hired her before you hired him.

He would be right.

When did you hire her?

Why don't we go ask her?

Alright.

Finish your coffee.

What about the fire?

Granger threw back the dregs in his mug. What about it? he said, wiping his mouth with the back of his hand. She'll still be burning when I get back.

They walked past the slow churning windmill. The stocks creaked while the sails flapped against the breeze. The cattle sauntered up a small hill, shaded by an immense oak. Sheep babbled in their huddle. Chickens roamed freely among the grounds. Evelyn Chambers held the reins of a tall chestnut stud outside the gate while the quartet studied the horse, making notes and smoking thin brown cigarillos. She looked up to see the two men approach.

Morning, she greeted.

Morning everyone, Granger replied.

The men nodded and exchanged pleasantries.

How's he doing this morning?

He had a good breakfast, she reported. Slept well too. I think he's ready to run today.

Good.

He turned to the men. What's the status with Lee?

He said he's coming to get Signatures sometime tomorrow afternoon, Redson said.

So, that means early evening.

They all chuckled.

Is everything ready for him?

Si, Javier said. They'll groom him before he leaves. Make him look pretty for the ladies.

They laughed.

Are any of them still in there? Granger inquired, nodding towards the stables.

Golden Wheat still might, Evelyn answered. She was being a pest this morning. Still cranky from all the traveling.

Alright. We'll catch up later.

They nodded to one another and went their separate ways.

Granger and Landon walked into the stables. The former grabbed a carrot from a bag on the wall and walked down to the stall that held the blonde mare. The sheen along her mane and coat glowed an ethereal white. Umber eyes flecked with cerulean, shimmering in the morning light. Her legs were shielded by black padded sleeves. Granger fed her the carrot and ran his hand over her slender head. He crossed to the far wall and took down a circular hand brush and came back and handed it to the young man.

Slip this on, he said.

He tucked his hand under the strap. Granger opened the stall door.

Go ahead.

Didn't they say she was cranky? Landon replied.

She is.

We need her un-cranky.

The horse whined and snorted, throwing her head back and forth violently. As if challenging him to approach.

Go on.

He shook his head then made his way to the stall.

The mare followed the nervous man with her eyes.

Take your time, Granger croaked. Go slow. Make sure to stay out from behind her.

He nodded and hesitantly placed the brush against the mare's neck and began to slowly stroke. She snorted and threw her head. He recoiled, then tried again.

Granger turned a bucket over and sat.

She thinks there's a fly on her, he said. You're going to have to brush harder than that.

He nodded and followed his instruction. He felt her large heart beating against the hide. A thin smile formed along his lips. Stray hair curled into the air. He moved about her slowly, section by section, as if detailing a car. It took him took two hours to fully brush the horse. When he finished, Maple lay beside the old man. He was reading a scrap of newspaper he'd hid on his person. An intense concentration plastered along his face. Stone still.

I'm done, he said, wiping his sweat drenched forehead with his shirtsleeve.

Get her a drink, the old man said without looking up.

He exited the stall and latched it and walked down the and replaced the brush. He fetched a bucket and ran water into it from a hose and toted it back to the stall and lifted the bucket onto the railing and titled it towards her. The mare drank, sloshing the water with her long pink tongue, dribbles slapping flatly on the ground. She shook her head and licked her lips, turning in her confines to peer outside.

Let's see if she'll come out now, Granger said, standing up. He folded the piece of paper and slipped it into his back pocket. Maple stood and stretched cat like. He took down a rope hackamore and fitted it around the mare with no trouble. He opened the stall and handed the rope to the young groomer.

Take her.

Landon took the rope and led the horse outside. Granger leaned against the stable door, watching. The four men on the table observed this wonder. Evelyn was gone. He opened the gate, led her in, half turned and latched it. She stood there, staring through those dark galactic eyes. What next? He inspected the hackamore then proceeded to slip it off. It came easy and the horse shook her head once free. She huffed, turned and ran towards the lake. His gaze following her into the distance.

Well done, Granger said.

Landon jolted with surprise.

The old man leaned against the fence, his arms draped over the railing.

She always reminded me of the horse I had when I was a child. When I first saw her, I thought she was.

How old were you at the time? Landon asked.

Seven.

What was her name?

Charlotte.

The young man nodded.

She was a good horse. Always good to me.

What happened to her?

Time. I put her down myself when I was fourteen.

I'm sorry to hear that.

Granger clicked his tongue. Nothing to be sorry for. It was part of a reality long before you were born.

Did you get another afterwards?

No. My father went shortly thereafter. My brother and I helped my mother sell the place. Once we did, I left.

Where did they go?

California. She had a brother out in Sacramento that they went and lived with.

Did you ever go see them?

No. I never saw them again.

He opened his mouth to respond, but realized he had nothing worth saying.

I like talking to the horses, the old man went on. They enjoy conversation as much as any other person. They don't judge you for what you've done. Or those you've abandoned. Neither those that'd come to pass or those that'll come within your orbit. They never judge. I don't believe anything as beautiful as a horse has the ability to judge one on any merits that make a man. You can see it in their eyes. Deep in there. In that wholly unknown, they understand. They forgive. Even if you never speak a word of it. They know the truth within your soul long before you ever did. I never could recall the last thing I ever said to my brother. Maybe I thought I would see him again. I didn't think our last time together would be slated as such. I don't think anybody ever does.

Afterwards, his face faded from my memory. Then one day, I saw him. As clear as the sky is now. As vivid as you before me. It must've been thirty or forty years ago. I was crossing the Tennessee plains in a pickup that needed to be put out to pasture yesterday, with a load on I thought tolerable at the time. Heading to Nashville for some damned book signing, or something. The sight was nothing to behold, for all there was was dirt, clay and dust. The sky, opaque. Shrouding the blue beyond it. Along that black stretch of ebony asphalt, a man and his young son, ten or thereabouts, were waving me down on the side of the road. At first, I took them for a mirage. Hell, I still sometimes think they were. I pulled over and spun the window down. They weren't going far, but the mustang they were driving gave out and threw them before falling into the ditch a ways up. They were scuffed a bit but were fine overall. I asked if the horse was still alive. They told me she was. So, I got out of the truck and followed them to where she lay.

The ash gray equine lay to one side. Her wheezing was faint, and fading. I looked her over for any sign of serious injury, but there was none that I could tell. I patted her and took her head and gently spoke to her and looked into her eyes and saw a tinge of amethyst deep in her retina. Almost extinguished. She did not look at me at first. Probably couldn't tell I was there, or didn't care that I was. Finally, she did. Her eyes grew wide, fixing on me. Her somber breaths ticked down in that shallow gulch as I held her tight against my chest to comfort her. Then I saw him, for a moment, in the centerpiece of that dusty old mustang eye. He was older. Tall, skinny. Well dressed and plain with a thin patchy beard. All he did was stand there, looking at me. No smile, no sense of motion. I never heard news of his death but I knew then that he was. Perhaps he wanted to see how I ended up. Pitting his final illustration of me against the boy he once knew. Then he was gone.

The two writers listened to the hissing wind through the fence posts and postulated the world before them. All that had been, all that was. And all that was yet to come. One of the horses took out running along the fence line, chasing phantoms. Landon toed the dirt and peered at the old man.

What happened afterward?

Gave the man and his son a lift to town and moved on, Granger replied.

Do you still think about them? Your family?

No.

But you remember them?

Yes.

That's good.

Yeah. That's a word for it.

He sat on a rickety chair, leaning against the windmill. The slow cadence of the fan had a relaxing quality about it. He'd been writing in the blue notebook Granger had given him since midday. The grubby pencil scratched against the paper in a cursive that had clearly not been used in years. His palm tightened, fingers curling crablike. The pencil fell into the grass. He turned and pressed his hand against the windmill to relieve the constricted pressure that beset him. The muscles relaxed, allowing the fingers to open and breathe.

Evelyn rode up on a mountainous black beast that was unlike anything he'd ever seen before. A mythical monster with hair along its feet like flames. The chest, an easy eighteen hands high. His tail was knotted in an Indian braid. Veins stretched across his chest, legs and neck. The ground sank beneath the polished hooves as if to bow.

What is that thing? Landon awed.

This is Signatures, she replied. He's one of our main attractions.

He's massive.

Clydesdales tend to be.

Are they usually that color?

Most of the time when you get a horse with black coats they'll have subtle gray or white hues to them. Blackouts are extremely rare. That's why Harrison paid a king's ransom for him.

Really?

Yes.

What's he for?

Other than intimidation?

He laughed.

Breeding. We make a lot of money on this stud, she said leaning down, patting his side.

He's a traveler?

Big time.

How long's he here for?

Few days. Gennady Leeson's coming by tomorrow to fetch him.

Who's that?

A breeder from Kentucky we do regular business with.

He nodded.

Dom told me to come look for you.

He did?

Yup.

Where's he at?

By the barn, she gestured with her head. Looks like you got some wrangling coming your way.

Wrangling?

Yup.

Like cow wrangling?

Cattle.

What?

It's cattle wrangling.

Oh.

Looks like you got some coming your way.

Swell.

She laughed. You'll be fine. As long as you do as he says that is.

And if I don't?

Then you're likely to get thrown.

He picked up his pencil.

What're you writing?

Nothing. Just some thoughts. Observations.

How's it coming?

It's coming. I haven't done it in years, so I'm a bit rusty.

I'm sure it'll come back to you.

He looked up and saw a thin smile across her lips. A shallow dimple embedded on her right cheek. Stray black hairs fell from under her ivory Stetson hat, and gently brushed across her eyes.

The gravel crunched beneath the rolling tires. Chips of rock clanked like fat rain on a tin roof under the carriage. She moved Signatures next to the writer and he could feel the hot hide radiate against his face. Todd Childress idled the truck beside the couple. In the bed sat Frank, Stu, and Javier.

Takin him for a stroll, Chambers? Childress asked.

Yeah. He'll be off again, so I thought I'd take him out for a little while.

You know that storm's acomin.

Yeah, I know.

Landon looked overhead at the effulgent blue sky. Whipped white clouds that mashed into one another. There is? he said.

Sure is, Childress replied.

How can you tell?

We're up in the mountains. When clouds start to pack in tightly like you see em doin now, before long, they'll squeeze and burst like grapes.

Evelyn nodded.

Maryland weather's like that, Ferns said. It can be hard to plan a day around it, but you get used to it eventually.

That's strange since the sun's been out all day, Landon said.

Well, get ready to seek shelter.

Is that where y'all are headin? Evelyn said.

Sure are, Childress replied. We got some business Harrison needs us to tend to before Lee arrives.

I'll see ya tomorrow then.

Yes ma'am. Have a good ride.

The driver looked at the writer before putting the truck in gear and driving on. Javier lifted a hand and gave a small wave as the alabaster dust churned up behind them. The taillights faded down the long pathway into the woods, and disappeared.

You best be going, Evelyn said, kicking the horse into a walk. The rain will be here within the hour.

Where will you be?

Around, she called back with a smirk.

The horse walked down the back road, disappearing within the shadows of the trees.

He found Dom leading a drove of pigs into their pen. They squealed and cried in sharp, horrified shrills. Their ears flapped like pinwheels, their noses wet and begrimed with mud. Dom latched the pen and nodded to his pupil.

Señorita Chambers delivered my message, I see.

She did, Landon replied.

III

Bueno. Come around. We'll get started before the rains come.

He walked around the gate, opened the latch went in. He followed Dom towards a small Morgan, coat the color of gunmetal. Dom retrieved a rope from the saddlebag and held it out.

Get the knot ready, he said.

Landon took the rope and slowly recreated the knot he'd worked tirelessly into memory.

Dom inspected it and nodded. Bueno.

He mounted the horse and held out his hand.

Tu mano.

What? Landon replied.

Give me your hand.

What for?

We may need to wrangle a few if they don't want to be driven.

Wrangle?

Si.

I don't know how to wrangle, Dom.

You probably won't need to. These cattle know the drill.

Then why do I need to come along?

They may need a reminder, he said with a sly smile.

I don't know—

Andale, amigo. Before we get soaked.

Landon groaned and grabbed Dom's hand.

Dom lifted him enough to get a leg over the horse and he adjusted into position. He could feel the quivering muscles of the horse beneath him. They rode at a stern pace across the range. The cattle lowed and trotted ahead of their pursuers, stoking up dust and dirt, rounding back to their crushes. The sky blackened. Ranch hands secured the herd as the sun vanished behind antimonite clouds. The rain was cold and hit like pebbles. Intermittent sprinkles that Dom knew would crescendo into a torrential alluvion. He kicked the Morgan. Then again. The cattle laid at the far end of distant the treeline, oblivious to what was soon to befall them. They saw the horse looming like a hell spawn in its shadow gallop, the rain parting against its spectral being like a necromantic drapery. They struggled to their feet and dispersed onto isolated trajectories. Dark mud painted their legs and splattered their hides. Beams of cold breath spurted from their nostrils like volcanic combustions. One of the heifers darted wildly towards them. Dom reined the horse, causing it to buckle. Landon lost his grip and was thrown through the curtaining rain. He was drenched on impact, tumbling though the thick mud. He staggered to his feet. The lasso was gone. Blood rushed to his head, skewing his vision with adrenaline. Two of the livestock made their way back to the barn unassisted. Dom rounded the horse and drove the remainders in. He found the rope submerged like a sea dragon in meniscus indentations. It was soaked and filthy but the knot was still good. The rain fell in long, thick sheets. A wheezing bovine walked the fence line. He adjusted his grip on the rope and approached the exhausted creature slowly. The cow moved its head from the fence. Before he could swing the lasso, the cow turned and found the strength to charge the lone cowboy. Landon dropped the rope and dove in time for the cow to miss him. He stood and ran towards the barn. The beast rounded and charged after him in hard, chugging grunts.

Dom secured the cattle with the other ranch hands. The yelling was the first thing he heard. Piercing the veil of rain, was the odd spectacle of the chase.

Mierdo, he mumbled, then kicked the Morgan into a sprint.

The cow had gained on its target. Its eyes rolling wildly, mouth agape, the eggplant tongue lolling in a foamed mixture of rain and saliva. It thrust its head with surprising speed. The horn took to the runner's side and watched him tumble to the ground. The frantic rider's hollering gained enough control of the delirious beast to drive it in.

He was up and out of the mud, clutching his sticky, bloody side when Dom returned and sat the horse and dismounted.

Are you alright? Dom asked.

Yeah. She got me good, but I'll be fine.

Dom removed the fallen wrangler's hand, inspecting the slashed shirt through the rain. A five-inch gash ran across the right side of his abdomen. The wound was not deep but the blood seeped in long, dark brown streaks like rivers on a globe.

They rode to the house through the thickening rain. Landon rested on the porch steps while Dom rushed inside for bandages. He listened to the loud splattering along the gravel. Hissing symphony. Gouts of rain cascaded off the roof in one unbroken waterfall. The puckering pink wound began to coagulate. He laid back on the porch and tried to listen to his breathing but the rain was too loud, too loud.

Dom opened the door, towels in one hand, a first aid kit in the other. You need to remove your shirt, he said.

Landon nodded and carefully slid his shirt overhead. It slapped on the porch with a flat sucking sound. He dried himself with one of the towels then wrapped himself in the others.

We need to get inside once I get you cleaned up, Dom said.

Okay.

Dom opened the kit and tore open an alcohol wipe. He was quick about his work, experienced. He dabbed the wound with gauze, then went over it with sterilizer. He dressed the laceration gingerly with more gauze and secured its placement with medical tape.

How's that?

Seems good.

Alright. Let's get you inside.

The room was still warm from the morning fire, but the embers in the fireplace had long died. Dom sifted through the ashes with one of the pokers and stacked fresh logs in their place. He popped a match and lit the wood, setting the fire ablaze again.

Thank you, Landon said, feeling his temperature rise.

Of course.

Dom returned the supplies where he'd found them and made a pot of coffee and poured two mugs. When he returned, he pulled a chair next to the wounded and handed him a mug and sat.

Gracias, Landon said.

Dom chuckled and raised his mug.

They toasted and drank.

Some lesson today.

Si, Dom replied. A little too much excitement.

Do you think I'll need to go to the hospital?

Best that you do. You'll need stitches. I can do it myself, but I think you may want to get them professionally done. Better safe than sorry.

Alright.

I'll take you once you warm a bit.

Thank you.

Of course.

Landon drank the coffee and studied the fire. The climbing flames whipped and darkened the back brick. The rain grew louder and sounded like an onslaught of pellets. He thought about the horses. How many of these rains had they seen in their lifetimes? Is it always new to them? Do they understand

In all honesty, were you hoping I'd wrangle today? Landon asked.

No.

Really?

Yes.

He rubbed his side, the throbbing wound caused him wince.

Why did you try to wrangle the cow? Dom inquired.

He shrugged. I thought I could do it.

And if you had been right, what then?

He fell silent.

You don't know, do you?

I guess I don't.

Loco hombre, Dom chuckled.

What does that mean?

Nada.

Landon sat and listened. He did not hear any stirrings from within the house, only the cracklings of the burning cedar, the rain on the roof. Where is everybody?

In a rain like this? They're either at the guest house or in the stables keeping the horses calm.

Stables?

Si.

Where's the other one?

Up the back road, next to the training track. *Señor* Granger built it so we didn't have to rush the horses back when these kinds of spells came.

That's smart.

Si.

Is he here?

I haven't seen him.

Probably in his study.

Probably.

How long do you expect the rain to last?

Could be an hour. Might be more. It's hard to tell at this time of year.

Does this kind of unpredictability make work here difficult?Sometimes.

But we are high up, and the rain tends to not stay long. Landon nodded.

When I lived in Durango and Texas, Dom explained, we would have several month-long dry spells. Sometimes in the same year. When the rains finally came, we worked in them graciously.

Isn't that dangerous?

It is if you're not paying attention.

But you pay attention.

Si, Dom chuckled, always.

The rain echoed against the brick like tittering mice. A log detonated. Bouquet of embers, whisking up the chute in elegant pirouettes. Orange transcended to white.

Do you have any family? Landon asked. Of your own?

Dom nodded slowly.

Where are they?

La casa.

What?

Home.

In Texas?

Durango.

How long have you been married?

Six years.

Do you have any children?

Si. Two girls.

He smiled. I bet they're beautiful.

They are.

Do you miss them?

Todos los dias.

He didn't know the translation but he knew the emotion. He nodded silently.

I talk to them every day, Dom said after a while.

What do you talk about?

I talk to them about my day. About the trees changing colors. *Señor* Granger, and the lovely words he says, trying my best to recite them. Sometimes I read aloud as if they were lying in my arms. Some days I sing.

Do you ever see them?

No.

He nodded then sipped his coffee. How's your side?

Stings, but I'll be fine till I get sewn up.

Bueno, he said, leaning back in his chair, stretching his legs before crossing them. He watched the fire and watched the smoke. He held his mug with both his hands, resting it on his lap. Sweat beaded along his brow. He drew in a long breath. *Bueno.*

Gennady Leeson arrived the next day with a posse that seemed to never end. The crimson Dodge Ram 2500 pickup leading the fleet, towed a luxuriously large horse trailer. Cars sporting Mercedes-Benz, Lincoln, and BMW insignias filed behind. They waved to the gathered crowd standing by the stables as if they were royalty from afar. Lee's driver pulled the hulking truck up to the fence line and shut off the engine. The cars parked along the grass, stretching far down the road they came in on. They exited their vehicles in a myriad of metal door slams, taking in large lungfuls of wet mountain air. He was a short, stout man born and bred in Hattiesburg, Mississippi. He'd made his fortune by successfully operating string of fried chicken restaurants throughout the state, which he eventually sold. Since then, he earned all his money playing the stock market. In the throes of an early mid-life crisis, he entered into the world of equine breeding. He'd purchased several plots of land in Kentucky and quickly became a known name in the industry. He wore a four thousand-dollar Stetson black hat atop his naked dome and a pair of nine thousand-dollar alligator Lucchese Baron boots. He was cleanly shaven, and slathered in French aftershave. His pearl snapped shirt glistened in the late afternoon sun.

Been some time, old timer, Lee said as he closed the truck door.

How are you Lee? Granger said.

Better now, after all that winding and weaving it takes to get this tank up here. My driver sure as shit didn't know what he was in for till he saw it. I told him about the roads, but he insisted on driving like some maniac who'd just flew the asylum.

Granger laughed. Well, I'm glad you all got here unharmed.

We'll make sure the descent is smoother since we'll have precious cargo, he said, nudging the driver.

I'm glad to hear it.

Where's he at?

Granger looked towards the fence and pointed. Yonder he runs.

Signatures galloped across the grounds to the gawking delight of the visiting crowd. Friends, family, investors. They fetched their Kodaks and Canons and snapped pictures of the towering stud. Granger retrieved a sugarcube from his back pocket and held it over the railing. The horse walked along the fence line. Cameras clicking away. Signatures lowered his enormous head, taking the treat from the old man's hand.

What a striking creature, Lee exclaimed.

Indeed he is, Granger replied, patting the horse's head.

Lee turned to Evelyn. You ready to show us that speed of his, Miss Chambers?

Evelyn laughed and stood from the bench. I'm ready if you are.

The track was freshly raked, the lawns mowed. The air cooled as the sun's intensity waded. Across the track stood the stables and a small house. Several workers leaned against the fence at the far end, getting ready to watch the show. The crowd chattered loudly as they took their seats on a set of wooden bleachers.

What did you say your name was? Lee asked.

Landon Cassidy.

You new?

In a way.

What way would that be?

He's a writer I invited to stay with us for a while, Granger said.

Well then, you're with one of the best. When I first met Harrison, I could hardly believe he was a writer. A Pulitzer Prize winning one at that.

What? Landon exclaimed.

That's right. A friend of mine told me a few years back.

He turned to Granger.

You loaned me a couple of beautiful mares, remember that?

The old man nodded.

When the guy asked me where I got the horses, he looked at me funny when I gave the name. He'd no idea such a recluse was secretly breeding horses. It seems no one ever knows what you're up to. You keep yourself holed up here, all quiet and dead to the world.

It's no secret what I do, croaked Granger.

Right. Well, I did some research, and sure enough, I found his whole catalog. Every last one of em. I bought em all, read em all, and Christ above, if they ain't some of the best goddamned stories I've ever read. Pardon my French.

Landon stared in bewilderment at the old man.

Don't tell me you had no idea? Lee said, laughing.

I knew he was a writer. I read some of his stuff the other night and it was wonderful. But I had no idea that—

That he's arguably our greatest living writer? He laughed louder. That's something else. Modest doesn't even begin to describe you Harrison.

Let's just enjoy what we all came out here to see, Granger said.

Yes. Let's get this show on the road.

He tried to put this newfound information aside and focus on Evelyn, but the revelation knotted his stomach. What am I doing here? How did it come to this? The voices tried to answer but he shook them away. He climbed the bleachers and took his seat amongst the crowd.

They began to cheer as Evelyn, now clad in rider's gear, walked Signatures onto the far side of the track. She took a small bow and mounted the horse and slowly rode past. Camera clicks and applause. She turned and waved to the appreciative crowd once more before taking off, slamming her legs against the muscular hide, sending Signatures into a canter that flurried his mane like black fire. His gait began to widen. She lifted in the stirrups and brought the crop down on him several times. Her immaculate posture seemed to float as the hooves propelled powdered dirt skyward in its colossal wake. They were at full gallop now. The crowd rose to their feet as they rounded the final turn. Evelyn's crop flapped back and forth throughout their thunderous sprint. Signatures' muscles were on full display, pressing against the skin, veins bulging obsidian along the neck and legs. A horror out of Greek mythology. Warhorse of destruction. The crowd cheered loudly as they flew by. A flurry of camera flashes captured the horse's brilliance. Evelyn slowed him to a trot. She leaned forward and spoke to the horse before dismounting and leading him to a galvanized water trough. A ranch hand paid her his compliments and took the reins. She smiled and thanked him and patted Signatures' torrid hide and headed back to the crowd.

Gennady opened the gate and ran towards Evelyn. He cheered her name and took her delicate hand in both of his and praised her as if she'd won the Kentucky Derby. The crowd filed in behind, echoing his sentiment before heading over to the horse.

He watched her for a long time from his seat. Her proud smile. The inaudible words she spoke to those who beckoned for her attention. Signatures stood by, nonchalantly eating a bundle of hay. He stood, descended the few steps and headed back.

He heard her call his name and when he turned he saw Evelyn walking towards him. They stood on opposite sides of the fence, her with one leg hiked against the railing.

Where might you be off to? she asked.

Just heading back before the crowd does.

Why don't you stay? Introduce yourself to some of the folks.

That's alright.

You sure?

Yeah. Thank you though.

Okay.

Nice riding.

Thanks.

I'll see you around.

He turned and walked on.

The quarter mile through the woods filled his lungs with damp pine, wet earth. Upended trunks now supported by their neighbors. Leaves yellow like banana slugs, decorated the forest floor. He came across a thick uprooted elm and stepped off the path for closer inspection. He knelt, and examined the inner workings like an engineer. Wooden coils, hollow chambers. Like a light post with its scrambled cables pouring out of it. Dirt crumbled off, plump earthworms danced like suffocating fish in the crater left behind. He wondered about its age, the things it had seen.

The windmill was on its final revolution. The two housekeepers were finishing dinner preparations when he walked in. He made a cup of coffee and took it to the front porch to drink. He sat in one of the rocking chairs, rubbing the stitches in his wound. Maple sauntered up the steps, shook and jumped onto the swinging bench. She stood until the pendulum ceased and laid down. The sun was fractioned by the mountains. A flock of geese conducted their routine flyover, barking towards the lotus sunset. The subtle rolling of the wooden legs settled his mind, and after a while he thought of Evelyn and the horse. He sipped his coffee and held it in his lap. Then he shut his eyes and fell asleep.

After dinner, Signatures was loaded into the trailer. The vehicle engines each churned to life and filed out one by one. Gennady signed all the paperwork shook hands with Granger, Evelyn and the other ranchers in attendance. He climbed into the truck and slowly backed out. He gave them one last wave then was gone.

Good work today, Granger said to Evelyn.

Thank you.

He was making his way to the house when she clutched his arm.

Harrison, she said.

He looked at her hand, then at her.

Sorry, she apologized, releasing him.

Something on your mind?

She looked around to make sure they were alone.

Why did you bring him here?

Excuse me?

Why did you bring him here? she repeated.

Who?

You know who.

Granger's back straightened.

Why do you ask?

I'd like to know your reasoning. I know you haven't explained it to the others.

Because that's my business.

It's all our business, Harrison.

He canted his weight to one side, exhaling impatiently.

Ever since Meredith left, she said, you haven't been yourself. We're all worried about you.

He said nothing.

If you're not going to say anything, then you need to at least tell him what's going on.

Granger leaned and spat. He bent down, adjusted the cuff over his boot and brushed a lick of dirt from his pant leg. He straightened, studying her concerned expression. After a while he gave her a gentle smile and patted her shoulder.

Alright, he croaked.

Then turned and headed in for dinner.

Evelyn stood there in the azure twilight, shaking her head, twisting her boot tip in the dirt. She looked up, viewing the early night. A plane silently outran the chiffon exhaust trailing behind. A memory of her father came to her. Something he'd told her when she was young, but could not remember when or why he had said it. He spoke of Atlantis, stating that all the planes we see above were not actually planes but ships. Enormous ships on an oceanic surface high above. Exhaust guised as wave breaks against the hulls. He told her that they were underwater, fathoms below a greater civilization. That those lucky and rich enough thwarted a great flood by developing top-secret flotation technology, only to later look down from their expansive observation decks, pondering about those less fortunate. Her father would yell at the sky, telling it that they were thriving. That they did not need the rich and advanced to survive. That all they needed was each other. Then her father would laugh and kiss her on the head, telling her that he loved her.

Sometime in the months that followed, Landon's writing was interrupted by a faint knock on the door. He closed his journal and crossed to his door, finding Ben leaning in the doorframe.

Good morning Ben, Landon greeted.

How are you?

Can't complain.

What can I do for you?

We just got off the phone with the mechanic down on the mile. Apparently, someone's interested in your truck.

Really? Landon exclaimed.

Yes. They're coming by in about an hour to check it out. I told him we were on our way.

Let me grab the registration.

Maple jumped in the back seat before the Bronco roared to life. Ben pulled out of the garage, put the truck in gear and headed down the gravel driveway.

Harrison isn't coming? Landon inquired.

He's busy.

The drive felt new to him. He'd forgotten about the outside world in the time he'd been here. The fact that he rarely saw civilization, if such things still existed. The curves in the road were foreign, the green hills, the chintzy houses. The cloud's shadows slid along the spired mountainside. Drifting shapes that shifted and sundered. There was no one on the road. Maple held her head out the window along their descent. Her jowls flapped wetly while her hazel eyes thinly shut from the oncoming wind. A post office came into view. Ben turned into the parking lot and idled the engine.

Wait here, instructed Ben.

Alright.

Ben got out and shut the door and opened the informational laden door and went in.

He watched Ben unlock a P.O. box through the window and take out a handful of envelopes and looked them over and stuffed them under his arm. Ben checked the box again then closed the door, locked it, came out, and got in.

Here, he said, handing the envelopes to Landon.

What's this?

Your mail. You've got checks from your old publisher. I guess they've been floating between your old addresses.

He gave the envelopes puzzled look, then took one up and tore it open. A check for two hundred and seventy-five dollars slid out. He opened another for three hundred dollars.

How come these are here?

Harrison told me to set up a P.O. box in your name right after you arrived, Ben explained. He said you should have some money coming your way, since you've been on the road.

He sat there, processing the information.

Pretty stupid if you ask me, Ben added. Not setting up a spot for your money to go.

Landon looked at the driver.

Till you decide to change it or move on, your mail will be delivered here. I usually gather it twice a week, unless there's something important Harrison needs me to get.

He looked down at the envelopes.

You're welcome, Ben said, smirking.

The truck sat in the corner of the parking lot, coated in a dry bilious powder, courtesy of the surrounding trees. He'd not seen the vehicle in months and was shocked to see it bootless. They left the engine running and got out. Maple watched after them from the passenger window. Landon rounded the truck, inspecting for any irregularities. He found none.

Nothing new to this sorry sight, a voice distant behind them shouted. They turned and saw the mechanic walking toward them. His hands were riddled with oil and grime. His gray jumpsuit was stained and faded from years of repeated washing. The red-stitched name tag pilled, frayed.

Sorry. Had to move her.

That's alright, Landon said.

Has he showed up yet? Ben asked.

No, not yet, the mechanic replied.

Ben looked at his watch. We're still early.

You're welcome to wait inside. We got coffee.

That swill you have in there isn't coffee.

The mechanic laughed.

I appreciate you doing this for us.

Yeah. I hope this fellow takes it because it probably wasn't going to last much longer.

Did you tell him the problems with it? Landon said.

Of course.

Did you offer a price?

No. Just told em there's a truck here a fellow's looking to sell because the engine's shot, and he can't pay the repair costs.

Landon looked towards the Bronco and thought about the checks. Even if they all contained two hundred dollars each, he still wouldn't have close to enough to pay for the repairs.

I'll get the rest of my stuff out, he said discouragingly.

He unlocked the truck and was hit with a potent, musty odor. He coughed and began to gather his belongings. Clothes and papers. Trash and empty bottles clattered onto the pavement. He wiped the crumbs off the seats and unhooked the cloth floor panels and beat the dust and dirt from them with his palm. He went through the truck again, picking between the seat cracks for spare coin, nubby pencils, then closed the door.

A green Expedition drove into the parking lot. The long black hitch peered from beneath the rear bumper. The woman behind the wheel drove slowly passed, eyeing the truck and men standing there and pulled into an empty space and shut the truck off and got out. She was short and skeletally thin with sunken eyes and wrinkles around her mouth that made her lips seem as if they were trying to squeeze off her face. Her faded beige Tractor Supply t-shirt was tucked into her oversized jeans, which were then tucked into a pair of tawny steel-toed boots. Her brown hair was long and wiry, colorless and worn out.

Howdy, she said with a heavy accent.

Hello, Landon replied.

You tha owner?

Yes.

She don't run?

No.

Since when?

A couple of months.

What's a couple?

Three. Almost four, I'd say.

You'd say?

Yeah.

You don't kno how long you been witout transpertation?

It all blends together after a while.

She spit. So, she's just been asettin here?

Yes, ma'am.

I ain't no ma'am. Not tha old yet.

He gave Ben a side glance.

She inspected the truck several times over.

Tires look good, she said.

They are. Got them before I left Texas.

When was tha?

A year ago.

The woman nodded.

The person I spoke to on the phone was a man, the mechanic said.

Yeah, she replied. Tha'd be my son. I tol him to call on account I was in tha field. We need a new truck fo our farm, and we need it yestaday.

Your son told you the engine doesn't run, right? Landon said.

Yeah, he tol me.

Do you plan to tow it back?

Depends on wha you sellin her fo, she countered.

How about five?

She looked at the truck, toting figures in her head. She looked at the owner.

Alright. I'm easy. I'll do five. Wait here.

She walked back to the Expedition and opened the glove compartment and took out a stack of cash bound by a thick rubber band. She licked her thumb and began to count out the bills on the seat.

I wish all things were that simple, Landon mumbled.

Ben nodded.

Thank you for your help, he said to the mechanic.

Sure thing, the mechanic replied. Looks like you boys got this.

Yeah. I appreciate it.

Take care now.

You too.

The mechanic turned and walked back inside, the door jingling faintly behind him.

The woman came back with the cash.

Here ya go, she said, handing it to the owner.

Landon took the thick stack and looked at it.

Thank you.

Ain't you goin ta count it?

No. I trust you.

A thin smile sprouted across her lips.

She backed up the Expedition. Ben secured the truck to the hitch with the metal chain she'd given them. Landon climbed into the driver's seat and dropped the shifter into neutral and closed the door one last time. They shook hands through the window and she towed the truck through the parking lot and pulled onto the road and was gone.

They lunched at a diner across the street. Elderly regulars and men on their work breaks were seated at tables and booths with cherry red leather, glitter sprinkled. Photographs of veterans lined the wall behind the cash register. Low murmurs, clanking porcelain. The table had a faint sticky film from the rag the busboy had cleaned it with. The waitress set menus in front of them and took their drink order. They opened their menus and scanned the options.

Have you been here before? Landon asked.

Once, Ben replied.

What's good?

It's a diner. As long as you don't order steak or fettuccini alfredo, you should be good.

The waitress returned with their beverages and set them on the table. Do you both know what you want yet?

Not yet, Ben replied. Take your time.

They flipped through the heavily laminated pages. Breakfast and lunch options only. A small plastic sleeve contained the daily specials. Landon sipped his orange juice. The glass was cold, a small chip in the rim. The bitterness gave him a familiar feeling of home when he was a child, when his family would go to Denny's after Sunday mass.

Do you know what you want? Ben asked, closing his menu.

Yeah. I think so.

Then close your menu.

He did.

Ben took up his coffee and blew the steam away and sipped, wincing immediately. He set the mug down and tore the lid from a creamer and stirred the coffee as he poured the cream in.

It's my understanding that you learned something about Harrison when Lee was here.

Landon looked at him. Yes, he replied. You could say that.

You really didn't know?

That he's a two-time recipient of one of the most prestigious honors to be given to a writer? Or that he's heralded as one of the greatest writers who's ever lived? No, I didn't.

Ben smiled. He tapped the spoon against the mug, then set it down and drank.

When did he get them?

The last one, almost ten years ago, Ben replied, wiping his lips with his napkin. Once the book came out, he was in the spotlight for a long time. He didn't like that, but he had Meredith. That made things easier.

Was that the last time he published anything?

Yes. I delivered the manuscript to the post office myself.

You did?

Yes.

He must really trust you.

We've known each other a long time. He sipped his coffee.

Where is she?

His wife?

Yeah.

Not sure, Ben said. I assume with her sister down in Florida, but I don't know.

Why did she leave?

That's a question you'll have to ask the old man.

Alright.

You really didn't know?

About his wife in Florida?

No. About the Pulitzers.

I said I didn't.

Ben nodded.

What?

It's just strange is all.

How so?

Well, you're in that world. Wouldn't you be on the up and up on that of news?

If you pay attention to it, I suppose.

But you don't pay attention.

I try to focus on my own writing. Or, at least I did at the time.

Ben shrugged.

Would you say Harrison pays attention to those things? Landon quipped.

Point taken.

Landon drank his coffee.

Does anybody know what happened?

You mean Meredith? Ben said.

Yeah.

No.

Not even Dom or Evelyn?

No.

So, what is it you do know?

Ben set his mug on the table, pinched the corners of his mouth and sighed.

I was leaving for the night, he said. As I was going to my car, I heard them quarreling. Loudly. All the way from the third floor.

Quarreling?

Yes. Arguing.

I know what it means.

Oh. Well, it sounded bad. I'd never heard them like that before.

He drank his juice, peering at the other tables. Subtle mumblings. Men in overalls and checkered long sleeves. Black hats with battleship embroideries, names like U.S.S. New Mexico, service records, and dates. A woman reading a magazine. Everyone either drinking coffee or Coca-Cola, slurping fried eggs, buttering toast.

The waitress came by and took their orders. She departed with the menus, placing them in front of two empty stools at the end of the bar.

After the fight, Ben continued, she was gone. Took one of the cars and hasn't been seen since. Harrison was in real bad shape. I'd never seen him cry before. It's strange seeing an old man cry, I find. Rolls your skin. He shut himself up for weeks. Eventually, and that's long eventually, he got back to his routine and since then he's been back to his old self. Only—

He cut himself off. As if afraid of being heard by furtive ears.

Only what? Landon said.

Only he's not himself. I can tell that there's something thrashing about inside of him. It's as if he's remedied the symptom but not the virus.

How can you tell?

When you've known someone long enough, you grow certain instincts.

Landon nodded.

Maybe you can talk to him. He's taken a real liking to you.

I'm not sure about all that.

It's true, Ben said warmly.

I'll see what I can do.

Thank you.

You all must really love him.

Everyone at the ranch loves him.

The waitress came by with a pot of coffee.

Need a topper? she asked.

Yes, thank you, Landon said, pushing his mug towards her.

How 'bout you, handsome?

Not yet, Ben replied. When the food comes.

Should be out shortly.

They nodded and sat silently for some time.

You need a haircut, Ben said.

What?

Your hair looks ridiculous. I'll take you to get that mess cleaned up.

What if I like it this way?

You don't.

But if I did?

I don't.

He laughed.

Do you think differently about Harrison now? Knowing what you know?

Wouldn't you?

Ben shrugged.

I don't know, Landon said. It's all still surreal to me. Whenever I try to get a grasp on it, something else happens. What do you make of that?

Ben shrugged. It's just the way things go, he said.

Maybe.

The waitress came back with their plates swinging in her hands. Here we go boys, she said, smiling. She set down the steaming plates in front of them and refilled Ben's coffee. She asked if everything looked correct and they said it was. They thanked her as she turned and left.

Ben salted his potatoes.

Landon peppered his eggs.

They ate.

He ran his fingers through his cropped hair. The erect follicles tickled his palm. A small plastic bag containing a black tin of pomade rested at his feet. He examined the light scruff outlining his jaw along his weak chin in the side view mirror. The back of his neck itched incessantly.

They returned to the ranch at dusk. A pallid light outlined the crest of the mountains. The buildings were dark prisms in the faded clearing. He could see the horses strolling lackadaisically into the stable. Ranch workers finished placing equipment into the sheds and headed inside for supper. They rounded the gravel path and parked in the garage. He folded the envelopes and stuffed them into his jacket pocket and opened the glove compartment and retrieved the five thousand dollars and put that too in his pocket and shut the compartment and opened the door and got out. Maple jumped into his seat and dropped out of the Bronco. She stretched catlike then went inside.

Thank you for your help today, Landon said.

Sure thing.

Do you accept tips?

Ben laughed. That won't be necessary.

You sure?

That's your money, Mister Cassidy. Keep it under your mattress for a rainy day.

Good advice.

Enjoy your night.

The lasso glided through the air and landed around the calf's neck. He pulled it taut and led her in. He slid from the mustang, shuffled to the calf, rapidly reeling in the rope. He loosened the loop, freed the calf into her pen, and shut the gate behind her. The pasture was clear for the evening. He walked beside the trotting mustang to the stall. He opened the door and Dom led her in. They secured the stall and walked to one of the benches and sat on the tabletop. Dom pulled the pack of Winston Reds from his shirt pocket, shook a cigarette loose, and pluck edit free with his teeth. He slid the Zippo lighter out, flicked a flame, and lit the end.

Want one? he offered, blowing white smoke from his teeth, his nostrils.

No, Landon replied. Why do you always ask?

Maybe one day you will.

I doubt that.

Have you ever smoked?

A little in college. I never liked it.

Maybe it wasn't the right tobacco.

You might be right.

He stood and rounded Dom upwind, watching the tip-toeing transcendence of the evening. Stars scintillated along the white terminus that guided the night. Wind shuttled through the pine needles, sounding like distant traffic. The effigy of day's long past.

You have not spoken with *Señor* Granger in weeks, Dom said.

It's more like he hasn't spoken to me.

Si.

He's locked in his study.

He gets that way when he writes.

Was he like that before I arrived?

Yes. But you must understand that I've only seen him this way with the last book he wrote. All of his other stories were written long before the ranch existed. So, I can only confirm these habits based on that one experience. If *Señorita* Meredith were here, she could tell you more.

Landon nodded.

Señorita Chambers seems to be warming up to you.

I guess.

You should watch her train the horses. There's nothing quite like it.

I bet.

She would never admit it, but she enjoys an audience.

When that Gennady guy was here, I saw the joy in her face when she rode Signatures for everyone.

Si. Si.

It was something else watching that horse run the way he did, Landon recalled.

Signatures is a diamond in a vast desert.

When will he be back?

End of the month most likely, Dom said, thumbing the thin black hairs on his chin. *Señor* Lee tends to return our horses early.

And yet he's always late on arrival?

Si, Dom laughed. He has a peculiar punctuality problem.

Landon chuckled.

But *Señorita* Chambers—

I know, I know. I'll go watch her.

Dom smiled and pulled at his cigarette. The bright burning ember breathed a subtle glow in that darkening world.

How's your writing coming?

Good. It feels good to write again.

Bueno. Señor Granger gave you one of his books to read, no?

He did.

Do you like it?

It's incredible. I'm almost finished.

He is a gifted writer.

That's putting it mildly.

I wonder how his new book will be, Dom pondered.

Do you think it will be the last book he writes?

Dom shrugged. I suppose that is up to him.

He's getting up there.

Si.

I wonder.

Si. Yo tambien. Yo tambien.

What will happen to this place after he's gone?

Let's not talk of unpleasant things. There will be a time when that future becomes the present. Then we can ponder your answer.

Landon nodded.

Let us enjoy the night.

Si.

Dom chuckled and drew in the remainders of the tobacco. He closed his eyes, as seldom was his tradition, enveloping himself in this minor ecstasy. Then he exhaled.

The following morning, Landon returned the book to Granger after breakfast. They made small talk for an hour before the old man got up and disappeared into the capacious house. He returned with another of his books, another blue notebook.

For your continued writing efforts, he croaked.

Thank you, Landon replied, taking the items.

How're the finishing touches coming along?

The old man sat and bit into a blueberry muffin, ignoring the question.

I'm happy to read more excerpts for you.

Read what I gave you first, he said chewing.

Alright.

He finished his muffin, licked his fingers, wiped them dry with a cloth napkin, stood, brushed his hands against one another, picked up his plate, walked to the sink, and handed the dish to the maid there. He opened the back door without a word and began shutting it behind.

Harrison, Landon called out.

The old man turned, opening the door.

When does Evelyn do her training?

Granger squinted at the clock on the far wall. The slow brass pendulum swung back and forth below fat black Roman numerals. She might be there now, he said. Are you going to go watch her?

I was thinking about it.

Granger nodded, turned and closed the door behind him.

He rubbed his chin and picked up the book and examined the stained, bent pages. The torn book cover. The cracked binding. He bent the book and held it to his nose and flipped the pages with his thumb and inhaled the musty vanilla and ancient wood notes. The maid gave him a concerned look. He chortled and put the book down.

The sun sat in a cloudless sky while a cold breeze tickled the trees. He heard faint conversation from the workers afar in the fields. Horses whined in the stables. A lawnmower rumbled to life beyond the sheds. In the middle of the track were several fencing hurdles and timber logs. He did not see Evelyn.

He climbed the small steps and sat on the bleachers. He set Granger's book down and leaned back and closed his eyes and canted his head to the sky. The sun felt warm and refreshing. Memories of Texas skies returned to him. Drinking bourbon or wine on the balcony as vast skies displayed warmer shades of the color palette, painting the landscape below. Winds singing in whippoorwill notes. He opened his eyes to the sound of the creaking gate hinges to see Evelyn aboard an auburn thoroughbred.

She had on tall black paddock boots, leather riding gloves, and a helmet.

The ebony crop rested in her non-riding hand. Taupe pants and an ivory button-down. The horse walked onto the course and circled each obstacle, familiarizing itself with them, listening to her secretive whispers. They leaped over each obstacle with steadfast accuracy, freezing in midair like a Polaroid. The hooves hit the ground softly, gracefully. The horse trotted with ease, never faltering its stride, easily clearing the wooden fencing, the well-placed lumber. After two hours, Evelyn dismounted and walked the horse through the course once more, talking quietly in its ear.

He stood against the stall while she rode the horse through the gate.

What are you up to, stranger? she said, approaching.

Came to watch you.

The whole time?

Yes. Did you not see me there?

I was a little busy.

Yes, of course, he laughed.

Did you enjoy the show?

I did. You were wonderful.

He was wonderful, she said, patting the horse. I just held on for the ride.

You seem to work well together.

Thank you.

How long have you training him?

Four years. Five in December. He was put out to pasture, but Harrison saw he had something left in the tank and brought him over from England. Sure enough, he was right. He competed for another year before we officially retired him.

Did he place in anything?

Second was the highest.

Now he's out to stud?

Look at you and the lingo.

He chuckled.

Yes, he's out to stud.

Has he had many offspring?

Several. One was a runner up in two events at Chio in Aachen last June.

What is that?

A prestigious equine tournament.

Were you the rider?

No. I don't compete anymore. But I was there for consulting.

He nodded.

Would you like to ride him? she asked.

I don't think so.

Let me show you.

I don't think that's a good idea on a horse like him.

You'll be fine, she reassured.

Evelyn scooted back in the saddle and extended her hand to him.

I don't think so, Landon implored, backing away.

Hurry up, she said, the sweetness in her voice gone. I have other things to do today.

He gave her a surprised look, sighed and grasped her hand and hoisted himself into the small space reserved for him in the saddle.

She handed him the reins.

Just a light snap and he'll go, she said. Don't worry. He's a good boy.

Landon nodded, following her direction. The leather straps slapped against the horse's neck, and he started off in a slow walk. The pair rounded the course and made their way back to where they started.

Good job, Evelyn said. Now let's do it again, but faster.

He looked over his shoulder at her. You're sure that's a good idea?

Slap the straps a little harder and he'll trot. It's easy.

Alright.

The reins made a flat whap against the hide and the wind immediately rushed against his face. He lost his balance but she gripped his waist with her hands and steadied him. The horse rounded the track and returned within minute. They rode for hours. She told great truths about the horse and about other horses she'd ridden in her lifetime. After a while he was convinced she was talking more to the horse than to him. She dismounted and watched him ride solo for the better part of an hour. The horse bucked a few times but he was able to save himself. When he finished, he slid from the saddle for her to take up the bridle reins. They led the horse back to the stable.

Evelyn went inside the small ranch house and changed out of her riding gear. When she reappeared, her hair was down, and he could smell the florals from her conditioner. She walked with an erect posture that encouraged him to do the same.

What are you doing the rest of the day? Landon asked.

I have to work with another horse after lunch. By the time that's done, the day will be pretty much spent.

Takes a lot of time it sounds like.

Sure does.

Have you ever been bored of it?

Of training?

Yes.

Never.

He nodded.

Once you find your passion, you must never give it up, she said.

I suppose.

Is writing your passion?

I'd like to think it is.

Yet you gave it up when your last book didn't do so well?

He looked at her.

Harrison told me. Said you lost your way.

That's a nice way to put it.

How would you put it?

I gave up, Landon said bitterly. Like you said.

Why?

I don't think I'm as good a writer as I think I am. I think my skills are limited, that that's all they'll ever be. Limited.

How do you know?

I don't, he said, shrugging.

Then why do you continue writing if you don't?

Therein lies the struggle.

I see, Evelyn said.

Do you?

Yes.

How?

Whatever you're passionate about, no matter who you are, you always have a stretch of self doubt, if not several bouts of it throughout your life. One memorable failure is usually the harbinger of it.

Well, mine was pretty memorable then.

That's good, Evelyn said, smiling.

He turned to her. That's good?

Knowing why you failed is what baffles most people. If you don't know why you did what you did then you continue to fail at the same thing.

Makes sense.

Do you know why you failed?

Yes.

Why?

I lost interest.

In what?

My story.

Just your story?

He looked at her.

She raised her eyebrows. The small smirk morphed into a long grin, the dimple on her right cheek glaring at him. Maybe what you think you failed at wasn't what you failed at at all, she said. Perhaps what you failed at was something else.

What could it be then?

Only you know that.

They walked in silence the remainder of the time. He never wanted to face the voices. Up until now, he did everything to quiet them, bury them. But now, he began to wonder, to speculate. The sun winked though the thick tree tunnel. Sounds of falling leaves landing atop one another. Low, hollow creaks from a distance one could not gauge. He glanced at her. The sun streaked across her warm Indian skin, highlighting the full, obsidian luster of her hair.

Was it your riding that made you doubt your abilities? he asked.

I've been a competitive rider all my life, she replied. When I was a little girl, my mother moved us from the reservation to Colorado. One day, some equestrian competition was on television. I was hooked immediately. I begged my mother to sign me up for lessons. It came so naturally to me that I attended equestrian school. I thought I could be one of the best, and what's worse was that people told me I could be. But when you start to hear that at a young age, you begin to lose your perspective. And when you start losing competitions, it messes with your head. You question everything that you thought you had the answers to, but your answers, no matter how many times you repeat them to yourself, were the ones that pointed you in the wrong direction. That's how I rode for years afterwards. I would enter so many competitions, only to always come up short. Years of this. Years of misdirection. What is one to do when the path that you've walked your entire life is riddled with signs directing you further into darkness?

I was lucky when Harrison showed up in my life when he did. I'd taken up drinking since I was eighteen. Entered competitions sloshed. Fell off my horse a time or two. I was twenty three when I met him. He's the only one that held a matchstick, the only one that led me out of that cave. Out of the dark. He encouraged me to look at my life from a different perspective. I, being the drunk I was, wasn't able to do it. But eventually, little by little, my confidence returned. And I was able to compete again. And win again. Granted, this took years, and I never became the second-coming of Reiner Klimke that I was lauded to be when I was a girl, but I found something greater. My passion, reignited. Brighter than before. After I found that, I never turned back. And here I am today, all these years later. Happier than I've ever been.

How long were you in the dark? Landon said.

A long time.

And you're still happy that you're not the best?

She looked at him and smiled. Depends on your definition of happy. The regular definition.

There is no such thing as a regular definition. All definitions are the works of those that wish to interpret the word based on the current point one finds themselves in. Words and definitions were made by man, and can be manipulated by man, as is all things created. If you want to stick to what was taught to you in elementary school, by all means, but when you decide how the foundation of your life is established, all else will cease to matter outside of it, and all you're left with is the knowledge of how you got to where you're standing. And that the only person that put you there is yourself.

You mean now?

I mean always. I am the best because I can happily look at my life and see it for myself. And that's all who needs to see it. All who needs to know it.

He pondered silently about this for the reminder of their walk, listening to the low crunching leaves beneath his feet.

The dusty gray pinto shook its large head as flies swarmed the dark, hairy ears. Dom replaced the lighter in the Winston pouch and canted his smoking head as he watched Landon mount the old horse and kick her into atrot. His head followed the rider owllike, twin beams of smoke slithering from his black nostrils.

Someone's discovered a newfound confidence in their riding, he said.

Thanks to you, Landon replied with a wry smile.

You joke.

Only a little.

I feel betrayed.

Hey, now we can wrangle together like real ranch hands.

Are you calling yourself a ranch hand mi amigo?

Maybe.

Well, if that's the case, we need to get you to control your horse at a slightly better pace than that stroll.

Do you usually have a specific way you train people how to ride?

Everyone does.

But the goal is the same.

The rider has to understand why they're riding the horse. They have to respect the horse. The only way a rider can do that is to take their time.

How long does it usually take?

Seis meses. Podría ser más largo.

Six months, Landon exclaimed.

Could be longer. It takes time.

I was thinking more like a week or two.

Do you have someplace to be? Dom said, smirking.

I must be ahead of the curve then. He leaned forward and patted the pinto on the underside of her neck.

You're not, Dom chuckled. Come down from there and walk her to the lake. Water her. Then, we'll begin our next lesson.

He dismounted and grabbed the bridle reins and clicked his tongue at her. Come on girl, he said. He walked the pinto across the grounds and opened the gate and closed it behind her and walked her among the trotting mares and thoroughbreds. They watched them pass. The lime stained grass bent beneath their feet. An invigorating wind brushed by, smelling of wet earth and pine. Other than the occasional nicker, there was silence. They came to the lake. Slow moving bass and pumpkin seed sunfish swam like ghosts beneath the blooming pale water lotuses. Minnow pods tested the surface, rippling like raindrops. The pinto lowered her head and slowly drank while her flanks shook to rid herself of the constant irksome of the black flies. He patted her hide and left her to walk the perimeter of the lake. The late morning sun glared back at him. The bright, white hole waved along the surface, never coming to full symmetry. He looked back towards the ranch. Alone, save the pinto. He removed his shoes and tucked his socks into them and tossed them aside and walked in. Mud smoked from his footsteps. The water was cold and felt good as it grew up his body. She lifted her head, the water dribbled from her gunpowder muzzle as he lowered into the bright glare. He felt the fish bump into him and scurry away. Stringy grass caught between his toes, twigs and other assorted mysteries underfoot. He came to the edge of the sunspot, his body half submerged. He reached out and touched the edge of the surface. The warmth comforted him. The pinto watched her rider with blinking placidity, then lowered to drink. He came to the locus and stood crucified in the enveloping white. Rogue sprinkles kissed his cheeks, his lower body warmed, and he could see the bare circumference of the sun through his red veined eyelids. He pushed off the bed and laid floating there in outstretched glory. He could hear the subtle motions of the fish beneath. Sometimes curious. Never bothersome. He began to cry. Tears leaked from their enclosures and vaporized within seconds. His throat tightened, letting out painful wallows of which no juncture could be made. And yet, he did not move, he dared not move.

Dom sat his horse at the fence line watching the dim figures materialize.

He saw that the young rider was wet, but decided not to think much of it. He eyed the sun and measured it against his arm to obtain the time. He plucked out a cigarette and lit it and drew in a long and silent lungful, awaiting the pupil's approach.

Is she full? he asked.

She ought to be, Landon replied. Drank damn near half the lake.

Dom laughed. The heat must be getting to her. It only gets worse as the summer carries on. We must be careful with them when that happens.

Right.

He took another long pull of the cigarette and extinguished it on the fence post and flicked it into a nearby trash bin and wafted the smoke away.

Bueno, he said, clapping his hand against the young man's shoulder. Let's get started.

He was over eight months on the ranch when he became confident in his riding abilities to wrangle the livestock from his own mount. When he wasn't working the farm, he rode or maintained the mares with some of the more experienced hands. He fell into a daily routine that suited him well: Wake up at six, shower, dress, eat breakfast, write until noon, take lunch with Granger and then others, work the horses and finish with the livestock until five. He grew fond of October, a seasoned chestnut Appaloosa. The muscular horse had long since gone gray in the muzzle, but he still drove fast from time to time. Every night after they rode, Landon would spend an hour brushing the Appaloosa's coat. He learned to speak to the horses, love the horses. In the evenings, he would eat and laugh and talk with Granger, Evelyn, Dom, and the rest of the workers. The large family setting delighted Granger, and he told old tales while everyone would quietly listen as detailed frescoes painted in their minds. Afterwards, they'd play pool or cards. A few nightcaps. He would journal for an hour before turning in, snuggling beside the snoring Maple.

A late autumn evening began to settle when Granger called out to him from the fence line. He halted October, sat him, and swung his leg over the muscular backside and slid to the ground. He hitched the bridle reins to the fence post then wiped the sweat from his brow with the back of his shirt sleeve.

You hollered?

You're getting better, Granger complimented.

Thank you.

Is he treating you well?

He is, he replied, patting the Appaloosa's hide.

Good.

Granger peered at the bright auburn coated stud. He looked like he could still compete based on his size, stride, and strength. But the old man knew such desires garnered false realities. That the only place the horse would ever see the full magnificence of competition again would be in his dreams. Dreams of glory, dreams of defeat. These are the things dreams tell us. At one point or another, each glory has its equal defeat. Not knowing which is upon us is the greatest cruelty, but also the greatest victory.

Something on your mind? Landon said.

I have a favor to ask you.

Ask away.

Put him up. We'll walk to the study.

Alright.

Landon walked October to his stall and stripped his saddle and reins. He watered and fed him two carrots, a sugar cube, and set a square bale and told him he would be back to brush him. Then he headed out and met Granger along the gravel path.

He'd not been in the study since the first days of his arrival. The inviting odors, the bright light from the windows hit him anew. Granger opened several of the windows, letting in the symphonic birdsong, the rustling trees. He shuffled to the kitchen and made a pot of coffee.

What is it you wanted to discuss, Landon said, sitting on the leather armchair, sliding his boots off.

I'd like you to write a foreword, Granger said, pouring the coffee grounds into the filter.

An immediate perplexity slapped him across his face. He dropped his boot and sat up.

A foreword? For what?

My book.

It's finished?

Yes.

The maintenance and everything?

That's right.

And you want me to write the foreword for it?

Yes. Would you be up for it? Granger said walking with the two steaming mugs by the handle in one hand, two coasters in the other. He slapped the coasters on the table and set the mugs atop them and rounded the table and slunk into the couch and removed his boots.

Landon pinched the bridge of his nose and took up his coffee and drank.

Wouldn't it be best to get someone with a higher stature to write something about the book that took you over twenty years to write?

Frauds, you mean? Granger said with a dismissive wave. Those childlike detectives have nothing else better to do. They always believe there are hidden messages in my words. It's ridiculous. What I have to say is on the damned page. All one needs to do is read what is written. Did you know they teach lectures on my work?

I did not.

Lectures, he exclaimed, shaking his head. It's maddening.

Maybe it's because you're the last of a dying breed. There are no other works like yours out there. Nor equal.

There's your foreword. Jot it down and be done with it.

Landon laughed.

I can't write about something I haven't read. Especially something so monumental.

Granger leaned and set his mug down. He stood, walked to his desk, slid the large drawer open, took out a tall stack of papers, walked back, and set the papers down with a hard slam. The mugs shifted, spilling black coffee over the rims.

There you go, the old man said.

Landon gazed at the ivory block of paper as if seeing the Ark of the Covenant.

Are you sure?

Yes. It's ready.

I don't know, Harrison, this is—

Read the damn pages Landon, the old man chided. Then tell me what you think. We can go from there. It's just a book for Christ's sake. Nothing more, nothing less.

He patted the young man's shoulder, crossed to his bookshelf, and pulled a book. A clicking sound reverberated across the room. Landon looked around and saw the wall come slightly ajar.

You're welcome to read upstairs if you like, Granger said.

He slowly stood and walked over to the wall. He pulled the hidden door open, seeing the wooden staircase to the second story.

A secret door? Landon said, astonished.

Ever since I saw *Young Frankenstein*, I've always wanted one. You can read up there if you like.

Thank you.

Granger patted him on the shoulder. Happy reading.

The second floor was surrounded by glass. The exposed beams overhead was varnished in a dark walnut. Brass hooks secured the thick, mauve curtains. A bar, stocked with unopened bottles of fine liquor, was flanked by two wooden stools with hickory leather cushions. A couch, matching the one downstairs, sat beneath a large painting of a sunset forest. He set the manuscript on the table, unlatched the deck door, slid it open, and walked outside. Each side of the deck had three powder blue lounge chairs and a white, steel table. Dead leaves and twigs had crept into the crevices. A whispering breeze. He looked out at the land, observing the hustle and bustle that had come to be his life. He went in, slid the door shut, and latched it. He walked to the couch, sat, and stared at the bright block of porcelain paper. The couch creaked when he leaned forward and thumbed to the last page, finding the final count: *640*.

He was over sixty pages deep when he saw the ironclad clouds move in. He stood and walked to the bar. The bottles, perfectly spaced apart. A thin film of dust across the shelves. He took a glass from the cupboard and washed it. He broke the seal on an amber bottle of Jefferson's and poured a generous amount. The spicy oak notes made his eyes curl into his head, like the welcoming fragrance of an old lover. He crossed to the window to witness the rapid darkening of the afternoon. Tiny droplets began to smear down the window. A faint clap of thunder. He returned to the couch and continued the story.

The rain had been falling steadily for three hours. He'd become quite drunk. His empty stomach growled in sluicing intonations. He made his way downstairs and explored the pantry. Canned goods and boxed cereals. He peeked out the window and saw the gravel path completely underwater. He poured a hefty bowl of Raisin Bran and filled the bowl with milk until he saw the cereal shift. His stomach bellowed haphazardly after a few bites, causing him to beeline it to the bathroom.

The study had turned icy cold. He found a heavy rust colored jacket and matching knit hat in the closet and put them both on. He saw that the rain had turned each building into its own private island. Lightning flashed in the distance, but the thunder did not come. He could not tell if the storm was journeying closer or venturing farther. The wind had picked up. Leaves slung through the sky like comets. His stomach continued to growl. He cranked the can opener until the lip gave way. He poured chicken noodle soup into a pot and turned the gas stove on. A soft hiss then the pop of blue flame. He stirred the contents with a fork then set the utensil aside. The soup heated quickly and he poured it into a bowl and stood by the far windowed wall and cooled the soup with his breath and ate while watching the trees thrash wildly.

The rain still fell when he finished the manuscript at six in the morning. His head was pounding. He set the last pages down on his chest and exhaled in celebrated exhaustion. His eyes began to water as he thought about the ending of the story, the words settling into his mind like sediment at the bottom of a wine barrel. Then he closed his eyes and fell asleep.

You finished it? a voice said.

He almost fell off the couch in fright. The throw pillows he'd stacked for a foot rest tumbled to the floor.

Granger was sitting across the table, the newborn sun beaming through the fissured curtains. His legs were crossed, his hands calmly settled in his lap.

How long have you been there? Landon asked.

About ten minutes, the old man replied. Why

didn't you wake me?

I just did.

Right.

You finished it?

Landon yawned and rubbed the back of his neck. Yes.

All of it?

Yes.

Without stopping?

Yes.

Why the hell did you do that?

I had to finish it, answered Landon. It's incredible.

Granger nodded.

What time is it?

Almost noon.

Landon groaned as he stood. The whiskey left a foul, dry taste in his mouth. He stretched his arms over his head, then bent over and stretched the backs of his legs. Two audible pops sounded from his hips. He picked up his glass, walked to the bar, and washed it in the small sink there. He opened a drawer and found a cloth and dried the glass and examined it in the sharp glow of the intruding sun and placed it back in the cupboard and walked to the bathroom and relieved himself. When he walked out, Granger was still there.

Can I ask you something? Landon said.

Of course.

Why didn't you tell me who you were when we first met?

How do you mean?

You know what I mean.

Why would me telling you my credentials be of any importance to you in a time of need?

Because you're a big deal.

Says who?

Never mind, Landon sighed.

Granger chuckled. Throughout my life, I've found that when I told people who I was, our relationship was never the same. I saw the change in their faces so clearly. So many people I loved. Respected. Gone now. I've burned more bridges than I've built. All because of that shift in expression. The realization of ulterior motives they thought they'd never conjure. It was not surprise I saw in their faces. But greed.

Landon sat back on the couch in that silent room.

What about Meredith?

What about her? replied the old man.

What ever happened to her?

She's with her sister in Florida.

Yeah, I know. But, what happened between you two?

Granger took a deep breath and stood. He walked to the cracked curtains and looked out, rimmed in white light, eclipsing the room with his silhouette.

We had a fight, he said sullenly.

About what?

Something we did not need to fight about.

Did you apologize?

Mhm.

And she still won't come back?

Suffice it to say.

Do you think she will forgive you?

Granger turned and looked at his inquisitor. That's her decision, he said. All I can do is wait.

Landon looked at the manuscript.

Will you write it?

The foreword?

Yes.

I'd be honored.

Granger nodded.

He turned back and stood in the window, looking out on the land. His shadow stretched across the floor, dark as oil. A pressurized stillness in the room. Silence purloined from infinity.

A cold snap came in the form of quarter-sized flakes. The sky was the color of stone. The hills and the river sand the trees had evolved into a bright, cold wasteland. Predators circled overhead hoping to spot their prey scampering through the deep snow before beginning their dive with outstretched talons.

A plump squirrel exploded in a twist of intensities, limbs and gore. Splintered bones. Purple viscera. Eyes black and lifeless as the critter twitched through its final moments. The snow steamed from the hot, pulpy mess. Then the bloody remains was taken up by the hawk and flown into the gray beyond. Vultures shortly began to wheel overhead, eyeing the bits of tissue that remained.

Did you see that? Dom called out.

Yeah, Landon replied. That was something else.

They usually don't blow up like that.

Must've been a real fat one.

Sí, lo era.

They rode the horses past the bloody grave, dressed in heavy coats with long johns and salopettes, their head swarmed by wool scarves and fur hats. The snow had ceased, but the chill kept cutting at them. Dom shouldered a chocolate coated Jarrett Standard hunting rifle. Landon adjusted his gloved hands, making sure the skin on his wrists stayed covered. He enjoyed the cold, but did not care for the wind. He found the snow enchanting when he was a boy, but found it irritating in his older years.

The horses plodded along, pulling hard as their hooves sunk into the powdery ground. Hot air poured from their nostrils. They walked cautiously so as to not lose their footing.

What are we doing out here, Dom? Landon asked.

One of the workers told *Señor* Granger that there's a fox stealing the chickens.

How do you know it's a fox?

It was confirmed this morning when they found the tracks in the snow.

We looking to kill it?

Lo tienes.

Y si se escapa?

Dom turned and looked at him.

Luego lo perseguimos.

They rode through the tree line. Slow and steady, the snow crunching beneath the hooves. After ten minutes, they emerged on the other side of a tall hill that brought them high enough to where they could scout the land better. Dom slid the Jarrett Standard from his shoulder and unlatched the scope from the barrel and laid the rifle across his lap and glassed the land. His partner sat watching him, huddled tightly in his coat. He tried looking out across that desolate plain but the snow shine stung his eyes to the point he had to look away. He looked back at the trail they'd forged. Their circular tracks like some archaic form of Braille. Tips of green grass erect like wild parakeet feathers. Granite smoke poured into the sky beyond the thick forest, the hot chimneys from whence they came. Dom's head swiveled slowly back and forth. Once in a while, he would lower the scope to see with both eyes or to rub his sockets warm. Then he would bring the scope back and scan again. They sat for a long time. The wind whisked sharply around them. Nothing skyward moved, nothing below made a sound.

How many do you think there are? Landon asked.

Not sure, Dom replied. Could be one, could be many.

Have you had this problem before?

Once, many years ago.

Do they tend to come out in this weather?

No. Not this far, at least.

They must be pretty hungry.

Landon looked out on the white hills. He thought he saw something move far off to the left, but could not be too sure. Check over there, he said, pointing.

Dom glassed the area and caught sight of something heading into the woods. He picked up the rifle and attached the scope and shouldered the rifle and kicked his horse toward sits new trajectory. His partner fell in behind.

The snow billowed like waves crashing into a rocky shore. The slow, steady fall of snow reddened their cheeks as they steered the horses towards flat ground. They brought them to a trot and inspected the tree line. Nothing moved. Wooden limbs crackled faintly from within. Snapping twigs caused their heads to spin around, but all that stirred was the great white silence.

Maldita sea, Dom mumbled.

Any tracks? Landon said, looking beneath the horses.

No. *Nada.*

I'll check around.

Landon sat his horse and dismounted. His feet crunched through the ice and he could feel the cold already wet on his toes. He walked to the tree line and gripped an ivory trunk for balance and peered into the thick woods.

Anything? Dom asked.

No.

He ventured through the thin trees, checking his distance from the horses to make sure he wasn't straying too far. He inspected the ground, finding beige pine needles peeking through. A crimson maple leaf fell from some unknown location. The snow hadn't been disturbed. He turned and headed back.

When he returned to the horses, Dom was not there. The rifle was gone. An odd feeling of isolation began to flutter in his gut. He looked around but did not spot his companion. A few feet away, he caught sight of his trail and followed as quickly as he could.

Dom was crouched behind a large boulder, checking the rifle chamber. He saw his panicked partner come through the trees, and signaled for him to stop. He held a finger to his lips and slowly waved him over.

What is it? Landon whispered, crouching beside the rifleman.

Keep quiet, Dom said. They're on the other side.

They?

Two of em. I found their tracks near the horses. You went the wrong way, he chuckled.

Is their nest nearby?

They shelter in dens.

Alright, he said, rolling his eyes. Is their den nearby?

I don't know. I just saw them come this way.

You're going to shoot them?

Si.

Both of them?

Si.

Landon sidled along the boulder and peered over the edge.

Two foxes with tangerine coats were in the midst of devouring the stolen chicken. Their ribs quaked against their auburn pelts, their emaciated stature like a peculiar breed of canine. Their ears and tail looked overgrown compared to the rest of them. They ate the chicken furiously as what could be their first meal in weeks, the small razor teeth flaring beneath their black, blood-coated lips. Feathers furled into the air. One of them sneezed.

Dom cocked the rifle as quietly as he could.

Their ears perked at the sound and they stood frozen, scanning with their bright almond eyes. They must've heard Dom get up because one of them grabbed the remains of the chicken and took off into the woods. By the time Dom got into position, they were gone. Faint trickles of snow fell from the branches they passed.

Demonios inteligentes, Dom cursed, lowering the rifle.

Si, Landon exhaled with relief.

Did you see how frail they were?

It looked like they're starving.

Dom got up and walked to the feathery blood plot. Crimson feathers, strands of viscera. He kicked at the snow then looked in the direction they ran to.

Do we give chase? Landon asked.

We have to, Dom replied. Otherwise, they will keep coming back as long as they know they can get away with it.

What time is it?

Dom looked at his watch. *Casi diez.*

Cuánto tiempo deberíamos estar en esto?

Veamos hasta dóndenos lleva el mediodía.

Bien.

They made their way back to the horses, mounted up, and rode through the woods at a slow trot until they got to another clearing. The fox's tracks were easily noticeable, thanks to the dribbling blood from the chicken. They saw the bandits across a distant clearing. Dom dropped the reins and swung the rifle from his shoulder, cocked the chamber, sighted and fired. The sound cracked sharply and echoed far off into the abyss. The muzzle smoked as if it were breathing. They looked for signs of contact but saw none. Dom shucked the brass shell from the chamber and placed it in his saddlebag and fitted in a fresh shell and cocked the chamber and shouldered the rifle. They kicked the horses faster and found no other sign of impact where they'd last seen them. The woods ahead were thick and difficult to navigate. They rode the perimeter, following the small green compass on the rifle before turning the horses west. They were two hours into their pursuit with no sign of their target. On the other side of the woods, any prints would have been long buried from the increasing winds.

Anything? Dom asked.

No, Landon replied. Nothing from what I can see. They might not have come out.

You might be right.

Dom looked into the woods. Nothing moved. He dismounted and opened his saddlebag, and came out with a can of chicken. He looked around the clearing for the highest rise then proceeded to shape out a bowl in the snow.

What are you doing? Landon said.

Baiting, Dom replied. You said so yourself, they're starving. So, if they're still in there, which I believe they are, they will get the scent of the meat and investigate. When they do, our efforts here should be over.

He peeled open the can and poured the watery contents out. He returned to his saddlebag, retrieved another can, and added it to the bowl. He placed the empty cans in a separate sleeve then remounted.

That should do it, Dom said. Let's get up that hill and shovel out a vantage point.

They rode up the hill, sat the horses and dismounted. They dug until they found the grass and shaped a bunker with the disturbed snow. Noon quickly approached. They followed the circumference of the woods with their eyes. Nothing came.

Maybe they went out the other side? Landon whispered.

Possibly.

But you don't think so.

No.

Do you think their den is in there?

There's a good chance of it.

How much longer do you want to wait? Dom held his finger to his lips then pointed.

He looked down and saw in the shallow tree line the subtle movements of the foxes. They were heavily shadowed, but he recognized their auburn manes slithering about the trunks. The hen was gone. They paused to sniff the air. Then they finally emerged. First, their heads, looking back and forth across the clearing, then their malnourished bodies. They orbited the bait with sloth-like caution, extending their thin cone snouts for better identification. They stepped closer. One of them nuzzled the pile and jerked back, ready to flee. But they did not flee. The other opened its mouth and nibbled at the pile and chewed and swallowed. Then they both laid on their bellies and ate. Dom cocked the rifle and fired without saying a word. The sudden wail of the first falling caused the other to freeze in place. Dom quickly reloaded, cocked, sighted and fired again.

They stood in the remnants of the rifle fire. The echo rippled throughout the pale landscape. Gazing down, they saw the quivering, bloodied bodies. The thin burgundy spray along the snow from the exit wounds.

When they arrived, one of them had struggled next to the other. He was already dead. She'd made a drag mark in the snow to rest her head on his neck. Her low cries of pain as if to say she was sorry. Landon dismounted and crouched down to beside her. Her eyes looked up at him, still crying. Apologizing. She nuzzled into her dead lover's fur once more as her onlooker watched the last ember in her soul flicker out. He knelt beside them for a long time. Then began to weep. A cold streak ran from his nose. He wiped it away with the back of his gloved hand then cleaned his glove in the snow. He'd never been a part of something like that before and he'd hoped he never would again. He ran his hand against their bristly fur then stood and walked back to his horse and slid the shovel from the rucksack and proceeded to dig.

What are you doing, Mister Cassidy? Dom asked.

I'd like to bury them, he sniffled.

Why would you do that?

He didn't answer.

The day had rounded two o clock. The sky was as barren as the land. A small pile of muddied snow and hunks of grass sat beside the hole.

Do you think this is deep enough? Landon asked.

Si, Dom said, smoking a cigarette. That should be good.

Landon nodded.

He pulled himself out of the grave and walked over to the dead foxes and carefully moved the female from the male and placed her aside and took up the already stiffened male and walked him back to the hole and gently laid him in. He retrieved the mate and placed her as best he could to replicate the way they'd gone. He stood over the grave, staring down at them. Remembering. He took up the shovel and casted the earth over them, that these lovers entwined here never see such evils again. They did not speak on the way back. When they rode through the shaded tunnel that connected the track to the ranch, Dom stopped dead still.

Landon turned and halted his horse.

What? he asked.

Are you alright?

Yes.

Are you sure?

I think so.

I'm sorry how things went, but there was no other way.

Is that right? Landon said, still unsettled. There was no other way?

We could have set traps or they may have been hit by a car. Either way, they would have suffered a more painful death than the one we gave them.

You gave them.

Si, Dom said, nodding. I gave them.

I'm sorry. I've never seen anything like that before.

Why did you get down from your horse?

What?

Why did you get down from your horse? When they died.

I guess I had to see them.

Why?

To apologize.

Dom nodded.

They sat there quietly. A plane hummed beyond the shrouded gray clouds. Several flocking geese barked from the opposite end of the treetops. Over thirty of them, lined magnificently. Their long V in a state of continuous evolution. Their wings flapped inches apart from one another. He watched them best he could through the thick branches above, until he lost sight of them. Their callings now cold and gone.

It's that time of year again, Dom said.

Yeah, Landon agreed, turning his horse. It sure is.

IV

Ben plowed and salted the paths up to the main road early that morning. Landon, Dom, Evelyn, and the rest of the ranch hands set up small pathway lights and secured the horses at the racetrack stables. Evelyn stayed behind to finish preparations while the others secured the livestock and equipment. They fought the thickening snowfall for hours. By the time they'd finished, they were coated in sweat. Landon could feel his heart beating against his chest, his breath tight in his throat. His bruised red hands were stiff, beet red and slow to straighten. He ran them under hot water, feeling the blood burn inside.

Está bien, Señor Cassidy? one of the men asked.

Si, he replied. *Gracias.*

Este clima es inusualpara esta época del año, Dom said.

Tengo todo asegurado, another man called, coming through the door.

Bien. Ahora esperamos.

He'd made a makeshift bath caddy out of a fallen oak branch, sawed shy of three feet, varnished in a thick maple. He set it across the tub rim so he could write while he soaked. Outside, the wind whipped mercilessly. Sharp and serene.

He been in an exhaustive slumber when he was awakened by the telephone around eleven. He reached across the bedside table and lifted the receiver.

Hello? Landon answered groggily.

Were you asleep?

I was.

Sorry.

It's alright. What are you doing up at this hour?

I couldn't sleep.

How are the horses?

Fine. Taking the storm like champs, Evelyn chuckled.

That's good to hear.

How's your writing coming?

It's coming.

That's good, she chuckled.

Yes.

Can you read me some?

Right now?

If you don't mind.

Sure, hold on a second.

He flung the covers over and got out of bed. The floorboards were cold and piercing. He walked to the desk and picked up one of the notebooks. He flipped through the pages and read a few inscriptions. As he was turning, his eye caught something out in the azure glow from the lamplights that outlined the gravel pathway. Through the phantasmagoric blizzard, he saw them. Heads erect, ears alert, tails downcast. He leaned forward as if to better his vision. They stood, watching him.

He ran to the phone and told her he would call her back. Before she could answer, he hung up and was getting dressed.

Maple snapped awake from the sound of the receiver being replaced. Stay here, girl, he said, stroking her head.

He fitted his shoes on and tied the laces and opened the door and ran down the hallway and into the stillness of the living room. He looked out the window to see if they were still there. But they weren't. He opened the door and the wind immediately crashed into his body as he worked the door shut. Ben had plowed an hour before but the pathways were already covered with about two inches of snow. All was dark except for the illuminated path bulbs. All silence filled with the sound of the howling wind. He squinted through the translucent snowfall as he made his way towards the main house. Two figures darted across the path towards the back road. He walked cautiously towards them. Within a few feet, they stopped, turned, and sighted him. He froze. Their cerulean silhouettes trotted up the back road, provoking him to give chase.

The icy wind lashed at his face. His cheeks burned, his nose constantly dripped. He stopped and tried to catch his breath, but the cold made it excruciating. Each inhalation pained him. Each time he looked up, they watched him. He tried calling out to them, but the words did not emit. He started after them again, but they turned and ran. His footing gave way, causing him to tumble in the snow. He got to his knees, wiped the frost from his face and continued on. When he emerged from the woods, the light in Evelyn's window was on. To the right of the track, behind the bleachers, stood the foxes. They were wet and speckled white. Black eyes, ears and nose. The gray along their bellies glowed against the blue hued pathway lights. They stared at him for a long time, unmoving. A heavy gust whipped the snow in flurried tirade. He looked towards the window and saw Evelyn standing there. The female slowly stepped towards him. Her breath plumed from her nostrils. He reached out his open hand in hopes of touching her, but she stayed well out of reach, canting her head in confusion at his offer. The male watched him, slowly breathing. The female sniffed his outstretched hand. He could feel her hot breath. Then she recoiled. Her black eyes unblinking.

Forgive me, he pleaded.

The door to the ranch house opened and Evelyn came running out in a thick black coat.

He turned to see her fighting against the wind and the snow. When he looked back at the foxes, they were gone. Their tracks had already been filled by the mercurial snowfall. All trace of their being there gone.

Evelyn called out inaudibly.

He ran to her.

Landon? she yelled.

Yes, he replied. It's me.

What the hell are you doing?

I'm not sure, he said, peering about for the foxes.

Come on, let's get inside.

IV

They turned and ran, shutting the door behind them.

The wind shook the small shelter. They could hear the snow pelting the windows like exploding firecrackers. She'd made a small fire in the chimney. Black smoke emitted from the bright orange flames. Dancing embers extinguishing. The room reeked of fresh cedar, as if the house had just been built. The decor was a replica of the larger guest house. Furs along the walls, an expansive floor length Persian rug. Leather couches and sofas. A large black-box television displayed a muted meteorologist, showing images suggesting the storm would last until late morning. The pendulum clock over the mantle chimed midnight.

I've never seen so much snow in all my life, Landon said, shedding his wet coat.

What were you doing out there?

I-I'm not sure.

Landon.

I thought I saw something.

You thought you saw something?

Yes.

Like what?

It doesn't matter.

Well, sit next to the fire. You need to warm.

Yes, he said crossing to the hearth.

He sat in front of the whipping flames, their heat already upon him. His outstretched reddened claws slowly opened and regained their feeling. Evelyn slid behind the small bar there and proceeded to make him a drink.

I suppose it was stupid I was out there, huh?

Your words, Evelyn replied, pouring the shaker full with contents unknown to him. She made the cocktails and poured them into two mugs and crossed to him and sat alongside, handing him the drink.

What is it? he asked.

It'll warm you up.

Smells good.

Yes.

They touched glasses and drank.

It's good, he complimented.

Thank you.

He drank the cocktail rather quickly.

She laughed, stood and made him another.

When he was warm enough, he told her of their hunt a few weeks back. About the pursuit of the foxes and how he wished he'd never offered to go with Dom. He said he'd never seen anything shot nor buried. It was as if the idea of their existence brought everything into full understanding, and that man's only pursuit in life is to take what he knows is not privileged to take. The ideas our mind tells itself over and over again comes to fruition when the day finally aligns with the situation it was looking for, assimilating for. Whats the only way to rid oneself of inconveniences? Extermination. What is the only way to rid the world of interference? Destruction. There is no other absolution, only the finite. But how can such fatalities be our only answer when we see them in our sleep, at the plains of our judgment? Is the only cure for such atrocities merely reproduction of further atrocities? All history of man's existence is brought back to it. Back to death. The unconscious fascination. The trait that binds us into network. When suppressed, it lies in wait, as if we believe it to be eradicated forever. And when it finally decides to emerge, we gladly take ahold like the hand of an old lover. What repercussions to follow is of no concern to the instinct. All that there is is the moment, the materializing present. Naked roads hidden beyond further roads, awaiting those amaurotic steps.

Am I a bad person? he asked, watching the fire.

What?

Am I a bad person.

No, she said gently.

Have you ever been close to death?

Sadly yes.

What happened?

My mother and my sister.

Both gone?

Yes. Together?

No.

Oh, good.

She chuckled.

I'm sorry, he said. I didn't mean it like that.

It's alright.

They drank quietly as the fire crackled.

How did you move on? Landon asked.

What?

How were you able to recover from their deaths?

I just did, Evelyn said. You have to. The dim reality is that the world keeps turning. There is no tragedy big enough to slow the turning of time. Sorrow has no say in such matters. She sighed and gave him a small smile. Perhaps the rhythm that controls all things it the correct rhythm. Perhaps any adjustment to that rhythm would bring matters into a territory too slow or fast for our grief. For grief has its own rhythm.

Landon Cassidy unzipped his second jacket, and the notebook fell out. The cover was damp, but the pages were not damaged. He picked it up and looked it over, not remembering how it got there.

Here, he said, holding out the notebook. This was what I was going to read you.

She smiled and took the damp book. She opened the cover and flipped through the ivory pages, reading over the bleeding words.

Nice penmanship, she said.

Thank you, he chuckled.

He stood and added three logs to the fire, enhancing the blaze.

She laid back on her elbows while he laid a large crocheted blanket over her.

Thank you, she said.

You're welcome.

They drank their cocktails while she turned back to the beginning.

Can I read first?

Sure.

Have you had anyone read you your own work before? Evelyn asked.

Nope. Can't say that I have.

She smiled and began to read in a low, sweet voice.

Are you cold? she asked a few minutes later.

A little.

Evelyn wriggled up the floor to the leather sofa and dragged large quilt off. She flung it over Landon and sat beside him. The notebook splayed prone next to them. The empty mugs stood against one another, their pale porcelain faces refracting the dimming flames in delicate metronomes. A log silently split, birthing forth a cluster of topaz sparks. She looked at the notebook.

How much more do you think you'll write? she said.

I'm not sure, he muttered. You never know with these things.

How long do you plan to stay?

He cracked his eyes at her.

She sat like a child, legs drawn in, arms hugging them tight. Her head rested on her knees, one supple cheek pressed to her bone. In her eyes was the distant reminder that this life he'd undertaken was not entirely his own.

I don't know. I've got nowhere else to go. If I'm a bother to anyone, I'll leave.

No, no, she said. That's not what I was saying.

What are you saying?

I'm just asking how long you'll stay. That's all.

He sat up and looked at the fire.

I don't know, he muttered.

Okay.

Okay?

Yeah.

Okay.

You still want me to leave? After almost two years?

Not at all. You've proven to be quite helpful around here.

But you don't trust me.

I called you tonight didn't I? Evelyn reminded. You ran through a blizzard to see me.

That doesn't answer anything.

It doesn't?

No.

Maybe you're asking the wrong question.

Or you're afraid of the answer.

Evelyn chuckled. Maybe.

Then answer.

What was the question again?

He chortled and shook his head. It doesn't matter, he said.

No, it doesn't.

Have you ever thought about leaving?

Me?

Yes.

A few times.

A few times?

There was never a valid reason why I wanted to.

Is there ever such a reason when one decides to leave a good place?

If there is I've never heard it, she laughed. Everything I ever wanted is here.

Right.

She set her chin on her knees and watched the fire. Her spine curled like a tortoiseshell. Her hair laid in delicate layers over her shoulders, her back. The orange glow paling upon her face. As if in reading words formulated there for her private comprehension.

A mechanical growl sounded in the distance.

Landon sat up as the purring quickly drew closer. He looked at Evelyn.

Ben's snowplow, she said.

He shucked the quilt and stood and crossed to the window and peered out into the cold night. A bright, circular headlight beamed like a Cyclops' eye. The yellow plow split the snow in bifurcated geysers. It rounded the house, splattering the exterior. Marble sized salts shot out against the bare ground. The truck rounded the track and faded through the trees, the light disappearing like a specter.

How long will he be doing that? Landon asked.

All night most likely.

The whole ranch?

He's dedicated when these things happen.

I'd say so.

He stood there a long time. Finally, he walked back and picked up the mugs and set them in the bar sink and laid beside her and flung the quilt over their legs. The emerald throw pillow was hard and barley cradled his head.

What were you were thinking about? Evelyn said.

When?

At the window.

I was watching Ben.

Afterwards, she explained further. You stood there, lost somewhere.

I did?

Yes.

He looked back at the window, as if he'd never seen it.

You don't remember?

No, he said slowly.

He laid his head back on the pillow and stared at the white ceiling, the hickory beams. He could hear her breath in his ear. So close, that heart. With the wind howling on sonorous notes, the scores of creaks in the wooden structure shifted all around them. Are we the detached? The far flung? Are these the times that play prelude to cessation? I have not seen his hand before yesterday. For it comes in the visage of friendship, as the cloaked one seemingly tends to do. The mechanical growl, the pang of a rifle. Tools to which the wielder contends. All beckon the same result. Where will you be when the end times come, you ask? Hopefully, in your arms. As I watch the last light of this world fade atramentous, and all is lost forever.

He wrote three separate drafts for Granger over the span of three months, each one longer than the last. He showered, shaved, dressed, grabbed the newspaper from the entryway table and walk into the kitchen for breakfast. He gave up his personal writing to dedicate his undivided attention to the foreword. Nothing much came. When something emerged, he would scribble it on a piece of paper and keep it in his pocket to come back to later that evening. Then he would wake in the middle of the night, walk to his desk, throw everything he'd chanced at writing in the wastebasket and go back to sleep. This was his new ritual.

This particular morning, Granger was lying on the couch, reading the new Stephen King. He flipped a page when he heard the front door close. He peered over the edge of the couch, and smiled as the writer passed.

Good morning, he called.

Landon walked back and peered in through the doorway.

How are you today?

Doing well, the young writer replied. How about yourself?

Can't complain.

I need to read them again.

Read what again?

Your books.

Which ones?

All of them.

Granger laughed. He set his book down and waved the young man over.

Landon crossed into the expansive room and sat on the armchair beside the old man.

What's the trouble?

I'm having a hard time with the foreword, Landon explained.

Why?

I'm not sure.

Well, what are you trying to say?

I'm just trying to honor you and your history of work up until this novel.

That's what people like to hear, the old man mused. The artist's journey.

Right.

I don't need some eulogy.

What?

I didn't ask you to pen a eulogy. All you need to do is write one near perfect sentence and be done with it. The greatest forewords do that. It sets the reader up for what to expect without boring them. That's all your doing.

Landon ran his hand through his hair.

What did you think of the story? Granger said. That night when you read until morning.

In a word? Haunted.

Then write that.

Landon laughed. He looked at Granger and saw that the old man was serious.

I can't just write one word.

One word may be all it needs. I don't mind that.

Landon shook his head.

Think simpler, Mister Cassidy. All you need to convey is how the story made you feel.

Alright, the young writer sighed.

Granger nodded and picked up his splayed book and continued to read.

Landon rose and left for breakfast, confounded by how to proceed.

He trekked over the frost coated gravel back to the guesthouse. Maple was still in bed, scratching her back when he came in. She stretched her back legs across the bed, elongating her spine, and slumped to the floor. Her collar jingled wildly as she shook. Her eyes smiled at him before she headed out the door, disappearing down the stairs. He walked to the desk and peered out the window to watch the dog run jovially in the snow. Her legs kicked frost onto her back. A ranch hand came up behind her. She played in the snow for a while longer before following the man through the back door. He'd kept one of Granger's books on his bedside. He picked it up and sat and opened it to the beginning and brought his feet up on the bed and read.

A full month passed by the time Landon Cassidy had read each of Granger's works cover to cover. Each new draft of the foreword grew slimmer and slimmer. The voices he'd find himself turning his head to in the corners of the room began to vanish. One evening he'd narrowed it down to half a page, and that was as good as he was going to get it. He rushed over to the main house and found Granger rocking on the porch, a Churchill cigar smoldering wildly from his lips. When the old man asked him what he was excited about,

Landon dropped to his knees and cried.

In the morning they drove down to the post office. The roads were slick, and they could feel the tires skid several times. Black snow and gray slush had built up along the shoulders. Groups of deer, speckled by the wet leaves they brushed against, grazed on the side of the road, not a care in the world. The trees and mountains stood white and undisturbed. Black birds cawed through the silence, flapping into the east.

Ben turned the Bronco into the parking lot and kept the engine running. Landon helped Granger out of the truck and to the front door. Everything was slippery. They stomped their feet on the doormat and walked to the front desk. Two people stood in line. One worker on duty.

I'll go check my mail while we wait, Landon said to the old man.

He inserted his key into the P.O. Box and turned the lock. Several envelopes, flyers and assorted junk mail were shoved tightly into the steel box. He nudged them out, spilling most of them on the floor. He set everything on a blue counter that held postal information, boxing prices, a trash bin. He threw away the magazines, credit card approval scams, and other nonsense he never signed up for. All that was left were four white envelopes that contained the royalty checks. He stuffed the envelopes into his jacket pocket, closed and locked the mail box door, and headed back.

The manuscript was wrapped in an ivory cloth with two black ribbons tied at the top in an elegant bow. Granger had placed it in a sealed brown box addressed to the attention of his agent. He paid the overnight shipping cost. The postal worker took the box and handed Granger his receipt.

They had a late breakfast at an upscale cafe on the north side of Market Street. The veneered oak tables were half full with an inviting solace filling the air. The floors were covered with long sheets of tile, the color of black currants, and the light fixtures reminded the young writer of a subway station. They were greeted by a short haired girl who showed them to their table, overlooking Main Street. They ordered coffee and an assortment of pastries. When they arrived, they were warm and very sweet. Cherry and peach filled. Powdered sugar coatings. Chocolate croissants. When they bit into them, the pastries would crack and flake. Audible moans of delight spilled from each of them. They drank the coffee black and ate silently as if they were a trio of monks on their day off.

I think this calls for a toast, Landon proposed, licking cherry from his fingers.

Granger looked at the young man and sipped his coffee.

Landon dried his fingers on his already chocolate stained napkin and held up his mug.

To a marvelous accomplishment, he said. Forty years in the making. Ben held up his mug and smiled thinly.

Granger seemed unmoved, but Landon sensed pride in the old man's eyes. A soft rose bloomed in his old, cracked cheeks. Then he extended his mug.

To you, Landon concluded.

They touched mugs and drank.

Ben smiled and nodded. He dunked a frosted doughnut into his coffee and bit into it.

Granger took up a piece of rye toast and slathered it with a beige cinnamon butter. He brought it to his mouth then hesitated. You did good on the forward, he said.

Thank you, Landon replied.

The old man took a small bite.

How far are you on your own story?

I tabled the second draft until I finished the forward, Landon replied, doughnut crumbling from his lips. I'll get back to it tomorrow.

I would like to read it when you're done.

It may be a while.

That's alright.

You sure?

Of course.

Okay.

Evelyn told me a little about it. It sounds wonderful.

Thank you.

They ate quietly.

Have I ever told you how I found the ranch? Granger asked.

No.

Would you like to hear it?

Absolutely, Landon exclaimed excitedly.

Ben reached over, picked up an almond croissant, halved it, and placed one end on his plate while biting into the other. The waitress returned and filled their coffees. They ordered another assortment of pastries with toasts and jams. She smiled and departed.

Back in nineteen seventy-nine, Granger began, I was on a cross country road trip with Meredith, and doing a little research along the way for a book I was planning to write. We saw many breathtaking places, experienced a variety of establishments, even came close to buying a spot or two.

Where were they? Landon asked.

One was in Montana. The other was in Colorado.

He nodded.

We made it into Maryland and bivouacked along the mountainside to watch the horizon glissade violet and pink. An empyrean we'd come to gaze upon each night before turning in. I surveyed the skirted blue mountains. Far off in directions we were not traveling, but I wanted to take a day and see them. Meredith indulged me. The next day we drove towards the Appalachians. The road took us higher into the mountains. Meredith saw an old trail off the main highway, riddled with weeds and overgrowth. The trees were shaped like a tunnel, as you see them today. We parked on the side of the road and got out and ventured down the path. Whatever there was before seemed to have been abandoned long ago. When we got to the clearing, all we saw was tall grass. Miles upon miles of tall grass. We found the highest point of the clearing and looked out on the sprawling landscape. I hadn't thought of Marfa in many years, but I did then. That's when we decided to ensconce here for the rest of our lives. We found the county office and purchased the land that day, it was simpler in those times. Afterwards, we continued our trip, discussing what we wanted to do with our new future. That was all we talked about until we broke ground a few years later.

That's incredible.

Ben nodded in agreement.

The waitress returned with their order.

The grass was yellow like wheat, Granger mumbled. The wind weaved through it as if it were talking to us.

They ate in silence and after a while the waitress brought the check. Ben paid in cash and they asked for another round of coffee. Landon stared out the window, watching the traffic pass by. Teenagers skateboarded through the gentle snowfall, families entered and exited shops. Children chased the snowflakes with outstretched arms and tongues. The subtle sound of silverware clanking against porcelain.

What are your plans? Granger asked.

I'm not sure, he replied, still looking out the window.

You know you're welcome to stay as long as you like.

He looked at Granger and gave him a soft smile. Thank you, he replied. I appreciate that. Then turned to look back outside.

Granger nodded and sipped his coffee, eyeing Ben.

Ben looked around the restaurant. The occupancy seemed to not have changed in the hours they were there. But the relaxing mood still lingered. Then he sipped his coffee and chewed the last half of his croissant.

The glare of the sun rimmed the pallid clouds. Heavy winds made working twice as cumbersome. The horizon was ominous one hour, lapis the next. Cold, drizzling rain emitted from each passing cloud. All would dry as the sun emerged. Then the heavy winds would rage again, blowing dark clouds of rain. That was October.

When he finished the last pages of his second draft, a knock rapped at his door. He stood, crossed the room, and opened the door. Evelyn was there, her hair wild from the wind, her clothes filthy from working with the horses.

A bit blustery outside? Landon asked with a smirk.

This weather is awful, she replied.

She came in and sat at the desk. He laid on the bed, looking at her. She glanced at the notebook on the desk, scanning the few pages there.

You're almost done? she exclaimed.

Yes.

She fell silent, reading to herself.

I found a nice place downtown that looked—

I was thinking about that too, she interrupted.

Excuse me?

Evelyn turned to him. I want to take you somewhere.

Take me somewhere?

Yes.

Are you free?

Am I free?

Yes.

Yes, he chuckled. I'm free.

I would like to take you somewhere. You can ask me out after that, if you still decide to.

How forward of you.

We can go Saturday. The weather is supposed to clear up by then.

Saturday it is.

Okay.

Okay.

She drove them in her sandy Toyota Camry across the state line into Virginia. They crossed the Potomac in Brunswick, and watched the sunrise blossom off the river. The water flowed calmly, tenderly. Undisturbed. He watched it disappear from sight beyond the bend. They stopped for gas in a small town outside of Fort Royal. He looked about the small crossroads made of brick, eyeing the dying town that would soon be deserted entire in five years. Old paintings of business signs long succumbed to a history faded and forgotten. Spray painted insignias on the sides in tar black. No car passed, no person stirred. Evelyn went inside and paid. When she came out, he was standing in the street looking up at something she could not gauge. She called to him. They got in the car and drove on.

They dined in a decrepit Mexican restaurant in Charlottesville. She told him the significance of the establishment to her upbringing, but that did not make the food taste any better. His meal was lukewarm and the tortillas stiff as cardboard. There was hardly any char to his steak and peppers. The beans cold. She spoke in Spanish to the owners while he waited outside. There were several cars in the parking lot, but he didn't remember seeing anyone else inside while they were eating. The door rang as she came out and crossed to the car.

Are you okay? she said.

You used to come here often?

Yeah, why?

He made a disgusted expression and shook his head.

Evelyn laughed.

The clock on the dash read 2:38. They parked on a dirt lot with a white picketed path that led to an assortment of white barns and buildings. Lush autumn colors of the brightest variety. She led him to a sign that read: Whitcomb Equestrian School.

This is where I learned to ride, Evelyn said.

They walked down the path and entered the first building. Portraits of thoroughbreds graced the walls. Some with jockeys, most without. They wandered amongst the silent rooms, viewing the various trophies and framed newspaper articles. He found a portrait of a teenage Evelyn Chambers with an alabaster thoroughbred. She held her helmet in one hand while stroking the horse with the other. She gave the camera a sideways look with a soft smile, no teeth, her tan skin blended lovingly with the sapphire blouse she wore. White buttons, one open at the top. Her black hair blew gently with the wind, and her eyes glowed with an almond perimeter.

This is you, he whispered.

She came up behind him and rested her chin on his shoulder.

Yes, she replied sweetly.

How old are you?

Thirteen.

You're beautiful.

Still am.

He turned to her and smiled.

Come on, she said, grabbing his hand. There's more to see.

They walked down a long corridor, walls lined with portraits of horses.

IV

White light beamed through the windows and pooled on the floor. Subtle coos from pigeons in their high wooden perches. They opened a door at the end of the stable and were greeted by the pungent scent of freshly mowed fields. Acres of riding ground encased by white picket fences. Horses trotted about, enjoying the cool air. Landon did not see any riders, nor anybody else for that matter.

Where is everyone? he asked.

It's the weekend. Only a handful of workers stay on until Monday.

What sort of riders do they train here?

Girls. As young as seven, as old as eighteen.

Looks expensive.

Oh yes. But some riders get a scholarship or a sponsor, like I did.

How'd you get that?

They thought I was going to be a great rider someday, remember?

Well, they were right.

She smiled and nodded.

Let's head to the stables, she said.

They walked through a massive white building that held the horses in nouvelle stalls. Their names, lineage, and class were etched above the doorframes in exaggerated scrollwork. There were four long rows of them, color-coded by coat. Like a paint palette in a hardware store.

This is a bit extravagant, he said.

Isn't it? Evelyn replied. The place is known for how they house the horses.

Are any of them the same since you've been here?

No. The ones I knew have been gone a long time.

What do they do with the plates? Seems expensive to engrave new ones for each horse.

That's where the hefty tuition costs come in, Evelyn giggled. They retire the horse, auction off the shoes, then put the plaque on these enormous black walls in the Remembrance Garden. It's a big tradition.

Really?

Yes. They reach out to alumni and have a big party. Raise a ton of money.

Shoes? Landon said, puzzled. As in horseshoes?

Yes.

They auction those?

It's for fun.

Have you attended any?

Once.

For the horse in the portrait?

Yes.

What happened to him?

He got old.

Do you miss him?

Yes. He was a beautiful horse.

What was his name?

White Jacket, she recalled with a slight smile, flashing back to her memories.

Can we see the garden?

Sure.

They walked along the picketed pathways, Evelyn serving as a tour guide. They entered the garden where the retired plaques stood glimmering in the afternoon sun. Primly trimmed rose bushes lined the stone pathways. A small court with four wood benches, etched with donor names. They sat and she spoke of the gala she'd once attended. She pointed out White Jacket's plaque among the assortment. Landon shielded his eyes with his hand and looked up the black wooden slab at the name.

A young girl straddled a small blonde thoroughbred. Beside her was a tall, portly woman, who seemed to be giving the child instructions. Evelyn and Landon stood against the fence, watching the private training take place. The child pointed to them. The woman turned and waved, then gestured to the child to ignore them and to get back to work.

Why did you bring me here? Landon asked.

I wanted to share it. This place.

He nodded.

I learned a lot here. Met a lot of friends, acquaintances. I've lost contact with all of them since, but I do think about them now and again. About our time here. Sneaking around, getting into trouble. Riding the horses when we weren't supposed to.

Did you ever get caught?

A couple times, she chuckled. They came down hard on us.

I bet.

Some weekends I would be allowed to stay and take the horses out. I'd ride them for hours. Losing track of the day. Those were the best times. When I could ride and not think about the world outside this place, even if it was just for a few hours. I think that's what made me who I am.

Do you do that at the ranch? Landon said. Ride away for hours?

Yeah, sometimes.

That sounds nice.

It is.

They watched the child gallop the horse into a small jump. The trainer applauded, telling her to do it again.

I'm glad you came, she said. It means a lot to me.

Thanks for bringing me.

Will you stay on?

Landon looked at his feet, his lips pursing in thought.

I'm not sure. I don't know where I'd go.

Evelyn nodded.

Well, I hope you stay on, she said, rubbing his arm.

When I got here you wanted me gone.

Perspectives change when you let them. I was wrong about you.

I don't think so, he said.

You don't?

I thought I didn't belong here either.

You still believe that?

I still have my doubts.

Everyone does when you pick up a life you never thought would be your own. The roads we take are never the ones we planned to set foot upon. One day you end up finding yourself wandering them. Then along comes a dirt road, and you've one opportunity to take it before it's gone forever. You took it.

When does it end? The road.

It doesn't matter, Evelyn said. Not when you're traveling it. If you look for the end, you'll find it. But that is not the point of the road. As long as you continue to follow, you'll get to where you were always meant to be.

So, we have no choice, is what you're telling me?

Yes. We walk these roads because the questions we cannot answer will reveal themselves based on how we walk them.

Landon didn't speak.

She smiled and set her head on his shoulder.

For now, Evelyn said, slipping her fingers between his and gripping his palm, let's just enjoy this moment together. However brief, we can make it long in our hearts.

They watched the young girl's lesson, remembering a time distant, but ever so near.

When they returned, a soft coral twilight painted the sky, the mountains. The ranch hands were leading the horses back to the stables. The herded livestock was secure in their pens. Granger rocked back and forth on his porch chair, Maple asleep at his feet.

The truck rounded the gravel path and parked in the garage.

Evening, she said, walking onto the porch.

How was the trip? Granger asked.

Beautiful, Landon replied. You couldn't have asked for a better day.

I'm glad to hear it.

What have you been up to? Evelyn asked.

Nothing much. Lee stopped by and dropped off Signatures. Told us he performed well.

That's our boy, never letting us down.

Indeed.

Anything else going on?

Just a beautiful day. Did you all eat? Supper's still hot.

We ate on the way back.

Anything good?

She looked at Landon, daring him to answer.

Don't let her pick the restaurant, he said.

They laughed.

Maple yawned and blinked her eyes at them, but was too comfortable to move.

I see she's doing well, Landon observed.

She's been good girl, Granger said, scratching the dog's back. Kept me company. Helped with some of the work around here.

Is that right?

The old man chuckled.

I'm going to grab a drink, Evelyn said. Do you all want anything?

No, thank you, Granger replied.

I'll come with you, Landon said.

Okay.

Evelyn went in.

He was starting after her when Granger called to him. He stopped, looking at the old man from the bright doorway. He'd stop rocking and was looking up at him with a concerned expression about his darkly wrinkled face.

What is it?

Come out here, the old man said. Shut the door.

He came out and leaned against one of the columns, crossing his arms.

What's up?

We haven't seen Dom today.

What do you mean?

I mean no one's seen him. He's not here.

He was yesterday. I was with him all day.

I know it, but the men told me he's nowhere to be found.

Landon peered towards the last vanishing light. He sucked at his teeth.

What are you telling me?

You were the last to see him, Granger said. I thought you'd know where might've got off to.

I haven't seen him since yesterday.

Granger stood from his chair, leaned over and spat over the railing. Is
it bad? Landon asked.

It's concerning.

What do you plan to do?

If he's not back in the morning, Ben and I are going to head into town and look around.

I'll come too.

Do you think Evelyn should join us? Granger said.

It couldn't hurt.

Alright.

Granger let out a long sigh.

Has he ever done this before? Landon asked.

No.

Not once in the time you've known him?

Not without us knowing about it.

Alright. I'll go in and tell her.

Thank you.

Sure thing.

He crossed the porch and opened the screeching door.

Landon, Granger called out.

Yeah? he replied, hanging in the doorway.

Keep it quiet. I don't want anybody to worry.

Yes sir.

Thank you.

Of course. He went inside, the door shutting behind him.

Granger studied the unblemished night, his breath slow and tranquil. He stroked Maple gently across the back. Gently. Watching the darkness cackle in the silence.

She sat up in bed, the blankets held tightly against her naked body. Her hair streaked past the middle of her back. She was very beautiful. The moon reflected off her round shoulders, pooling into her collarbone, paling upon her face. A queen of moon bleached tenebrosity. She thought about going to him, but she didn't. She could feel it, beyond the woods. Beyond the spired and naked limbs that foraged forth to the barren sky and worshiped the unknown climate that befell each day. Never complaining, never a question asked. Somewhere nearby an old acquaintance waited. How long they loiter is never certain, only that their presence be known only to those of prior experience. She laid back in bed, still clenching the covers to her cool skin, as if to stop them from being ripped away.

He stood in front of Dom's door, contemplating going in. He saw no movement cut across the bar of light seeping beneath the frame. The dim hallway light casted sinister shadows down the walls. Few men still awake downstairs. A mucous-embedded fit behind one of the doors. He lifted his hand to the doorknob, then relaxed it back at his side and waited. He stilled his breath, grabbed the doorknob, twisted it, and cracked it open. Then he stopped. He could hear his heartbeat, the rapidity of it. The uneasiness of it. He closed the door and walked back to his room and disappeared silently within.

Ben stood outside the garage warming his hands in the cold early light. The horses were out stretching their legs and trotting along the fence line. Ranch hands came out with cups of coffee and hot tea, the remnants of their breakfast.

Buenos días, they said in passing.

Buenos días, Landon replied. *Está el Señor Granger ahí?*

Si. Él está terminando su desayuno.

Gracias.

The workers nodded to him and went on their way.

He went through the back door and found two others eating. The older woman and gentleman were busy cleaning and putting dishes away. The house was quiet, save the Spanish mumbling between the workers at the table.

He came out and walked to the garage. Ben was still there.

Morning, Landon said.

Good morning.

Have you seen them yet?

Not yet.

He looked around, searching the cold, quiet grounds for their manifestation.

Did you get something to eat? Ben asked.

Not hungry.

It could be a long day.

Can't be any longer than twenty-four hours, unless there's something you know that I don't.

Ben chuckled, shaking his head.

Do you have any idea where he could be?

A few places come to mind, but I doubt he's at any of em.

Why's that?

Ben shrugged. Just my doubt.

The front door opened. He turned to see Granger and Evelyn stepping out from the front door. Ben helped the old man into the Bronco while Evelyn and Landon jumped in the backseat. Ben got in, turned on the ignition, and blasted the heat. They sat there silently, waiting for the truck to warm. Ben put his hand on the gear stick, but Granger gently tapped it away. Ben looked at him.

Granger sat stock still, eyes ahead.

Evelyn shot Landon an uneasy glance then looked at the old man.

Dom was killed last night, Granger said mournfully.

What? Landon exclaimed.

Evelyn gasped, holding her hand to her mouth.

A drunk driver struck him while he was walking back to his car.

How do you know this? Ben said, surprised.

The police called me this morning.

The car was unsettlingly silent. Even the idling engine seemed dolorous.

Do we need to drive to the station? Ben suggested.

Granger nodded slowly.

Ben let out a loud, long exhalation and put the truck in reverse.

They drove down 40, listening to the engine's mechanical oscillation, the rolling cacophony of the road. They stopped at a red light along the Golden Mile. Only a handful of vehicles on the road. At their idle, Landon's trance was broken by an odd movement along the grassy island that separated the traffic.

A groundhog, brown and portly, his body waving like an earthworm, its jaw full of the grass, chomping rapidly. The white teeth looked as if he brushed twice daily. His head jerked around but was not bothered by its dangerous location. He continued moving about, eating.

They pulled into the police parking lot in downtown Frederick. The doors hissed open on their horizontal frames as they approached. Officers at every turn. A desk clerk was writing in a ledger when Granger walked up and asked for directions. They spoke, nodding to one another. She pointed to a hallway behind her and gestured with her liver spotted hands a series of turns in concert with her directions. When she was done, Granger shook her hand and nodded for the others to follow.

The sitting area was barely at capacity. Granger approached the plexiglass window and spoke to the officer sitting opposite.

How can I help you, sir? the officer asked.

I was called about Dominic Garcia.

The officer looked through his papers, finding the name.

Yes sir. He's here.

Granger nodded.

We needed someone who could identify him.

Alright.

You can have a seat. I'll let them know you're here.

Thank you.

Granger sat next to Ben and waited patiently, his head lowered to his chest.

They heard a buzzing sound and another officer came out holding a clipboard. He called for the group to follow. Ben stayed behind. The officer asked each of them for their names. One by one they told him. The officer wrote. They walked down a series of hallways until they reached door labeled: Morgue.

I just need one of you, the officer said. If you like, the rest can wait here.

No, Landon replied. I'd like to go.

Me too, Evelyn added.

The officer looked them over, nodded and handed each of them a pair of blue latex gloves and a K95 mask.

The room was white, made brighter by the fluorescent tube lighting.

Formaldehyde and other various chemicals thick in the air. Steel walls, mortuary cabinets. Fingerprint smudges. Their footsteps echoed off the linoleum floors. A sharp quiver ran down the back of Landon's spine. Gooseflesh bubbled along his arms. He was suddenly cold and uncomfortable. His throat was very dry. When he licked his lips, all he got was the sharp taste of iron as if he tongued stack of pennies. A coroner draped in white came through the doors. He wore thick black frame glasses and a tight haircut. He introduced himself and offered his condolences. The coroner and officer led them down the room to one of the steel doors. A low creak emitted from one of the hinges as he opened it. He grabbed the handles and pulled the table out. The black bag lay centered. The coroner looked at Granger. He nodded.

The man slid the zipper down and slowly peeled the bag away from the mangled head like a cocoon. Lying there was the halved face of Dominic Garcia. Part of his skull was exposed. Jigsawed pieces of white bone. The mangled flesh was compassed with dried and cracked burgundy blood. Lacerations etched about his face. His nose was shattered, half of his mouth caved in. He'd no teeth. The muscles in his neck laid in twisted variation, the skin stretched in peculiar fashion, as if sewed.

Granger took a deep breath and let it out slowly. That's him, he said. The coroner nodded. He gently folded the wrap over his face like a loving father tucking his child in for bed. He zipped the bag shut, grabbed the table handles, slid him back in and closed the door.

Granger looked at his feet and sighed. The officer brought them back to the waiting room where all was as before. He told them to wait while they finished up the last of the paperwork. Granger nodded as the officer went out.

Was it him? Ben asked looking up from last week's issue of Time magazine.

Yes, Evelyn said. It's him.

Ben sighed and crossed himself.

The officer returned with a clipboard containing several pages. He handed it to the old man, along with a pen he'd already uncapped.

We just need your signature on these, he said. Let me know if you have any questions.

IV

Do you have any of his belongings? Granger asked.

A few things, yes. We'll get those to you before you leave.

I appreciate it.

Granger sat down and read through each of the papers, signing the dotted lines at the bottom.

Twenty minutes later, the door buzzed and opened. An older officer came out with a box containing Dom's items.

Harrison Granger, the officer called.

Granger finished signing the papers, got up, crossed to the officer and traded as if at auction.

I'm sorry for your loss, the officer said.

They stood by the Bronco and waited while the old man quietly wept against a willow tree beside the small creek. A crooked thing there, hunched over the box of the wrangler who'd managed to cobble together very few representations of his lifetime. As the artifacts fade away, as all artifacts do in this world, memories remain. However long, until they too are gone from memory. And all whoever knew us, our personal historians, will be lost. As if we never were. The echoes of our existence, forever vanished.

The ride was as silent as the one that preceded it. The day was unseasonably warm. Gray clouds streaked across the sky in long baroque strokes. Clogged traffic patterns, fast food lines building for the lunch crowd. A family of panhandlers on the corner of the sidewalk. Their broken, bleary-eyed children crouched in the curb as the world around them drove past. Never an eleemosynary coin to rattle in their little palms.

They sat in the living room with Dom's box centered on the long coffee table. Granger sat at the head next to Evelyn and Landon. Ben sat opposite with his head on his hand, legs crossed, waiting. The old man leaned forward and slid the cardboard top from the box and placed it aside. One by one, he took out the items: A blood stained leather wallet, a mangled receipt, Dom's broken Stetson, an ancient and chipped yet still ticking Tissot wristwatch, a crumpled pack of Winston Reds with two remaining, and a large silver belt buckle. The lighter wasn't there.

Granger staged the items as if curating a small western museum.

Is that everything? Evelyn said.

He picked up the box. Something rattled inside. He reached in and pulled out a small locket. It had a long, thin silver necklace and a small cross engraved in the exterior, heavily scratched. He tried unclasping it, but it wouldn't budge. Here, Ben said, leaning forward and reaching into his back pocket. He pulled out his keyring, detached the small red Swiss Army knife and handed it to Granger. The old man opened the knife and carefully placed the tip of the blade in the tight lip and pried the locket open. He closed the knife and handed it back to Ben. Granger stared at the small photograph of a young man holding two little girls. The photograph was old and badly faded. Etched onto the opposite side were the words: *Amelia 6, Clara 4. 1987.*

He placed the locket in Dom's chest pocket and thanked the undertaker and turned and left the funeral home. They sent Dom's body to be buried with his wife and daughters and parents in Durango. His brothers saw to the arrangements. A week later, Granger, Evelyn and Landon returned from Mexico, where they pressed forth with their lives, knowing that the empty void in their hearts would never fill again. And that was that.

The cock crowed at the bruised morning sky. Layered clouds, flat and rounded, stacked like shale stones at a creek's edge. A beige haze in the distance. Cardinals and blue jays hid like precious gemstones in the thick woods, their calls sharp and sonorous. Red-bellied woodpeckers drummed in the distance. Passing finches in crying commotion. The trees whipped like fluid traffic, their chartreuse leaves giving off their final pigmentation before the autumn season bores down across the land. The horses galloped across the grounds, far from the eyes of their masters. Where esoteric whispers take place in territories of those privy to their whereabouts.

He'd spent the night and morning reading over his completed manuscript, plucking out anomalies, restructuring clauses. He felt good about this one, confident. Feelings he thought had long since parted ways with him. When he finished he stood, stretched, and quietly walked to the bathroom and took a long hot bath.

The coffee was rich and velvety. Hint of spice. He held the transparent glass to the light, to find no light breaking through. He drank while ascending the porch steps to the study. The door was unlocked. The room was empty. The wall that led to the second floor was ajar. Granger sat on the rear balcony, reading The New York Times. He was dressed in an olive button-down and faded Levi's. Bright red socks on his sockfeet. He looked over his shoulder and smiled as his long-term guest brushed the lemon lime leaves from the deck chair with his manuscript and sat. The coffee was still hot when he sipped it.

I can smell that from here, Granger said.

It's damn good, Landon replied. I could drink this for the rest of my life.

It's Colombian.

How'd you get that?

The old man chuckled.

I finished the book.

Leave it on the table, the old man said without looking up.

Landon set the manuscript on the table beside him. He placed a small pillow over it to keep the pages from flying away.

How do you feel? Granger asked.

I feel good.

Good.

He brought the newspaper together, thumbed the page and opened it again and continued to read.

Where were you thinking of sending it?

I'm not sure, replied Landon. I doubt the agents I've spoken to before I got picked up are still interested.

That's a bit closed minded.

We'll see. I still have their addresses somewhere.

I can send it to mine. She'll give it a look. Maybe ask around.

I can't ask you to do that.

It's no trouble. Think of it as payment for all the hard work you've done here.

You've already given me more than enough.

Let's just see what she says, Granger repeated.

Alright.

How much have you saved from those checks?

Around six thousand.

Do you know where you're going after this?

No.

Then stay until you do. Meandering aimlessly serves no one.

I don't know.

Then stay until we find out what Ricky says.

Is that his name?

Her name. And no. It's Rachel.

Gotcha.

The old man read silently.

Have you found out when they'll be releasing yours? Landon asked.

Sometime next year.

That's exciting.

He nodded disinterestedly.

Are they making you do any press for it?

They're trying to, but I'm too old for the circus.

Landon chuckled as he finished his coffee. The mug tapped his teeth, sending an irritating sensation throughout his body. He licked his teeth and ran his finger across them and set the mug down.

They sat quietly, enjoying each other's silence, listening to the sounds of the morning.

He thought about thirteen-year old Evelyn, riding youthfully along the green hills. The wind against her body, embracing a freedom few ever felt. He thought of her reading on the jade-washed grass, her alabastrine horse grazing nearby. That's what I'll do today, he thought. And tomorrow and the next day. He closed his eyes, took in a large lungful of air and slowly exhaled.

I'll leave you to it, he said, getting up.

Granger nodded.

He went downstairs and browsed the books on the shelves. He slid a few out and studied them, flipping through the pages before replacing them. He tapped on the shelf, listening to the quixotic metronome his fingers played on the wood. He took down a copy of Hart Crane's *The Bridge and Other Poems* from the top shelf, and looked it over, remembering when he'd read it years ago but had long since forgotten. The book was an older edition. Faded lettering. Yellowed pages. He held the book to his nose, flipped the pages with his thumb, and inhaled its aroma.

As the front door closed behind him, a black Lincoln was coming down the road. He'd not seen it before and he took it for a mirage at first sight. But the car continued forth. He watched as it rounded the gravel pathway, kicking up thick ivory dust in its wake. When he rounded Granger's house, the driver, a tall black man with a freshly shaven face in a black suit, was getting out. He nodded to Landon as he opened the trunk, then the rear door. An older woman with short chiffon hair, wearing a long burgundy dress emerged. She was draped in a luxurious black shawl. Her arms were finely toned for her age, but her hands were stalked by fine wrinkles. She had lavender toe nails peeking from beneath her thick sandal straps. She stood with a strong sense of purpose and grace, looking about the ranch. A thin, gentle smile grew across her rouge lips. The crow's feet shadowed behind her tawny sunglasses. The driver brought the luggage up the porch steps and through the front door. Two trips in all. Landon walked over, stopping suddenly as her head shot at him. She cocked her chin to one side, as if finding something out of place.

Who are you? she ordered more than asked.

My name's Landon Cassidy, he said plainly.

Are you new here?

No ma'am. I've been here a little over two years now.

Two years? she said laconically, as if to herself.

Yes, ma'am.

She looked him up and down several times.

Who are you?

She removed her sunglasses and set them atop her head.

I'm Meredith Granger, she said. Harrison's wife.

V

Signatures lay at the foot of the hill, his dark hair blowing gently against his neck. His tail flapped about, whipping away the flies. The sun brought out the richness of his dark chocolate undercoat. Landon's head laid along Evelyn's lap, the borrowed book shading the sun from his eyes as he read. She sat with her face canted to the sun as she always did on beautiful days like this. Leaves rustled like locust wings. Plump black clouds roved across the horizon. He peered over the book to examine the sky, then went back to reading.

Looks like rain, he said.

Evelyn opened her eyes and looked at the clouds.

No, she replied, they're moving too fast.

The sky is peculiar today.

It's a peculiar day.

You mean Meredith returning?

Yes.

Have you seen her yet?

No. I believe she and Harrison have a lot of catching up to do.

He nodded, flipping the page.

It's strange knowing she's back, Evelyn said. After all this time.

Aren't you glad?

I am. But it's still strange.

The timing's odd.

What do you mean?

I don't know. It's just odd.

V

Say what you mean.

He set the book down and looked up at her.

I just find it strange she's returned right as his book is announced. That's all.

So?

I don't know, he said, shrugging. Forget it.

You think she came back for money?

I don't know.

Then why say it?

You kept asking.

You don't know her, Evelyn chided.

He didn't reply.

They listened to Signatures' distant snorting, their eyes avoiding one another.

You're right, he said.

I'm sorry.

That's not how she is.

How is she then?

Warm and motherly. She knows all the staff by name. Cares about their families. Gives everyone gifts during the holidays. Cooks for them on their birthdays. She loves them. She loves Harrison. She knows him better than anyone.

They've been together for a long time.

Yes, but it's more than that.

Alright, he said.

The dark clouds had dissipated. The sun beamed across the periwinkle sky. A cicada hissed somewhere nearby. A long crescendo followed by an almost immediate silence.

You gave him your manuscript? she said.

Yes.

What will you do after he reads it?

He said he would send it to his agent. Shop it around.

Really?

Yes.

That's great.

Landon nodded.

Then what?

Well, he sighed, if anything happens it will take a long time. I'm sure there will be feedback, meetings, schedules, deadlines, that sort of thing. You'd think it would be simple, but before you know it, a year or more has flown by when its finally published.

I see.

It's strange having the future so close now. I'm kind of afraid of what it holds.

Afraid of what?

The unknown.

But we'll be with you.

He turned to look at her.

I'll be with you, she said, caressing his hair. You won't be alone. I promise.

Thank you.

She leaned over and kissed him. Soft lips. Honeysuckle fragrance. When they finally broke, he could still feel the sensation on his mouth. She smiled, closed her eyes and canted her head to the sun again. He held his book up and read. Her hand softly ran against his cheek, warm and loving. The sun sprang from the clouds, illuminating the world, heating their skin. Signatures lifted his head and watched them. Those eyes observing solace he would never forget.

The Camry winded down the mountain road. There was a chilled wetness on the air. Late grazers in white, deserted fields. A pair of does played a game of chase in serpentine patterns. He watched the amber sun roll like a coin along the jagged mountain peaks. It disappeared beyond the frosted tree line, its afterglow blistering the higher limbs in marigold. He listened to the metallic revolutions of the chain tires. There was no one else on the road. They picked up 40 and drove towards downtown. The traffic was light as early dark settled.

V

Where are we going? he asked.

I want ice cream, Evelyn replied.

Ice cream? It's freezing outside.

There's a great place downtown.

Landon laughed.

Downtown is beautiful this time of year.

I'm sure it is.

They parked in a garage, leashed Maple, and walked down an alley onto Market Street.

Christmas wreaths hung from every street lamp, each displaying a scarlet bow. A light snow started to fall, crowds started to grow as the evening wore on. They walked arm in arm with Maple leading the way. They shopped through various knickknacks and novelties, buying stocking stuffers for the workers. He sniffed an assortment of candles and hand creams, even purchasing small bottles of shaving cream and aftershave for himself. Evelyn looked through racks of clothes from local dressmakers. Peculiar designs. Loud patterns. He bought her an ivory, flat brim Montana hat that he carried in an awkward circular box. They toted their bags down the street, making their way to the creek, their heels clapping loudly along the brick.

The ice cream shop was tucked between a Mexican cantina and an office building, the line long out the door. Maple sat patiently as undecided customers swiveled between the two large menu boards. They inched closer, growing colder through their layers. Twenty minutes had elapsed by the time it was their turn. Evelyn ordered two fudge ripple cones. Landon paid. They wrapped their hands in napkins and indulged, walking back the way they came.

Do you like it? Evelyn asked.

I do, Landon replied. Creamy.

It's from a local dairy farm not too far from here.

Landon nodded, licking the dribbling cream.

He looked over and saw the red barn shaped grocery Granger had found him in two years ago. The windows were dark, an orange *CLOSED* sign hung in the window.

What is it? Evelyn asked.

That's the place where I met Harrison, he said, nodding to the store across the creek.

Really?

Yes.

What were you doing there?

He licked the ice cream, thinking back. He didn't answer.

They found a bench and sat, the ice cream melting in their hands.

Do you think you'll write about your time here? she asked.

I'm sure I will.

I hope you do.

Why?

So that you remember.

You don't think I will?

She shrugged. Our minds fade when we get older. It's best to write what you know right away. Before the details are gone.

I'll write about it. How could I not? This has been the greatest experience of my life.

She smiled and bit into the cone.

Over the next several weeks, he hardly saw Granger or Meredith. He worked and washed the horses, exercised Signatures when allowed, and wrangled the livestock each evening. He played cards and shot pool with the ranch hands every night. He even tried his first Winston cigarette, waking up the following morning with a sore throat. He watched Evelyn train the horses on the track while attempting to understand Joyce's *Finnegan's Wake*. Dinners were quiet. Spring winds replaced the winter cold. He grew accustomed to wearing Dom's old jackets. A week later, a bad storm ravaged the ranch. He worked vigorously through the cascading rain, securing the horses and livestock. He even had to run to the bunker beneath the windmill to restart the generator. The following morning, Granger visited him in his room and returned his manuscript. They exchanged a few words before the old man returned to the house. He found small red tick marks on the pages with feedback etched in the margins. He spent months making corrections before giving the old man the revised draft.

Getting there, Granger commended. Read it aloud to find the rhythm. It should be constant start to finish.

And it's not? Landon said in disbelief.

No.

He ate an early lunch and spent the reminder of the day in Grayson's study reading the manuscript in a low, controlled voice. He placed red ticks on sections that he stumbled over or repeated due to uneven structure. When he was done, he read it again. The workers filed into the illuminated house for dinner. He watched through the window, but never left. When he made the final changes and read the manuscript aloud once more, it was past one in the morning. He poured himself two fingers worth of Jefferson's and laid on the couch and drank, slowly fading to sleep.

In the morning he ate a large breakfast of four eggs, three pieces of rye toast, bacon and sausage, blueberry yogurt and several cups of coffee. No orange juice. There was no one in the house. He ascended the wide staircase and walked down a long hallway to Grayson's bedroom. A small table stood outside the large double doors. He set the manuscript on it, adjusting the skewed pages. He set his ear to the door. Then he turned and left.

At the end of the week, Meredith wrapped the manuscript in an ivory cloth with a black bow and placed it in a cardboard box. Ben drove him to the post office. He went in alone and waited in line and paid the overnight shipping cost to Granger's agent and collected the receipt and checked his mailbox and retrieved the three royalty checks and slid the junk mail in the trash and returned to the Bronco and rode back to the ranch. Two months later, Granger knocked on his door.

Taking a nap?

Yes, Landon replied, rubbing his eyes. This heat wears me out.

Don't I know it.

Come on in.

The old man walked into the room. The bed was messy, but everything else was kept tidy and neat. He sat at the desk, smiling at the several blue notebooks stacked in the upper left-hand corner.

We're having a big dinner tonight, he said, to commemorate everyone's hard work as we get ready for summer.

Wonderful, Landon exclaimed.

The staff will be gone for a few weeks.

Shift change.

Yup. That time of year again.

It comes quickly.

Granger nodded.

Landon sat up to better look at the old man in the late afternoon light. I got a call from my agent this morning, Granger said.

Yeah?

She'd like to call you. Said a lot of publishers are heavily interested in your book.

Really? Landon exclaimed.

Granger nodded.

That's amazing.

I suspect you'll be getting several calls in the next few days.

Does the phone in here have its own number?

Yes, It's an extension.

Alright.

Congratulations.

Thank you, Harrison.

Landon stood and extended his hand to him.

They shook firmly.

The story will always be there, son. Never be afraid to write it.

Granger stood, crossed to the door, opened and left without looking back.

The dinner was the largest feast he'd seen in years. Candle lights, crystal drinking glasses, expensive wines, succulent roasted meats. Freshly harvested vegetables. The smoke and steam from the kitchen pitched a muted haze over the crowd. Conversations loud and jovial. Everyone was finely groomed, strongly scented, nicely dressed. They passed bowls and trays around. Roasted pork with its charred honey skin and driblet gravy. The best food Landon had ever tasted. Wine continuously poured. Granger stood with his iced tea and called for a toast. The table quieted.

Tonight, is a night for celebration, Granger said. Celebration for another good year. A celebration for years to come. For those gone, those arrived. All, our family. I humbly call each of you one of our own. To everyone's hard work, we celebrate. To my wife, for without her, all this would mean nothing.

He leaned over and kiss Meredith on the cheek. The crowd agreed with nods and vocal confirmations.

To another great year, he concluded. Cheers.

Cheers, everyone cried out, touching glasses. The light clinking sounding like wind chimes.

They drank.

After the dinner was over, and the rich desserts consumed, Granger presented the table with a box of Cuban Montecristo cigars. The men cheered and proceeded to pass them around. They each took one with childlike enthusiasm, smelling the packed tobacco leaves. Everyone smoked along the porch. The cold night wind felt good against Landon's numb forehead. Each inhalation felt like a treasure, a true gift. Evelyn huddled against him, blowing thick gray smoke into the night. No one said a word. They all seemed to be in the same frame of mind. Indulging in a rare and blissful moment. One of the men whispered to another. The other chuckled. Slowly, the crowd began to disperse, heading back to the guest house for a final night of poker and pool, beginning the next day with hangovers of pleasant memories.

When all had left, the smoke still hung in the air like the whisked away remains of those never to return. Landon was halfway done with his cigar before he started to slow down, elongating the moment as long as possible. Evelyn's was barely smoked. She knew how to smoke a cigar. She took her time, holding her draws and emitting them slowly and methodically. The ash hung tightly as the char glowed within. The cold kept them pleasantly tipsy. He knew if he smoked the cigar faster that it would all be over. Goodbye beautiful dinner, goodbye beautiful cigar. He tapped at it, dropping the pewter ash into a porcelain tray. He looked at the stars in the opalescent sky. The twinkling that would be there long after his time was done. He stopped himself from taking another draw, resting his hand upon his knee.

Evelyn laughed.

You saw that?

Oh yes.

I always smoke these too fast, he said, coughing.

It's because you have an oral fixation.

A what?

She laughed.

Landon shook his head. This girl, he said.

You need to be careful.

I know.

She rested her head on his shoulder. Tonight was fun.

Yes, it was.

You'll be getting calls from agents tomorrow?

Possibly.

You probably should get to bed soon.

He drew on the cigar.

And miss a good night of poker? he said, smiling, the smoke emitting from his nostrils, his mouth.

She laughed. Alright. We can play a few hands.

Now you're talking.

The phone rang as soon as the clock struck seven. His mouth tasted awful, his head was in knots, and the sound of the telephone did not help. Maple looked around and went back to sleep. Evelyn was not there. He stood and shuffled across the same cold floor to the bathroom. He sat, rubbing his fogged head, and urinated. The cold water from the faucet tasted good as he swished and spat several times to alleviate himself from the ashtray embedded in his throat. He coated his toothbrush with paste and brushed furiously for ten minutes. Spittle ran down the drain in a dirty gray spiral, his eyes fixed drunkenly upon the hypnotic vortex rounding the drain hole. He stuck his tongue out then splashed his face with cold water, rubbing his dry and sore eyes. The phone rang again but he ignored it, closing the door for silence. The cigar aftertaste lingered, now with the minty undertone of a pack of Newport's. He sat in his underwear on the side of the tub, gently swirling his cold feet in the boiling water filling the basin. He stood, undressed and slid into the tub. He wet the washcloth and squeezed out the excess water and folded it and rested it over his eyes and dozed. As if by instinct, he lifted his leg and turned off the water with his foot. The water line was directly under the faucet. He was submerged and warm, his chin resting on the surface, his nostrils breathing in the hot steam. Better, he mumbled, as the water slightly trilled.

At ten to eight, he drained the tub and dried off. The world finally stopped spinning, and the taste in his mouth was fading. He wiped the steam from the mirror, brushed his teeth again, then slathered his face in menthol cream. He took his time, shaving one strip at a time before rinsing the blade. He lathered again and took a second pass in the opposite direction. A few cuts along his neck began to bleed. He wiped his face with cold water and slapped on aftershave to dry and sting. He looked at himself in the mirror one more time, running his fingers across his smooth and tired skin.

The room was ice cold when he came out. The phone had stopped ringing. He began to dress, underwear first, then socks. He put on a checkered button-down with brown slacks. Then he sat on the bed and waited for the call.

He picked up the receiver on the first ring.

Hello?

Good morning, a calm voice said. My name is Rachel Nelson, I'm with International Creative Management. Is this Landon Cassidy?

It is.

Good morning, Mister Cassidy. My client, Harrison Granger, told me to contact you about your manuscript. I have it sitting in front of me now. It's quite good.

Thank you.

Harrison said you've been living with him for a few years now. Is that correct?

Yes.

How has that been?

Wonderful.

I do love the ranch. It's quite peaceful there.

It is.

When Harrison told me about your situation, I grew curious.

Situation is a good word for it, Landon chuckled.

Sounds to me like you got a raw deal.

Something like that.

Makes for bad business. When representatives don't stick through the tough times.

It was tough. But I'm fine now.

That's great to hear.

Thank you.

He coughed away from the receiver.

So, how long have you known Harrison? he asked.

Well over thirty years now, Rachel said.

Wow.

And most of those were hard times. Long stretches between stories. Many nights where we argued, bickered, or fought until the sun rose.

Really?

Oh yes.

And yet you stayed with him?

I wouldn't trade those times for anything in the world. I love the man. I bet you were thrilled when you got his new book.

Thrilled is putting it mildly. But I want to talk about you.

Okay, Landon said, adjusting his position.

I see the potential for this book to be your biggest seller yet, after looking at the numbers of your previous book sales.

That shouldn't be too hard.

If I may be curt, I'd like for us to break your record sales in hardback alone. Afterward, we can talk paperbacks, e-books, etcetera, etcetera.

You think we can do that?

You wrote a good story that I think will appeal to a wide audience, she said. It's simple and well-paced. Perfect for any aged reader. And that's how we're going to sell it.

Sounds like you've already given this some thought.

Rachel let out a slight chuckle.

If you decide to sign with us, she said, we're ready to advance you forty thousand dollars.

Forty thousand dollars, Landon exclaimed.

That's right. When you get an endorsement from Harrison Granger, enough to where he asked you to write his foreword, which is wonderfully written by the way, then that is someone we want to work with.

I don't know what to say.

How soon can you get to New York?

I'm not sure. I'd have to check.

Please do. I'll call you back later today so we can plan on discussing the details further.

Sounds wonderful, he said breathlessly.

Are you okay?

Yes ma'am.

You'll probably get a lot of calls from other agents today. I can tell you that their offers won't be anywhere near ours, and the forty thousand is just the start.

I understand.

Good.

Wait, he said.

Yes?

How do they even know about my book?

Word travels fast in the big apple, Mister Cassidy. Do you think Harrison's manuscript got to me without a few birds chirping beforehand?

Right.

Like I said, I'll call back later today, say three o clock?

Three sounds great.

Excellent. Enjoy your morning, Mister Cassidy. I look forward to talking again soon.

Click.

Landon laid there with the receiver on his chest. After a while the dial tone sounded. And after a while, he hung up. He was paralyzed with ecstasy. He turned to Maple and rubbed her back.

Let's go get some breakfast, girl, he whispered. Today's a good day.

The hallway was empty. The small chalkboards that hung beside the doors were scrubbed clean. Small powdery piles in the floorboard beneath. All except for Evelyn. Her name was scrawled just how it had been the day he arrived. The laundry chute was ajar due to a clogged sheet. He opened the door and untucked the sheet and let it fall to the dark abyss below and shut the door and went down the stairs.

The living room was put together as if all the ruckus from last night had been a fever dream. Chairs were pushed in tight. Ashtrays, clean and polished. The countertops and the pool table were spotless. Fresh logs in the fireplace. The ash gone. He looked around the room and inhaled the cedar and pine scent he'd come to love. He saw a fold in the rug and walked over and kicked it flat. He looked at the gold pattern sewed there and followed it with his eyes. Maple scratched at the door. He walked over and opened it and she ran out. He turned and looked over the room once more. Then closed the door.

The gravel was be speckled by the morning frost. The frigid air made his breath plume in thick clouds. Along the distant tree line, the sun sat in front of a clear, aquamarine sky. He stepped carefully along the gravel, so as to not lose his footing.

Maple ran up the back steps.

He grabbed the railing, feeling the warm wood emit through his hand. He stomped the collected frost from his boots, opened the door, and went in.

He heard voices down the far hallway, followed by the sound of the front door closing. Several workers were finishing their breakfast. He closed the door and nodded to them.

Buenos días.

Buenos días, the men replied.

He got the dry dog food from the pantry and unclipped the harness and rolled the bag open and knelt holding the bag taut and dumped a generous amount into Maple's silver bowl then set the bag down and rolled the top closed and fastened the clip and set the bag back in the pantry. He fetched a clean plate from the drying rack and scooped two helpings of scrambled eggs onto it. He cut two thick slices of rye from the loaf, put them in the toaster, and slid the handle down before noticing the glass display of pastries, impossible to resist. He grasped the glass knob, lifted it off, and set it gently aside to examine the sugary treats. They were soft and still warm. Bleeding cherry Danishes coated in a thick layer of sugar that stuck to your fingers. Bloated croissants with glistening butter along their brown, flaky hull. Assorted cookies and blondie bars. The toaster popped, breaking his trance. He removed the toast and quickly dropped it onto his plate, feeling the heat scorch his fingertips. The butter was cold and curled like chiseled wood shavings. He set them on the toast and watched them melt into daffodil pools. He poured a glass of orange juice and another of water. Then took a mug from the cupboard and slid the coffee pot free and poured himself a cup.

Ambos se van hoy? he asked, sitting down.

Si, one of them said. *El camión está todo empaquetado y listo.*

Después del desayuno, nos pondremos en camino, added another.

A dónde vas? he asked, peppering the eggs.

Mexico, the first one answered.

He nodded.

Where will you be? asked the third man.

Not sure yet.

I hope to see you when I get back.

Landon smiled and thanked them.

The men wiped their mouths and stood. They walked to the sink and washed their plates and set them on the drying rack. He stood and hugged them as they passed.

Viajes seguros mi amigos, he said.

Tú también Señor Cassidy, replied the first man.

Adios.

They fitted their Stetsons to their heads and touched the brim and walked down the hall and out the front door. Landon sat and continued his breakfast in silence. Cars and trucks passed by the windows, their horns blaring as they passed their onlookers. The house was quiet. Somewhere a faucet dripped. Slow and singular. He forked eggs onto the toast and ate. He thought about several things all at once, then none at all. Where was that dripping coming from?

When he came out of the bathroom, Granger was in the hall, staring at the pictures along the walls. He body jolted in surprise.

This picture sums up most of my life, the old man croaked dressed in a white button-down and khakis. His sleeves were rolled up, exposing his dark, tan arms.

You scared me, Landon said.

Sorry.

It's alright.

Did you speak with Ricky?

Who?

Rachel.

Oh. Yes. She was nice. Polite and professional.

Good.

She said she'd call back at three.

What was her offer?

Forty thousand.

Granger nodded approvingly.

We didn't get into the logistics, but she did say to avoid other suitors.

Will you?

Yes.

Why?

Because she called.

Very loyal of you.

Landon shrugged.

Ricky is good at what she does. She's also patient, which, I'd venture to postulate, stems from dealing with me all these years.

Landon chuckled. She said you were tough.

I was. Granger said, looking at his polished boot tips, recalling long distant memories.

Meredith came in through the front door. She wore a rose-colored jacket and mustard pants. Her ivory turtleneck shaped her body well. White curls peeked from beneath her black fur hat.

Mister Cassidy, she exclaimed, good morning.

Good morning, Mrs. Granger.

It looks to be a beautiful day. That is, if you keep away from the wind.

Did you have breakfast? Granger asked him.

Yes. Just finished.

What are your plans for the day?

I was going to help wash Signatures before he leaves. Maybe work the livestock.

Granger nodded.

It's a shame that most of the horses are gone again.

That's how it goes.

Less horses, less workers.

The quiet will be nice, at least.

Always is.

Meredith laughed.

How've you been, ma'am? the young writer asked.

It's good to be home. Thank you for asking.

He smiled.

A peculiar air set about them.

He shot a look at the old photograph, then back to the old author's wife. Well I best be getting on, he said, giving her a gentle smile.

Come find me after your call, Granger said.

Alright.

He gave Meredith a smile as he passed.

Have a good day, ma'am.

Thank you, she replied. You too.

He walked across the blistering gravel, examining the various tracks from the tires. Dusty. Deeply imprinted. Maple followed him lock step to the fence line, her tongue lolling.

The wind was nothing more than a cool ray with a gelid kiss at its end. It burned his eyes to the point he had to lower his hat to deepen the shade over his brow. The ranch had gone quiet. No muttered conversation, no routine activity. The flowers along the gravel perimeter jittered as the sun beat down and purloined the tinct from their gossamer petals. Signatures and another dark-haired thoroughbred were out grazing. They wore beige socks and moved stiffly. Their tails whipped across their haunches. Droves of flies circumnavigated along broken patterns. The horses seemed unfazed by the heat. They stood and ate, swinging their manicured manes as if the weather was unlike any other. Perhaps they never did give it much thought.

The quartet, clad with their notebooks and pencils, sat at their same table in their same order. Todd Childress held a smoldering cigarette between two amber fingers. Stu Redson was the only one scribbling. Javier Graves and Frank Ferns watched the horses. He glanced at them and gave them a short wave. Childress was the only one who responded. They never had taken to one another. He always took them for lazy sycophants. They never spoke unless needed to, and even then, conversation was short and sweet. He heard Graves call out to him. He turned and saw their eyes on him, the caller waving him over. He sighed and spat and tucked his hands deep in his back pockets and walked over. The bitter breeze caused him to squint thinly upon approach.

Fine day, Graves said.

That it is, Landon replied.

Had a good breakfast?

Same as you.

Graves chuckled.

You all seeing Signatures off?

Childress nodded as he drew on the cigarette.

Landon turned to watch the horses.

What are you still doing here? Graves asked with a slippery grin. Enjoying the view, the young writer replied. What are you still doing here?Redson looked up at the young man. Working, he replied, eyes thin and defensive.

The young writer smirked, turning to the thin, graying man.

Is that what you call it?

Redson didn't reply.

V

Landon eyed Graves.

Is this why you waved me over? he said. To ask what I was doing here? Again?

That's right, answered Graves.

Two and a half years and you've only been able to muster up the same old question. Y'all should stop working so hard. Take more vacations. Read a book.

That's the problem, son, Redson interjected. You never answered.

Then educate me, *Señor* Redson.

Too late for that. Been too late for that.

Says who?

Let me tell you about a dream I had.

I don't want to hear about your dream.

In the dream, I'm wandering through a vast landscape. There are trees and woods all around me. I come to a city, but there is no one there. The elms and oaks and spruces and pines are all towering over these great skyscrapers. They bend and twist about them. Coiled together like some sort of art installation. I take a closer look and see that the trees are still growing, tightening against the steel and glass. Then it starts to shatter. Glass falls from the sky like triangular hail. I try running but the glass is already cutting into me. I crawl into a large hole that's carved into a redwood. The glass has long since turned to rain and the blood from my lacerations coagulate. I leave the redwood and walk through the city in the rain and come to a clearing. There is a large lake, placid and black. Barely a reflection casted upon it. At the center, the water slides open like a door, but the water does not pour in. What climbs from within, is a wolf. Big and gray. Hot, citrine eyes. He stalks across the water on dainty paws, barely a ripple emitting from them. He stands at the waterline and stares at me. Not hungry, but curious. Then the snow started to fall.

Landon didn't say a word.

Redson smiled and went back to his notebook.

The other men cackled like fiendish schoolchildren.

That's quite the humdinger, said Landon. My suggestion is you stick to laughing and scribbling. That's more your wheelhouse than gypsy speak.

And what is your wheelhouse, Mister Cassidy? Graves smiled. Besides being a lucky drifter? A man fallen from grace and rescued out of pity?

Landon looked at him.

You cannot respond because you know I'm right. We know what you are, and if you would have met Señor Granger back when we first did, he would have spat on you. Called you a disgrace. Never would've given you a second glance.

The young man bit his lip. His throat quivered with nervous rage. A red warmth ran down the back of his neck. He wanted to smack the man.

Redson looked up at him. They were all looking at him.

Where will you go when this is all over? Graves asked.

Someplace far from any of you, Landon replied through his clenched jaw.

Graves started to stand, but Childress placed his hand on his shoulder and brought him back.

I think it's best none of us wave each other over anymore, Landon suggested.

Ferns shook his head.

Safe travels, gentleman, he said walking away.

Mister Cassidy, Redson called.

He didn't turn back.

He wiped his brow with the back of his sleeve and rounded the barn, watching the livestock huddle in the diminishing shade. Two men sat stoically on their horses on the hilled horizon. Their arms resting over the pommel, the shadow of the oak tree cloaking them. He continued past the revolving windmill and the cold study and into the forest along the back road, listening to the crackling leaves underfoot. Overhead, he studied the naked limbs of crisscrossing branches. Nests once occupied, now vacant. Their twisted circular configurations uncommon to any blueprint ever seen or shared. Do they know the shape in which they create? Why not others? The fallen trunk he'd forgotten about, had become scabrous along its outer layer and infested with termites. A small pool of abhorrent, stagnant water. Flyblown and encrusted with a putrid yellow grime. An oily visage that obscured all reflection, sending false semaphores to breeders and bird alike. Soon the heat would take it entire. This bantam oasis. Sleep, fallen one. And take hold of these dreams that wrench away the eaters of the world. For the world you bed upon will be muted in your absence. And all your brethren will watch over you as the fires of the future scintillate around you. Never touching you. Never touching you.

The track was deserted, the stables barren. The small living quarters where Evelyn found him late that cold night was clean and empty. He opened the gate and walked along the track. The thin, browned grass cracked beneath his feet. The sky was ice blue to the point it was almost white. Only the sun was there to observe him round the track. Nothing stirred. He saw that the stalls had been scrubbed, all equipment properly placed. He came to the front door of the small house and turned the knob, feeling it click open.

The hinges creaked sharply as he entered. Nothing had been disturbed. It was cool, the air conditioner blowing on him as he stepped further in. He crossed to the bar and found the shelves freshly stocked. The bottles flared in the blue light casted upon them. His feet shuffled woodenly as he rounded the bar and plucked a glass from the cabinet and took down a bottle of Tullamore Dew and broke the juniper seal. He sniffed the liquor, tasting the spices in the back of his throat, then poured and replaced the cap and set it back on the shelf as neatly as he found it. He held the glass to the light then swirled it under his nose and drank. He set the empty glass on the bar and looked at the silent layout of the room. His hushed breathing was the only sound.

When he returned to the ranch, the horses were gone. He worried that Signatures had been picked up early but saw his silhouette through the stall window. He opened the stable door and went in.

Signatures stood in the far stall. Miguel, a short, boxy Hispanic with buzzed black hair and a cleanly shaven face, was hanging a blanket on a long hook. He walked to the stall and ran his hand up the massive head.

Buenos días, Miguel said, walking up to Landon.

Buenos días.

You come to groom him?

I'd like to, yes.

Bueno. Bueno.

Miguel walked to the opposite end of the stable and gathered the grooming supplies. Landon grabbed a rope hackamore and fitted it around the horse's head and knotted it to the post on his left. He walked down the aisle and took up a mustard-handled pick and walked back and opened the stall door and went in, shutting it behind. He clicked his tongue to grab Signatures' front right hoof. The horse lifted with ease. He straddled the leg and began to pick out the cold muck. He dropped the hoof and did the same to the other three, carving out the V shape until it all was clear and apparent. He cleaned the pick with a hose, then dried it off and placed it with the others. The ranch hand stood waiting with the supplies at his feet.

Are you ready? Miguel asked.

Yes, Landon replied.

I'm ready.

They flicked the dirt from Signatures' coat, what little there was, working their way with the hair. They passed the coat again in long sweeping motions. The ranch hand soaked a colorless sponge and gently washed around Signatures' eyes, ears and muzzle. Landon whispered in Spanish to him as he worked the soap into his hide. He replaced his brush, took up a comb and unfolded a small step ladder and placed it at his flank. He climbed up and folded Signatures' mane towards him like a sleeve of drooping pasta. He ran his fingers through the coarse hair, straightening any tangles. Then he took a section in his palm and ran the comb slowly through. He worked patiently, methodically, slowly. Miguel dropped the damp sponge into the pail and left the stall. He squirted several droplets of wash fluid in the bottom of a bucket then filled the bucket with water.

When he returned, Landon was brushing out his tail. He set the bucket down and picked up a fresh sponge, soaked it and began scrubbing Signatures' legs. Water slapped the concrete. His hands circled up the body with the hairline. Landon grabbed a sponge and started on the posterior. They met in the middle. Signatures shook, coating them and the stall in cold, sticky water. They laughed and patted the colossal horse on the neck. Landon wetted his mane and tail, making sure to keep the hair as straight as possible. Miguel took the bucket and tossed the water out the stall window and walked back to the hose and washed out the bucket and coated the base in shampoo and filled the bucket with thick white suds. It was going on one o clock when they began lathering Signatures in soap. The drain beneath gurgled with water and bubbles and hair. They coated him twice before rinsing him off. Miguel cleaned his immense head while Landon conditioned the tail using fresh brush to work in the potent almond-scented cream. Then he did the same for the mane. When they were finished, he gave Signatures a carrot and two sugar cubes.

Gracias Mister Cassidy, Miguel said.

Mi placer.

As he headed towards the guest house, he looked askance to see the four men gone.

The humming heater was all he heard as he opened the door to his room. The clothes he'd thrown down the chute throughout the week were folded and neatly stacked on the freshly made bed. He crossed to the desk and opened a drawer full of blank blue notebooks. He took one out, along with a pencil and pocket sharpener and left.

Wood shavings gyrated onto the gravel. The rough gnaw of lead as he twisted the graphite into a fine point. He inspected the sharpness and blew off the residue and tucked the pencil behind his ear then blew the grit from the sharpener and tucked it in his pocket. He walked through the stall door and down to Signatures. The horse looked at him and grunted. He turned a bucket over and sat. He leaned against a post and looked into Signatures' black eyes as if he was looking upon the Creator itself. The horse did not blink. His tail slowly whipped and settled, whipped and settled. He rapped his fingers quietly against his knee.

I guess one last ride isn't in the cards, huh? he said.

Signatures stared at him.

At least we have this time.

The horse grunted.

He smiled then opened the notebook, took the pencil from his ear and started to write.

He'd written six pages when he heard the sound of tires on the ruffled gravel. Granger, Meredith, Evelyn and the quartet were walking towards him as he emerged from the stable. The collection of gray Silverados had pulled in and parked, but no one stepped out.

Where've you been? Evelyn asked.

Here, Landon replied, nodding to the stable. Keeping him company.

How is he?

Tranquil.

Evelyn folded her hair behind her ear and nodded.

The truck doors opened and several men stepped out. They were wearing matching navy button downs and jeans, brown shearling coats. Even the boots and Dakota hats were the same. Only their skin tones gave them variety. They smiled and greeted Granger and the others. Everyone shook hands and exchanged pleasantries. Quips about the weather.

Is he ready? The lead representative inquired.

Just got done with a bath, Granger said.

Excellent, he replied.

The representative turned to the other men.

Open the stall boys, he shouted. Let's get to it.

The brown-coated army split into two teams. One man unlatched the trailer chains and opened the door. The interior was not as luxurious as Gennady Lee's but still spacious enough. One team prepared the trailer while the other opened the stable doors and entered. They fitted a hackamore over Signatures' head and gently led him out.

May I? Landon asked, approaching the man holding the rope.

He nodded and handed the young man the strap.

Landon led Signatures to the box stall, susurrating Spanish into his ear.

He came to the ramp and the horse went in without complaint. There was enough room to turn him and he did. He removed the hackamore and patted him one last time on the head, then turned and walked out.

As the representative finished the paperwork with Granger and the quartet, Landon watched the men close the stall door and slide the locking rods into place and engage the latch. They shook hands once more then got into their trucks and filed out. The truck backed up slowly, Signatures peered through the barred rear window at his family in attendance. Landon waved sullenly. *Buen viaje, amigo mío,* he mumbled lachrymosely. Then the truck drove down the gravel pathway and faded through the trees. He never saw the horse again.

Well, said Redson stretching, that about does it for us.

Y'all won't stay for dinner? Meredith asked.

No, no. We should get to the airport early. Traffic at this hour can be relentless..

You're right about that, Granger agreed.

We had a good year, sir, Redson said holding his hand out to Granger.

Yes we did, shaking firmly. You all did a wonderful job.

Landon rolled his eyes, looking away.

They shook Meredith and Evelyn's hands and thanked them.

When they saw Landon's back turned, they scoffed. The silence was brief yet potent.

The truck bed was loaded with their suitcases and other belongings. They opened the doors and filed in and sat in the same order they would have at their table. The ignition caught after a few coughs. The truck reversed out the garage and drove on. They waved as they passed. The red taillights nebulous in the galvanized gravel dust that trailed through the shaded tree tunnel. Then they were gone.

Landon turned around and saw their concerned eyes. Meredith opened her mouth as if to say something but no words manifested. Granger nodded, turned, and went back inside. Fifteen minutes later, the call came in.

Hello? Landon answered.

Mister Cassidy, it's Rachel Nelson.

You sure are prompt.

As are you.

He laughed.

How's your day been?

Serene.

Good word.

I'm ready to talk business.

I'm glad to hear that.

Yes ma'am.

I take it you didn't answer those other callers?

No.

Good. So, continuing from what we discussed this morning, we're ready to give you a forty thousand dollar signing bonus and a six-year contract.

Six years?

Correct.

Just like that?

Just like that.

How many books do you expect me to write in that amount of time?

In a perfect world, we'd like a book a year.

Like clockwork, he replied sarcastically.

Relevance is key in this business, as I'm sure recall.

Yes, of course.

But we can discuss that further when you come in.

Okay.

I sense hesitation in your voice.

No, he amended, just thinking.

What are you thinking? Rachel inquired. Remember, I'm here to help make you feel comfortable through this process. I'm looking to bring you on as a collaborator. Not to keep you under an iron fist. We want to do what's best for our writers.

I understand.

Do you?

He did not respond.

A faint voice on the other side of the room called out to him.

He turned to look, but no one was there.

Listen, Mister Cassidy, Rachel said, I know your situation. Harrison and I have talked at length about it. We're both excited about what's in store for you. But you have to want it. The gamut of a meandering life is not as romantic as history's most acclaimed stories make it out to be. Harrison lived it, he doesn't want that for you. Nor do I. You have the makings of a great talent, but you must nurture it. It is arduous, but now you have me. You have your family on the ranch. If you squander the opportunity to do what you were meant to, then what was it you were looking for in the first place?

I don't know, he said quietly.

Yes, you do.

He was silent for a long time.

Say it, she coaxed.

I was looking for the opportunity to be something great.

Well, here it is.

He looked back at the room. Nothing.

Right, he said, taking a long breath. Okay. Let's do it.

Say it again. So that you hear it.

Landon composed himself and took another deep breath. He looked out the window, studying the land he'd fallen in love with, and smiled.

I'm ready.

There was a long pause. As if both parties, all parties in the world, were finally at rest.

Welcome to your future, Mister Cassidy, Rachel congratulated. You have a plane to catch for New York at nine tomorrow morning. Your ticket will be waiting for you at the American Airlines counter.

Thank you, Rachel.

Congratulations Mister Cassidy.

See you tomorrow.

He replaced the receiver and sat looking at it.

He took a long shower and changed into a fresh set of clothes. He was the first to arrive for dinner. The table was set. The two-team kitchen crew were preparing the finishing touches as they'd done each night. He sat in the middle on one side of the table, waiting for the others. He heard a sort of commotion from upstairs. Shouting. A door slam.

Evelyn came in through the back door, thwarting his growing concern. He turned and smiled at her. She walked over and kissed him lovingly on the cheek. She rounded the table and sat opposite him.

How'd it go? she asked excitedly.

I fly out tomorrow morning to sign the papers, he replied.

She breathed a sigh of relief. That's wonderful, Landon. I knew you'd get it.

Thank you.

It's all moving fast now, huh?

I don't think I felt like this even when I signed with my first publisher. It's almost surreal.

I bet.

Will you come with me?

I can meet you in a couple of days. I can't go tomorrow. I have things I need to take care of.

Alright. I'll get you a ticket.

Perfect, she said, smiling.

Granger and Meredith came in. Their cheeks were flushed, the back of his hair tousled. They sat at the heads of the table, opposite one another and unfolded their napkins and set them in their laps. He was breathing rapidly.

How'd the meeting go? Granger asked after a few minutes.

I fly out tomorrow morning, Landon said. Sign myself up.

Congratulations.

Wonderful news, Meredith chimed unemotionally.

Thank you, Landon replied. Both of you.

Let's have a toast, Granger said.

The older gentleman turned around.

Four glasses, Granger told him.

The servant gave him a look of skepticism.

Excuse me, sir? he said.

Bring us four glasses.

The man shot Meredith a concerned look. She sighed and looked away.

He walked over to the cupboard and took out four red wine glasses and inspected them in the overhead light and crossed to the table and set them in front of them.

The good red, Granger ordered with a frenzied look.

Yes, sir, the servant replied hesitantly. He approached a door at the other end of the kitchen and retrieved a small keyring from his pocket and rifled through it and found the one he needed. He inserted it into the lock and turned the latch and opened the door and descended the stairs into the damp cellar.

Landon listened to the man's muffled shuffling underneath. The dining room was very quiet. He stole a glance at Meredith, who was staring with hard contempt at her husband. He shifted his gaze to Evelyn, who seemed apprehensive.

The older gentleman emerged with a dust-coated bottle of Penfolds, 1951. He crossed and stood next to Granger and turned the title to him for his examination.

Still as beautiful as the day I received it, he said, reading the bottle. What is it? Landon inquired.

A bottle of Penfolds nineteen fifty-one, Granger said. The greatest Australian wine ever produced. A true vintage.

How did you get it?

One of the horses we trained, well, Evelyn trained, won first in dressage at the Melbourne Cup a few years back. Remember that?

Evelyn nodded.

Really? the young writer said, looking at her.

Yes, she muttered.

The owners of the horse gave us a case of this as a gift for bringing them a champion.

That's incredible.

We only drink it for occasions such as this.

How many have you had?

Counting this one, one.

They laughed timorously.

The older woman set down a platter of thick pork chops, a large bowl of freshly pounded golden mashed potatoes, bowls of steamed rainbow carrots, cauliflower and succotash. She returned to the kitchen and gathered the rest of the meal.

The gentleman popped the cork and set the bottle to breathe on the counter. He filled their glasses with water then returned to the bottle and brought it to the table and poured a splash of the scarlet liquid into Granger's glass. Then did the same for the others. Meredith placed her hand over the glass, shaking her head.

The older woman came around and set a glass of lemonade in front of Meredith.

With glasses in hand, Granger toasted: To your good news.

Cheers, they muttered and touched glasses.

Granger stared at his glass with demoniacal possessiveness. He twirled it by the stem and brought it to his nostrils and swirled the wine for a long time, inhaling deeply.

Landon glanced around the table, seeing the others on edge.

Granger tilted the glass to his lips, the globule slithering down until it settled on his tongue. He closed his eyes, his mouth, and savored it passionately. Like a teenager in church. Like an exsiccated plant culling the last morning dewdrop. He swallowed with ecstasy, then set the glass down.

When he opened his eyes, it was as if he'd gone through metamorphosis. The gentleman sat the bottle down at the center of the table. Landon sipped the dry-aged wine. It was exquisite. He never understood the idea of vintage wines and the ridiculous prices they went for, but when he sipped, he knew then.

Do you like it? Granger asked.

Yes, Landon said. It's incredible.

It's very good, Evelyn agreed.

The old man smiled.

Meredith looked at him coldly. She didn't say a word.

Well, let's start passing, Evelyn announced.

Landon forked two chops onto his plate then passed it to Meredith. They scooped vegetables and wheeled the bowls around until everyone had full helpings. They filled their glasses with the wine and set to eating. He cut into his pork chop, porcelain and juicy. He chased it with the wine. A heavenly pairing.

Now that you're signing, what will you do next? Granger asked.

Probably get a car, Landon replied.

They laughed.

V

I was toying with the idea of driving to the coast to work on my next book.

The coast? Evelyn exclaimed.

Yes.

That's a good idea, Interjected, his eyes fixated on the wine bottle. He passed his tongue over his lips before taking in a spoonful of succotash.

Evelyn will be coming to New York in a few days.

Is that right? Granger said, turning to her.

Yes, she said. Not tomorrow, but the following day.

Good timing.

She nodded.

How long do you plan on staying?

Not sure, Landon said.

We'll see where the days take us, she replied, smiling at the young writer.

Well, whatever you decide, you kids have fun.

Thank you, Harrison.

Eat and drink. Today is a great day.

When she finished her plate, Meredith wiped her lips with her napkin, stood, and left without another word.

Granger watched her then set his silverware down and followed her.

The room went quiet.

Something's wrong, Landon whispered.

Of course, there is Evelyn snapped back. Where have you been?

What happened?

I'm not sure, but since she's been back, all they've been doing is fighting.

They have?

Yes.

I thought things were better between them?

I don't think so, Evelyn said, shaking her head.

He looked over at the old man's empty chair. Then he looked at the bottle of Penfolds.

The wine, he muttered. Do you think she's upset because he drank?

That'd be my guess. He's been sober well over thirty years.

A sip of wine won't do anything. No matter the vintage.

I think it's the principle of the matter.

He shrugged.

What do you think is wrong? she asked.

I don't know. They've been married a long time. Could be anything.

They slowly continued to eat.

He finished his glass and set it aside, restraining the urge to refill. Then the fighting started. Horrific emotional shouting from the second floor. Obscenities and accusations. Doors flying shut, fists pounding. His appetite vanished. He looked at Evelyn. A look of fright had come over her. He'd never heard a shouting match of such magnitude before.

This is bad, Evelyn whispered. Really bad.

What should we do?

I don't know.

We should go.

You think?

It sounds really bad.

I could go up and try to calm them down.

Do you think that's a good idea? Landon asked.

We only have two options.

Yeah.

Which do you think is better?

Landon shook his head, unsure.

I'll go, she said.

Are you sure?

Yeah. If they're still going at it, come up.

Alright.

They rose from their chairs and followed the shouts and screams down the hall. Doors slammed. Someone was pounding or kicking at the wall. The eyes in the pictures followed them, eager to see what was to unfold. He glanced at the photograph of Granger sleeping on the bus. They came to the foot of the winding ivory staircase. A moment of dangerous silence. They looked at one another. Then the shouting resumed, further away, it seemed. As if they'd become lost in the walls. Evelyn mounted the first step, grasping the banister.

She took a deep breath, then ascended. She reached the second-floor landing and was gone.

He listened to the calamity above. No word from her. He waited a long time. He looked down the hallway towards the front door. A scratching sound was coming from it. He looked up towards the shouting then ran to the door and opened it and watched Maple scamper in. She shook her body feverishly and ran towards the shouting and up the stairs. Maple, he called after her, but she was gone. He drew in a long breath and slowly took each step one at a time. There were impacts from fists in the walls. Pictures in all matters of proportions, none straight. A porcelain vase shattered in a doorway. He looked around but did not see anyone.

Hello? he called out.

Nothing.

He made his way down the hallway. All had gone quiet. Somewhere, someone was crying. The doors were in various stages of closure. He slowly peeked into each room to find everything in disarray. Their bedroom door creaked unobtrusively as his knock opened it further. Meredith's back was to the door. She did not hear him enter. He stood in the doorway, observing the decimated room. The bed was thrashed apart. Pillows gashed, their insides spilling out in feathery pools. Blankets thrown all over. Clothes balled up from being used as projectiles. Books splayed like fallen birds. Pages torn and scattered about. One of the curtains had been ripped away, the rail askew and naked. The outer dark and heavenly bodies audience to this great unraveling.

Meredith? Landon muttered.

She ceased her crying and turned to look at him. Her hair looked like a wild boll of cotton. Blurred cerulean eyes. Her mascara, black as turtle blood, ran down her wrinkled cheeks.

You, she sneered.

Are you alright?

Am I alright? What does it look like?

I'm sorry. I just—

What would you know of it anyway?

He fell silent.

We've been together for over thirty years.

I wanted to make sure you both were okay.

Okay? You wanted to make sure we were okay?

Where's Harrison?

She looked around the war zone, as if seeing it for the first time. She mouthed something he could not hear.

What?

This all started with you, she repeated.

Me?

When he told me that he met you in New York that year. I knew then that you cast some sort of spell on him.

I don't know what you're talking about. We barely spoke.

Then whatever few words you used must have been the right ones.

She sat up, wiping her black tears, staining her hands, the chair. She plucked two tissues from under the rubble and blew her nose.

You triggered something in him that sent him back to his old ways, she said.

How's that?

Do you know why I left? The real reason?

It's not my business.

Oh, silly boy, Meredith chuckled, it is.

He looked at her.

After he told me about your encounter, he began writing again. Picked up the book he started all those years ago and frantically went to work. I couldn't tell you the last time I saw him work so diligently on his writing. Some nights he would never leave the study. And some weeks, I'd hardly see him. Then one day, he stopped. All his momentum crashed, like a bullet train into a thousand-year oak. His rage, which we had worked so hard to quiet, returned.

One evening he came home, drunk and thrashing about. He didn't even ease into it. Just threw away all those hard-fought years of happiness and sobriety to reek of cheap whiskey. He came upstairs, stumbling into the walls. I was sitting right here when he came through the door. I watched him stand there with his hands in his pockets and his leg twitching badly, not a care in the world. Like a child who knows he'd done bad and accepts it. Just standing there, laughing hysterically. We tried talking, but that didn't do anything. What you heard now is just another result of your repercussions.

You're telling me all this is because of the wine he sampled? Landon said.

No. I'm saying you're the catalyst.

He was silent.

All this irrevocable damage began with you.

No. That's not true.

Voices in the ceiling began to quietly laugh at him.

Stu and the others told me their qualms about your presence here, Meredith said. I thought they were blowing smoke, but when I saw you, everything made sense. Everyone on this ranch has a purpose Mister Cassidy. You've learned a few things in the years you've adopted, but we still don't know your purpose. But I've finally come to see it. Your purpose, is disruption.

He shook his head. The laughter in his head growing maliciously now. He heard the floor creak. The laughter stopped. He turned, and saw Granger sitting against the wall on the opposite side of the room. He was holding a bloody towel to his head while getting his hand bandaged by Evelyn.

So, Landon said to the old man, the reason she left was because you relapsed?

Granger didn't answer.

He vowed to never drink again, Meredith said, staring at her husband.

Landon turned to her. Why didn't anybody tell me? I would have left.

Then his writing would stop.

I don't believe that.

It is not a matter of belief. It's a matter of reality.

I'm sorry.

Tomorrow you leave for New York, yes?

Yes ma'am.

Take everything with you, she demanded, getting to her feet. Whatever clothes you bought, the notebooks he gave you, your damn dog. Take it all and leave.

She crossed to him.

He kept his head lowered and could feel her quivering breath on his cheek.

You're not welcome back here, she sneered in his ear.

He looked over at Granger and Evelyn.

My job as his wife is to protect him. Something nobody else did. Ever. I protect him, his writing, everything. From outsiders like you. The workers are gone, now it's high time you follow suit.

He bit his lip and nodded.

I'm sorry for any harm I have caused, he said. It was not my intention. You can see yourself out. She walked back to the lounger and sat.

He thought about looking at them again but he didn't. He headed for the door and walked onto the landing and descended the stairs. Maple's jingling collar after him.

The table was clean and cleared. The dishes covered with foil, Saran Wrap. The wine was corked and stored away. The older gentleman and the woman were gone. He heard the front door open and shut. He peered into the hallway. Nothing. He opened the door and found Evelyn on the porch swing, swaying back and forth. He closed the door and sat next to her. They swayed quietly for a long time.

I'm sorry, Landon, Evelyn said.

She's right. It is for the best. I don't belong here. I'm just a distraction.

You're not. Don't believe her. She's always been overly protective of Harrison.

Rightfully so.

I'm sorry.

It's not your fault.

She ran her hand down the back of his neck.

Will you still come to New York? he asked.

Of course.

Good.

We can get a car and drive somewhere. That would be nice.

We can take our time.

Yes.

He slid his hand into hers.

V

Do you love me? she asked.

He turned to her.

Yes. I love you.

Evelyn smiled.

Good. Because I love you too.

They squeezed each other's hands tight as the moon vanished beyond the clouds.

Ben knocked promptly at five o clock. He handed Landon a small navy suitcase, told him to dress warmly, and that he would be waiting in the truck. He watched the driver's quiet, carpeted steps make their way down the hallway and down the stairs.

He sat on the bed, rubbing his eyes. Maple was fast asleep. He stood and unzipped the suitcase and packed the few clothes he had purchased. He showered then shaved with the sandalwood cream he'd bought downtown then packed the toiletries in a small leather bag and tossed it into the suitcase and set blue notebooks atop and worked the zipper around until it shut completely. He dressed in beige chinos and a blue button down. Maple stood and stretched and slinked to the floor. He made the bed and gave the room one last look. He extended the suitcase handle and whistled for Maple to follow and switched off the light and said goodbye forever.

The jean jacket and scarlet scarf did not keep him warm. He hurried across the gravel pathway to the Bronco. The exhaust flowed thickly in the bitter cold. He opened the trunk and tossed in the suitcase and shut it and opened the back door for Maple. She leaped in and laid down. He sat in the passenger side and buckled his seat belt.

Just us?

Yes, sir, Ben replied, putting the truck in reverse.

They pulled out of the garage. He looked up and saw Granger standing in the window. A faint hazel light behind him. They exchanged a small wave. Ben put the Bronco into drive and they headed down the road.

The traffic was nonexistent as they pulled into the drop-off zone.

Ben leashed Maple while Landon got the bags. He rounded the truck and handed him the leash.

Thank you, Landon said.

Take care of yourself, Ben advised.

I will.

I'll talk to Harrison. He'll want to see you again.

That's kind of you, but we both know that's not happening.

You never know, Ben shrugged. Life is funny.

Right.

Ben nodded.

Thank you for everything, Ben.

It was a pleasure getting to know you, kid.

They embraced.

Ben knelt and scratched Maple behind the ears. Be a good girl, he said, then stood and turned to the young man.

Good luck, Mister Cassidy.

Drive safe.

He watched Ben return to the Bronco and drive away. He looked down at Maple's excited brown eyes, smiled, and went in.

He purchased Evelyn's ticket for a late morning flight when he checked his bag. He used a payphone to call her room, relaying the flight information. No answer. The voicemail clicked and he left the message, signing off: *I love you.*

The wail from the orange siren jarred him. The carousel came to life. The steel panels slowly slid against one another. Maple's ears perked up when he closed the blue notebook and put his pencil in his chest pocket and stood. He watched as the motley crew of passengers bent over and grabbed their bags.

A driver stood by the exit doors holding a sign with his last name.

Late morning traffic was in full effect. The driver worked diligently to inch his way forward. By the time they arrived at the St. Regis Hotel, an hour and a half had elapsed.

The room was a brilliant blend of black, pewter, and walnut. An enormous square-cut mirror stood behind the chiffon California King. Wall length windows overlooked the city skyline. The World Trade Center and Empire State Building were so close he could touch them. The cars moved like insects below. Ashen clouds. Whorls of rain. Maple paced around the room, smelling everywhere. A knock came on the door. He turned, crossed the room, and opened the door to a waiter wearing white tails and polished black shoes, rolling in a tray. His thin salt and pepper hair slicked back and cemented with peppermint-scented pomade. He presented a sterling silver bucket with a chanted bottle of chilled Dom Perignon. He parked the tray at the center of the room then reached into his jacket and pulled out a card and handed it to the guest. His name was written in an elegant script. The waiter picked up the bottle, popped it and poured Landon a glass and handed it to him. Thank you, he said. The waiter bowed and turned to leave.

Wait, Landon called out, putting the glass and card down.

The waiter turned in the doorway. Landon took out his bruised wallet and pinched a ten dollar bill and walked towards the door, extending the tender. The waiter held up his gloved hand.

That won't be necessary, sir, he said.

Excuse me?

Everything's already been taken care of.

Oh.

The waiter bowed and closed the door.

He tucked the bill back into his wallet and tossed it on the table and picked up the glass and crossed to the window. Cheers, he muttered and drank. The champagne was cold and smooth. It bubbled all the way down his throat and felt good when it hit bottom. He threw back the rest. The bottle was ice cold and beaded with moisture like a basketball. The water dribbled as he poured his next glassful. He dried his hand on his pantleg and drank while exploring the room. He finished the glass and set it on the tray and unpacked his clothes and set them in the drawers and closet. He assembled his attire for the meeting and hung it on a wire hanger and went into the bathroom and hung it on the bar behind the door and turned on the shower to full heat and watched the steam billow in thick clouds. He shut the door and crossed to the clock on the bedside table and set an alarm for forty-five minutes. The champagne bubbled anew in the glass. He looked at Maple and thought to when she last ate. He ordered a lean sirloin steak with mashed sweet potatoes. When the food arrived, he removed the lid for the food to cool. He cut the steak into small pieces and set it on the floor. She ate ravenously. He poured another glass of champagne and picked up the envelope, turned it over to find no other words. He looked out at the New York skyline slowly indulging in the champagne. The alcohol was already working and he was feeling pretty good. He set the glass on the carpet next to a tall hickory chair, sat and broke the letter seal. The card was thick and as white as the envelope. The message was from Rachel Nelson.

Greetings Mister Cassidy,

I'm glad you've arrived safe and sound. This champagne is to commemorate the successful partnership I know will lead us far into the future. Please order whatever you like. If you are looking for any dining or drinking destinations, let the concierge know. I look forward to our meeting this afternoon. The driver will be waiting in the lobby at two thirty. He will know where to go.

Till then,
Rachel Nelson
Literary Agent | ICM Partners

The elevator doors slid open, and he walked out. He checked himself in an oblong mirror, smoothing out the rest of the wrinkles with his palms. He descended the ruby velvet stairs and stood in line for the front desk. The receptionist's smile revealed paper-white teeth.

How can I help you, sir? she asked.

My name is Landon Cassidy. I'm in room thirteen—

Landon Cassidy? the receptionist cutoff.

Yes.

One moment, please. She typed on the keyboard, turned, and walked into a back room.

He looked around the baroque lobby. Suit and tie businessmen in long, dark coats and fedoras, shaking off their umbrellas over the carpet. Families taking pictures. Guests dining at the bar and restaurant. He saw the pouring rain through the windows and sucked his teeth.

The receptionist returned and handed him an envelope. This is for you. He took the envelope and examined his name in the same impeccable script.

Thank you.

Is there anything else I can help you with today? the receptionist inquired. I seemed to have forgotten.

Well, let me know if you remember.

I will. Thank you.

Have a pleasant stay.

He found an empty seat at the far end of the bar and ordered an Old Fashioned.

The bartender made the drink then set it on a napkin with the hotel's insignia etched in red and gold. The liquor was dark and gave off a light mist. The dark cherry stove beneath the large, smoked cube.

What time is it? Landon asked.

The bartender looked at his wristwatch. One o clock, sir.

Thank you.

How would you like to pay today, sir?

Charge the room.

Yes, sir. What's the room number?

Thirteen four.

Thank you, sir.

He nodded and lifted his drink and sipped. The whiskey warmed him. His nervousness waned, and with one or two more, it would cease to be a bother at all. He took another sip and ordered another. He downed three glasses of water, used the bathroom and headed through the lobby to meet the driver. The streets were coated in an endless rain. Everyone wielding an umbrella as if it were everyday tool. He watched the myriad homeless bivouacked in their cardboard shelters and bleeding newspaper beds. The office building spanned several stories. It was modern and elegant. Sapphire mirrors on every floor. The driver pulled up to the entrance, got out, and opened Landon's door.

Here we are, Mister Cassidy, he said, opening an umbrella and escorting him to the front door.

He tipped ten dollars and thanked him.

Standing beside the front desk was a young black woman. She was thin with pinned-up hair and a gray pencil skirt. She closed her brown ledger as he came in.

Mister Cassidy? she inquired.

Yes?

She shook his hand and smiled.

Welcome to ICM Partners. My name is Kennedy, how are you?

A little wet, he joked, wiping the rain from his hair and sleeves.

Of course. Sorry about that. But if you follow me, we'll head on up.

They walked down a wide hallway, her Gucci heels echoed off the linoleum. A row of polished elevators opened, closed and chimed. She set the elevator button aglow on one of the panels. The doors behind them slid open.

How was your flight? she asked as the elevator ascended.

Fine, thank you, he replied.

Sorry again about the rain.

It's alright. It came out of nowhere.

She chuckled. It happens quite often here.

How's your day been?

Busy. After I drop you off, I have to get to a meeting. Then another one afterward.

What's the meeting about?

PR stuff.

Have fun.

Thank you, she chuckled.

The lights overhead blinked white with every new floor.

How long have you been working here?

Two years. Well, I interned my first year, then I graduated and got hired.

Where'd you graduate?

NYU.

Good school.

Yes.

What's she like? Landon asked as they reached the final floors.

You'll love her.

He smiled.

The doors opened. He looked at the mahogany walls, the navy carpet, the glass encased offices. Men and women dressed in button downs, ties, slacks, skirts. Clean cut hair and ponytails. Several carried stacks of paper. Others at their decorated cubicles reading and marking manuscripts. The mechanical whirring of copiers printing, pages turning.

Follow me, Mister Cassidy, the young woman said.

They walked through the halls, passing suspicious eyes. They came to a long hallway. The walls were lined with elegant black and white portraits of the clients. Harrison Granger among them. He must have been in his sixties. He was leaning against a wooden post, the sleeves rolled up. A cut, sutured by a strip of black coagulated blood, along his wrist. His fingers sat relaxed and intertwined over his belt, the thumbs kissing at the tips. The rugged belt, a simple silver clasp. Faded blue jeans. His face was calm, peaceful. The tracks along his forehead and cheeks like rivers on a globe.

The young assistant knocked on a white door at the end of the hallway.

Come in, a soft voice called out.

Kennedy opened the door.

The office was tasteful but not as gaudy as Dolores Stemper's. There were several pictures on the walnut walls, mainly of what could be deduced as family, friends, and colleagues. Awards. Beige carpet, black trim. The overhanging clouds cast an air of mystery about the room. The lights were soft with a tinge of yellow, as if in a library. Books lined the walls on several floating shelves. It reminded him of Merlin's room in Disney's The Sword and The Stone. Sitting at a darkly varnished oak desk was Rachel Nelson. She stood and walked around. She was tall with dark hair, ivory skin, and small feet. She wore a chocolate turtleneck with emerald bellbottom slacks, exposing her nude Prada heels. Her extended hand was soft and warm.

Welcome to ICM Partners, Mister Cassidy, she greeted.

Hello, Miss Nelson, he replied with a firm grip.

She dismissed Kennedy, and invited him to sit.

The rain streaked down the windows. A sudden flash of lightning, followed by the crack of thunder. She peered back at the window.

I'm sorry about the dreary weather on your big day, she said.

That's alright.

She nodded, opened her desk drawer, took out an envelope and handed it across.

What is it? he asked, taking the envelope.

A surprise.

He carefully tore the top and pinched the single page inside and slid it free. It was blank.

Turn it over, Rachel said.

He did.

There, in his scratchy handwriting, was the foreword Granger wrote for him.

When did he write this? he asked, exasperatingly.

A while ago. It must have been after he read a few of your drafts.

But that was long before we spoke.

Yes.

He knew I would come.

I'm sure he had a strong belief you might.

Landon looked at the words and read.

When writers write with unsullied beauty, the words hum in your head. Haunt your dreams. Beckon your desires. And in the rose brimmed dawn, the world becomes your own. Forever wholly. Forever conquered.

~

Harrison Granger

He read it again. He looked at the words for a long time. Then slid the paper back in the envelope and handed it back to Rachel. He relaxed his shoulders, leaned back and let out a long sigh. He tapped the envelope on his thigh.

Rachel chuckled.

Could you come in real quick, please, she said into the desk intercom. Yes, ma'am, the voice replied.

The door opened, and a short man in his late twenties entered. He had quaffed brown hair and a nice profile. He crossed the room and stood beside the desk, awaiting his orders.

Let's have a drink before we start, shall we? she asked Landon.

Sure. Coffee would be great.

Two, Stanley.

You got it ma'am, the short man said and left.

Thank you for the champagne, Landon said.

My pleasure.

I'd invite you to dinner tonight, but I'm kinda beat.

Understandable. Its been a long day.

Landon chuckled.

How's tomorrow sound?

I've got a special someone coming into town.

Who's that?

Evelyn Chambers.

Harrison's trainer?

Yes.

Evelyn's a beautiful woman.

Yes, she is.

Where are you going?

Not sure yet.

The weekend in New York? No reservations?

They laughed.

I'll make some calls and get you a table, Rachel said.

You can do that?

She raised his eyebrows and smirked at him.

The door opened. The young assistant came in with a small tray with their drinks. He set the drinks in front of them and removed the tray.

Can I get you both anything else while I'm here? he asked.

Rachel looked at Landon.

No, he said to the young man. Thank you.

Rachel shook her head.

He smiled and closed the door quietly behind him.

They lifted their glasses.

Shall we begin then? Rachel asked.

Yes, he replied. Let's begin.

They touched glasses and he sipped the best sip of coffee he would ever have.

The rain pelted at the windows as thunderheads roiled nearer. Outside the populace strode wet and lost. Foragers in search of coin or purpose. Diminutive dreams from bodies once worthy of cause, now driven by sludge and minimal significance. Their heartbeats tick in cadence with those that dwell in bathypelagic depths. Where fairer trials sunder the damned. And conquerors laugh in the void.

He was there two hours and when he left he had a copy of his signed, six-year contract and a check for forty thousand dollars tucked into his jacket pocket. Through the pouring rain, the driver headed uptown to the nearest bank. He spent the better part of an hour transferring his current funds into a new account and deposited the check into his savings and thanked the teller.

He asked the hotel receptionist if Evelyn had called but there were no messages.

Are you sure? he asked.

She refreshed the page.

I'm sorry, sir. I'm afraid I don't see any messages for you.

Alright. Thank you for trying.

He borrowed an umbrella from the hotel and took Maple out to a small patch of grass down the block. She did her business, and they hastened back inside. He dried her with a towel in the bathroom then himself. He washed out her food bowl and filled it with water. She lapped it dry. He refilled it and set it down.

V

The ice had turned to slush, but the remaining champagne was still cold. He filled an unused glass and drank it like water. He looked at the green, glowing bedside clock. 5:15. He poured another half glass and threw it back and set it on the cart and headed out.

Parfum de Page was quiet and soothing. He'd forgotten how beautiful it was. He shook the rain from the umbrella and set it in the stand beside the door and ascended the steps, inhaling the fine aged vanilla scent from the books. Tantalizing notes of black pepper and raw earth entered the air. He looked around the expansive lounge and saw two men drawing on torpedo cigars, the thick porcelain smoke sprouted from their mouths, their nostrils, and drifted amongst the Jacobean beams. The bartender was an older, taller man. He stood hunched like a bulldog and his cheeks drooped as if he held tiny weights in his mouth. His eyes were the color of parakeet feathers. He nodded to Landon and asked for his writing affiliate. He gave it, telling the bartender that he signed today and that he'd been there years ago under a different outfit. The bartender walked to a computer at the end of the bar and typed his name. He could not see around the hulking man, but he did see him nod in confirmation. The bartender came back and took his order and made a drink and slid it across the bar. Congratulations, the bartender said. On the house. He thanked the bartender and tipped him twenty dollars. He turned, sipping the whiskey. He observed the decorated fireplace. Spiraled garland. Velvet draping with silver bell trim. The distant murmurs of conversation. He turned and saw the chair and table by the window he'd sat in years ago. He chortled and walked over and looked at the chair. Slight creases in the leather. A small chip on one of the legs, exposing the beige flesh beneath the varnish.

He sipped the whiskey then set it on the table.

The curtains were cracked. He slid them open to view the dark rainy late day.

He sat down. The leather squealed under him until snug. He picked up his whiskey, sipped, and watched the world turn outside.

Night settled over the city about thirty minutes later. The lights of New York shimmered in every direction. Men and women made their way upstairs, ordered drinks, sat, conversed with one another. He ordered another whiskey and sat alone, becoming quite drunk. He nervously picked at the dry skin on his thumb. Then he heard it.

Hello Landon, the voice croaked behind him.

He turned and looked up.

Harrison Granger stood with his hand on the head of the chair, peering down at him.

The young man was wide eyed with petrification.

The old man smiled thinly and moved to the side for the bartender to set a chair down.

Thank you, he said, sitting as the bartender headed back to the bar. He wore a mustard long sleeve with a brown belt and dark denim jeans. His boots were new. Alligator Luccheses. His leather jacket was streaked with rain and his hair was thin, gray, and gone.

How did you find me? Landon murmured.

You were not at your hotel. I figured you would be at dinner, or here.

Landon picked up the glass and downed the whiskey. He let out a long, flammable breath.

Good guess.

The old man smiled and nodded.

What are you doing here Harrison?

He leaned forward and patted the young writer on the knee. He scratched at the sandpaper stubble on his cheek, licked his lips and drew in a long breath that equaled its exhalation.

Evelyn had an accident, he said. His voice was low, jagged. Like a rust riddled razor.

What? Landon exclaimed.

A bad one. A terrible one.

What happened?

Something spooked the horse and threw her. Her foot got caught in the stirrup.

No.

She was dragged some ways before they were able to get the horse to stop.

His chest tightened.

She's in the hospital now. We're not sure of the outcome yet.

He felt his breath leave him as if he'd been whacked with a baseball bat.

Granger waited, watching the young man process his new reality. They sat for a long time.

When did all this happen? he asked through constricted vocal chords.

Early this morning, Granger replied.

He couldn't hold on anymore. He curled inside himself and wept loudly. Conversations beyond them ceased and others in attendance turned and investigated the commotion with prying eyes.

The old man leaned forward and rubbed the young man's back. It's alright, son, he whispered. Everything will be alright.

No, Landon sobbed. It won't be.

Yes. Yes, it will.

Be quiet old man, Landon yelled, slapping the old man's hand away, looking through reddened eyes of pain and drink. What gives you the right to tell me that all is well in the world? You come here with this news and say everything will be alright? That jaded view of the world may have got you through your drunken prime, but what good is it when you cannot fathom the weight of reality?

Granger's eyes flickered with occluded tears. His jaw clenched, his nostrils flared.

His breath was heavy and hot. As if he'd just finished sprinting.

I'm sorry.

So am I, Granger replied.

He wiped his face with the back of his sleeve and picked up the glass and drank the remainder of its contents. He minced the ice with his teeth, the cold rang in his gums. But it soothed his clenched vocal cords as he let out a long, chilled sigh.

When does it end, Harrison? he asked. The constant running from the fading sunlight. The constant struggle that leaves me stranded on the high seas when the skiff has been banjaxed by endless typhoons. I see myself there again, working against the unyielding downpour. Right when I thought I'd found a light to guide me, was just the trickery of the storm. Prelude to the hurricane. Now I am as I was before. Waging a battle with predetermined outcomes. I thought my life would be different. I saw it so clearly.

It will be alright, Granger said softly.

How? How can you say that when we've lost those closest to us?

The old man leaned forward, his eyes blue as the Pacific.

You're here, he said. Right in the moment you need to be.

But where is here? What are my coordinates? What is my itinerary?

The myriad of people we meet along our individualistic odysseys are never the keepers of some secret that will bestow upon us the great knowledge we so seek. That is a cheap trick. A sleight of hand. We are the only ones who truly know what the end of the road looks like. We've seen it in forgotten dreams. Dreams we had when we were young. When innocence roamed freely, and the world outside waited at the gates. You have seen the end of the road. A sliver of it on the horizon. You wield the telescope. As we all do. You don't need to drift alone anymore, son. But I cannot show you your destination. For only you know where it is.

Landon gazed out the dark window. And beyond the streaks of rain that obscured the bright New York cityscape, past the flaring red car lights and winking turning signals, and past the citizens and tourists with their umbrellas that crossed the streets, the cigarette smoke and hot breath curling stale and bitter, was the outline of the great equine. His titanic silhouette over the horizon. His large, endless eyes upon the scared young man. Then he looked at the old man.

You'll be alright, son, Granger said placing his warm palm on the young writer's cheek.

But is that enough? Landon whimpered. Will it ever be enough?

Granger smiled gently. You'll see. You'll see.

He pinched his eyes and cried. After a while he sat up and wiped his cheeks with his palm and dried them on his pant leg. His throat hurt and he knew he would cry again. Granger stood and patted Landon on the shoulder. He looked up at the old man through glassy eyes and touched his hand in silent gratitude. Then Granger crossed to the stairs and descended. Out of his life. Forever.

He returned to Maryland a day later. He was at her bedside the full seventy-two hours until they pronounced her gone. He thought about attending the funeral but could not bring himself to return to the ranch. For three days he lived in a small hotel room in New York, dining at little cafes, bars, bistros, listening to talentless local singers and bands belt out covers well out of their wheelhouse. One night Rachel took him to a Michelin star sushi restaurant. He stayed up late in his hotel room filling the blue notebooks with the first act of his next novel. Anything to avoid the loss of her. He found a blue Ford Ranger from a newspaper ad and paid the owner in cash and drove it off the lot then and there.

Harrison Granger won the Nobel Prize for literature later the following year. Landon Cassidy's fourth novel did well, placing ninth overall on the New York Times Bestseller list for three weeks straight.

As the years passed, he lived in various northern coastal towns for long stretches of time. He worked on a fishing boat in Nantucket for five years, sleeping above a bar he helped tend on the weekends, gathered notes and ingraining himself in the town's history and culture. The voices never really went away. At the end of his stay he submitted his longest, and eventually, most successful story. With it, his name entered the mainstream. Various awards and film adaptations followed. Maple had been gone several years. Her ashes were stored in a small mahogany box that resembled a humidor. His truck had accumulated over two hundred thousand miles. Rachel Nelson died of a heart attack a week before her eightieth birthday. He attended the funeral and gave the eulogy. He never did open the envelope he'd received at the hotel. He drove south, sleeping in the bed of his truck under starblown skies. He dined at roadside diners and bathed in their bathrooms, remembering the times of his youth. Every once in a while, he would catch himself staring in the mirror at the long scar along his side. His fingers ran over it, feeling the artificial indentation, trying to recall his times as a would-be wrangler.

On his seventieth birthday, he pulled the prowling emerald 1965 Shelby Mustang into a rest stop in northern New Jersey. His knees were stiff, and his lower back throbbed. The stale taste of burnt coffee lingered in the back of his throat from earlier that morning. His bladder pressed against his belt.

He shut the engine off and opened the door and stepped out, checking his back pocket for his wallet. The door shut with a metallic thud. He combed his long, silver hair with his fingers and headed for the entrance.

The place was mobbed. Lines for food, coffee, bathrooms. His eyes had worsened through the years, and he could hardly make out the signs without his glasses. He massaged his lower back as he shuffled through the maddening crowds. He stood in line for the bathroom and almost lost himself before getting the zipper down. A small self-serve coffee station went by the goodwill of dropping a dollar into a large plastic tub. He slid the dollar through the slot and peeled off a cup and pumped it with hot coffee. When he got back, the Shelby was gone. He looked around the parking lot for half an hour but never found it. He went back inside, looked around and walked up to an officer at a small information booth.

How can I help you, sir? the young Hispanic officer asked.

It appears that someone has stolen my car, Landon said.

Are you sure, sir?

It's not where I parked it. And I just spent the last thirty minutes running around the lot looking for it. I think it's safe to assume I've been two timed.

How long have you been here?

Almost an hour now, he said, taking a sip of the lukewarm coffee.

Just a moment, sir.

The officer, dressed in a chocolate brown uniform and a flat brim hat with canary yellow tassels, left the stand and went through a door at the far end of the building.

He thought about the valuables in the Shelby, aside from the car itself. But there was nothing that couldn't be replaced, except for Maple's ashes and the journals with the few stories they contained. The important stuff was locked away in a storage unit outside of New York City. He pinched the bridge of his nose. Dry skin caught under his nails. He balled it up with his fingers and flicked it towards the ground.

The officer emerged, thin colored papers flapping in his hand. He stood behind the podium and slid the paper across the table.

Fill this out please, he said. What was the color, make and model of the vehicle?

Sixty-five Shelby. Green.

He whistled. Nice. Should be easy to find with the traffic cams.

Hope so.

Landon filled out the initial the information and slid the papers back to the officer and continued with the rest.

The officer picked up the pages and looked the information over. Looks good, he said.

Alright, Landon replied, writing.

The officer picked up a phone and dialed. He spoke to the officer on the other line, giving him the information. He paused, listening. He lowered the receiver.

Do you have anything of major value in the vehicle, sir?

My dog's ashes, Landon replied dryly. A couple bucks and some journals. Some outfits in the trunk. But the ashes are what I want back more than anything.

Is that all? replied the puzzled officer.

Of major value, yes.

Dog ashes?

What?

Never mind.

He went on repeating the information into the receiver. When he was done, he thanked whoever was on the other line and hung up.

We'll put an APB out for the vehicle. Is there a number we can contact if we find it?

I wrote it here, Landon said, tapping the paper with the pen.

The officer looked through over and nodded.

Make sure to sign the bottom, here.

Sure thing.

Landon signed the dotted lines and straightened the pages and handed the packet to the officer and clicked the pen shut and set it down.

The officer reviewed them page by page. When he was finished he tore the pink sheet off and handed it to the silvery long-haired man.

Keep this for your records, he said.

Landon took the paper, looked at the broken scrawl that barely got through the first page, folded it, and tucked it into his shirt pocket.

Any suggestions as to what I do now? Landon asked.

You probably should wait until your vehicle turns up.

You have my information. I'd prefer it if I moved along.

Okay, the officer said, slowly. Do you know where you were heading?Just down the coast.

Take a bus. It goes pretty far.

Where do I find out about that?

The officer pointed over Landon's shoulder.

He turned and saw the bus booth out the front doors. A small wooden circular structure in a fresh coat of maroon. A young woman sitting behind the tinted window.

Do you need money for a ticket?

Landon looked at the officer and smiled. No, he said. Thank you though.

We'll be in touch.

Thank you for your help.

He used his smartphone to call the agency to let them know about the car. He said he would call back in a few days to check in then hung up. He purchased a pack of Winston's, a liter of water and an assortment of snacks and protein bars and used the bathroom again and headed outside.

The bus shook violently before leveling off on the parkway. He gazed out the window at the passing rickety trees, the gray gloom of the clouds. He felt the bus shift gears, then sat back and slept.

When he awoke, they were parked in a small station on Exit 9. He looked down the bus aisle. Most of the passengers had departed. He used the bathroom in the back then returned to his seat in time for the bus to venture forth. They returned to the parkway where the exit signs ticked down. He sat up and peered over the seat in front of him to eye the road ahead, but there was nothing but pallid blurs. They passed Exit 8, then 7. At Exit 4, the bus turned and entered Rio Grande. The sun was high over rapidly moving clouds. He asked the driver for the time. One o clock, sir, he said. He stepped onto the pavement, rubbing his knees. There was a diner on the other side of the road and he remembered he'd not eaten a good meal since earlier that morning. He turned and asked the driver if he had time to order lunch.

You got time, sir. We leave in an hour.

The diner was slow for lunch. A long table with a portly father, his two young sons and their grandparents were eating quietly off to the right. Window shades canted at different levels and axis. Cobwebs in most of the light fixtures. Assorted candy bars, layered thinly in dust. Dry pie slices in an illuminated display. He sat at the counter on a wobbly black stool. He stood and bent over and tightened the screw and sat and swiveling slowly to check his work. The waitress came over, welcomed him and asked what he would like to drink.

Coffee, water and a large orange juice please, he croaked.

Any cream? she asked while sliding a large plastic menu to him.

Two please

You got it, hon.

He briefly browsed the lunch menu, then flipped it over and read the breakfast options. He involuntarily felt his back pocket for his wallet. He took it out and opened the flaps and rifled through the slots and folds and cash and closed it and slid it back in his pocket and returned to reading the menu. She returned with the three beverages and set them down gingerly and took his order.

He wiped up the remainder of the snotty yolk with the last piece of rye and ate while reading the local town paper. Small time crime. High school football victory over arch rival. Want ads. Political squabbles. He paid and thanked the waitress. As he placed his hand on the front door, he turned to see the family. But they were gone.

Had a good meal? the bus driver asked as Landon slowly stepped up the stairs.

I've had worse. Thanks for asking.

The driver chuckled.

The bus was filled with a motley crew of workers and families. His former seat taken. He sat directly behind the driver, next to the outdated medical equipment and a large tire iron. Across the aisle was a woman holding her infant son. The ignition caught and the bus roared to life. They took a long, slow turn onto Main Street and another long turn onto the parkway and continued south.

He saw the trees clear, revealing a flat bed of pungent swamp water. Several cramped fishing boats rocked in placidity. He could not tell from the distance, but he thought he saw a Ferris wheel on the horizon. Blinking chromatic lights atop the tree lined horizon. Houses on stilts. He was not too sure.

The bus crossed a tall bridge then slowly drifted into a single lane. Their pace lulled to a crawl. He looked out and saw gulls circling the bay. Lines of cars turned towards a sort of seafood market. Docked fishing boats waded like mallards. Sprouting a few feet further down the road were towering, historic Victorian homes. Beautiful and vibrant. They flanked the single road for about a mile until the bus took a right turn into a dated station.

Cape May, the driver announced. End of the line.

All the riders stood and disembarked.

Landon looked around and stood and followed the last passenger.

The sun warmed his clammy skin as he watched the riders go their separate ways. He thanked the driver and crossed the road at the traffic light and walked down the street towards some sort of mall. He studied the lackadaisical regulars, the garish tourists. All walking alongside their families, relatives and friends. An elderly couple took pictures of the massive, and out of place, cathedral on the street corner. Children ran amok with ice cream stains on their cheeks, hands, and clothing. Brace-faced teenagers with their tan, thin legs and bleached blonde hair walked closely with one another as their flirtatious eyes waltzed in tandem with their blossoming emotions. He strolled down the shopping center, his head on a swivel to take in all the elaborate shops. The buildings were freshly painted but he could see the age in some of them by the minor details modern cosmetics couldn't fix. He came to a dead end and made his way back to where he started.

He walked down Ocean Street, pausing to admire the sweeping hotels, the manicured lawns, the charming backroads. Efflorescent Roses of Sharon, worshiping the sun. He heard the crashing ocean. When was the last time I heard that? He thought of Nantucket, the boats. His ears followed the all too familiar signal to Beach Avenue, where expensive vehicles lined the road and bicycles polluted the racks. He crossed the road and mounted the sandy steps and followed the pathway onto the beach.

Can I help you, sir? the old woman said from her shaded shelter, as if she were some guardian to another kingdom.

I was hoping to see the ocean, Landon replied. Splash my face a bit.

Do you have a tag?

A what?

A tag. A beach tag.

No, why?

You need one to go in.

A tag?

Yes.

I need to pay to swim in the ocean?

It pays for the lifeguards and to keep the beach clean, sir, the woman chided.

Don't city taxes pay for that?

It's ten dollars for the day.

He guffawed.

She glared at him through her dark sunglasses.

You're not joking, are you?

It's ten dollars for the day, sir. Or you can watch it from the promenade.

He shook his head, retrieved his wallet, pinched out ten dollars and handed it to the guard. She didn't bother to lean forward to meet him halfway.

Thank you, she said. Have fun splashing your face.

He crossed the wooden slats that served as a walkway and sat on a hot bench and took off his shoes. Sand poured from the inside as if he'd been walking there all morning. He stood and headed towards the water.

His heels hurt, and he tried not to put a lot of pressure on them but his knees wouldn't have it. The sand eventually cooled. The salted breeze kissed his lips. He looked up and saw the Atlantic water clear and mint hued, like rust on a copper roof. He rolled up his pants and tucked his wallet and keys into his shoes and set everything in the shadow a lifeguard stand.

A cold chill shot up his body as he stepped onto the damp bank. He felt his long hair thicken from the rogue droplets that sailed on the wind. He walked forward, feeling the water pass across his feet. His eyes shut into baptismal euphoria. He slowly stepped until the water was at his knees, cleansing him all over. He opened his eyes and studied the horizon. A thin gray line separated the world from the heavens. He made a wrinkled bowl with his hands and submerged it. The water was clear and grainy with salt. He doused his face, exhaling anew. He did this several times, running his fingers through his damp hair. An unsuspecting wave knock him over and carried him up the bank. He laughed in his soaked clothes as the waves ran up his back. He sat up and hacked the salty taste from his mouth, as if he were a little boy. He reflected on his life, what was, what was yet to come. Then he stopped. He listened to the tide. Children chasing the foam line. Distant whistles from the guard stands. Gulls squawked overhead. Her smile. Her eyes. Her silhouette on that black, mountainous steed, the sun behind them. Are you the apparition I still see in my dreams? They silently stood there. Waiting. When he gazed back out at the thin gray horizon, feeling the cool, salty waves blanketing his lap as he basked in the sun, they were gone. But he knew she would always be there. Waiting for him.

Epilogue

She bent the thick white sheets delicately with her soft olive hands. The thin ivory bone slid smoothly along the crease. She opened them, folded them opposite, and slid again. She swayed them in the air like laundry on a hilltop breeze. Her palms secured both sides of the paper and tenderly split them apart. She folded them once more, sliding the bone to confirm it. All the pages lay to rest. She opened her desk drawer and took out a small tin of beeswax and removed the lid. A pungent sweet, succulent odor of lemon filled the room. She unfurled the porcelain silk from the spool to her arm's length then severed it with the scissors. Her fingers pinched both ends as she ran it across the wax as if buttering an ear of corn. She set the string on a cloth and shut the tin and placed it back in the desk drawer and took out a small, faded wood ruler. A silent zephyr snuck in from the cracked window. The sheets fluttered noiselessly atop one another. She grabbed four sheets, folded each into one another, checked their straightness and marked in two-inch increments with a light dash of graphite from her wilted pencil. She returned the ruler, the pencil and set a candle aflame. She heated the awl, then held it to the window to cool. The needle punctured with ease. She set it aside, picked up the needle, threaded the waxed string and knotted it off. She began at the bottom, passing through the signatures with deftness. When she was done she folded another four sheets, set them atop of the others and began again. And again. Then all was bound. She draped the tome in burgundy cloth, leaving the spine exposed. Twin clamps strangled the pages to the desk. She tapped the brush against the bottle to loosen the strands, then caressed the spine in delicate strokes of potent adhesive. She looked over her work before cleaning the brush. The sun emerged. Her olive skin warmed. Her aging almond eyes smiled at the gentle sight. She breathed in the musty fragrance of the room. Wet grass. Raw earth. She leaned back in her rickety chair, breathing slowly and evenly. Her hands lay folded across her thin stomach as she rocked herself slowly to sleep.

A Note on Type

Garabond originates from 16th-cenutry France, from its print creator Claude Garabond. The type resembled that of a calligrapher, rather than the traditional scribe. Due to this unique style, the print became clearer and elegant when sent through printing presses. Garabond's print was used in many Roman and Latin texts, as the style came about during a cultural transition. Garabond's, now famous, type caught the eye of the Greek goverment, and was comminsioned to design their own unique type, dubbed *Grec du Roi*, which, was only used for the county's text.

About the Author

Lucas Alves grew up in Houston, Texas. He studied film, theater and acting in San Francisco, CA, where he appeared in several productions. Aside from his passion for writing, he is a voracious reader and loves to travel the world with his family. He currently lives in Frederick, Maryland with his wife and daughter.

www.ingramcontent.com/pod-product-compliance
Lightning Source LLC
LaVergne TN
LVHW010609100826
845148LV00014B/2902

* 9 7 9 8 9 8 8 3 3 8 1 0 9 *